PRAISE FOR *CRAZY HORSE'S GIRLFRIEND*

"Erika T. Wurth's first novel, *Crazy Horse's Girlfriend*, is gritty and tough and sad beyond measure; but is also contains startling, heartfelt moments of hope and love. In my opinion, a writer can't do much better than that."

—**DONALD RAY POLLOCK**,
author of *Knockemstiff* and *The Devil All the Time*

"There's no horror flick or disaster movie scarier than a teenager's life. I found myself wanting to cover my eyes and shout, 'Girl, don't go there' while reading. Erika T. Wurth writes about a young woman's longing with such heart and soul, it made me want to cry. Here she chronicles the poor with compassion and respect, and depicts their moments of joy with the only language worthy of such heights—poetry. I hope this book is the first in a long series of this young woman's life. If so, sign me up. I can't wait to read the next volume."

—**SANDRA CISNEROS**,
author of *The House on Mango Street*

"Tough, tender, and funny as hell, Erika T. Wurth's unflinching debut novel *Crazy Horse's Girlfriend* illuminates the grim world of Idaho Springs. Wurth's raw, muscular writing takes the gritty story of a pregnant sixteen-year-old drug dealer and transforms bathos into a revelatory journey. Immensely compelling and readable. Couldn't put it down."

—**EDEN ROBINSON**,
author of *Monkey Beach*

"Erika T. Wurth's first novel is a knockout—packing a raw punch of emotional truth that makes an unforgettable impact. I fell for her narrator, the tough urban Native who is alternately wise-cracking and vulnerable, a smart, engaging witness with a big bad beautiful heart. Wurth made me care for everyone in these pages, singing a powerful honor song on behalf of our young people who are fighting their way through difficult times in order to survive. She writes with a voice of courageous, mesmerizing grace."

—SUSAN POWER,
author of *Grassdancer*

PRAISE FOR *INDIAN TRAINS*

"This is a funny, sad and powerful book. Each poem is lovely, and the cumulative effect is devastating."

—SHERMAN ALEXIE,
author of *Flight*

CRAZY HORSE'S GIRLFRIEND

A NOVEL

ERIKA T. WURTH

CURBSIDE SPLENDOR

CURBSIDE SPLENDOR PUBLISHING

Published by Curbside Splendor Publishing, Inc., Chicago, Illinois in 2014.

First Edition

Library of Congress Control Number: 2014945065

ISBN 978-1-940430-43-0

Designed by Alban Fischer
Cover image based on a painting by Douglas Miles

Manufactured in the United States of America.

CS

www.curbsidesplendor.com

"Survival = Anger × Imagination."

—Sherman Alexie

FOR M.

I hope you're in that blue, blue perfect place you always dreamed of.

CHAPTER 1

I was sitting around in the basement of yet another fucking drug fuck, when I decided to get nervous. I was pretty high myself, and felt like I was sitting on the edge of a lake, the sun setting hard and fast, like it wasn't the sun at all, but a wild, terrible stranger who was ready to take me down with him into the dark. Jake was holding a couple of dimebags out for inspection, and two of the guys were fine. It was the dude in the corner I hated. He was not a pot-head, he was a meth-head. And he looked sick. His face looked like someone had broken glass over it, but it was just what he had done to himself, just the goddamn meth.

"Jake," I said, and elbowed him.

"What?"

I looked over at the guy. Jake looked at him and back at me.

"I got it covered."

The guy was staring at me. His hair was greasy as shit, dirty blond, and the only time he moved was to pick at the acne on his face.

The two other guys I'd known since kindergarten. They were brothers, and part of one of the Idaho Springs clans, one of the families that was so large they put half the rez families I knew to shame. There were so many of them in this inbred, bullshit, crazy ass town. For fuck's sake, forty-five percent of the dumb broads in my grade had gotten pregnant by the end of the last school year. They had to send this counselor in from Denver to be like Jesus, wear a condom. But the thing I'll never forget is after that guy's speech, some dumb ass chicks going, but condoms are too expensive. Oh, yeah, much more expensive than a baby. I know why they say that, 'cause they know they can just get on welfare like everyfuckingbody else here once they pop one out. To be honest, I think half the chicks around here think that having a baby is gonna make them happy. And then when it doesn't, they get on meth, which is something that rots your soul from the inside out as quick as you can say clusterfuck.

Finally, the meth-head spoke.

"You're, uh," he said, grinding his teeth. "You're like, here to fuck us or what?"

Jake looked over at him and shook his head, just a little. The guy blinked, continued to grind his teeth, and looked at his pals, the two brothers. They were sitting on an old yellow corduroy couch, already smoking their newly acquired joints, their pale faces nearly featureless from the sad, grey light coming in from the basement window, duct tape crisscrossing the glass. I'd seen a lot of shitholes in this town, but this place could win a shithole contest. The couches were practically rotting into the floor, and cobwebs were everywhere, oddly the only semi-pretty thing about the place. The only natural thing. The rest was full of years of barely giving a fuck about living, full of garbage. Old GI Joe dolls with their khaki covered limbs broken off, destroyed video games, eight-tracks, tapes, parts of guns and, worst of all, old diapers. Every few minutes, I could hear a child, or maybe two crying the way a lost animal might. I was sitting on my jacket so that I wouldn't have to put my ass on about five tons of old fast food wrappers, which covered the place like a fungus.

The meth-head flicked his eyes over at my cousin. "What's it to you?" The two brothers tensed, waiting to see what would happen.

Jake stopped sorting the baggies, put them down, tucked his long, dark arms behind his back, sighed and leaned into the couch.

"If you even try to touch my cousin, I promise I will fuck you up."

The guy looked over at me and then back at Jake. He started laughing.

The two brothers looked real nervous.

"What's so funny?" My cousin asked, but he knew. We both knew. My family is Apache, Chickasaw, Cherokee, and white, but my auntie and her husband adopted Jake when he was a baby. He's Nez Perce, Arapahoe, Cheyenne, and black. And big as fuck. Whenever he feels like screwing with me, he palms my face in one of his hands.

"If you two are cousins, I'm—I'm—a pigeon," he finished lamely, raising his hand to pick at his face again.

"Hilarious," I said. "You're a regular Rodney Dangerfield." The two brothers started laughing, one of them choking mid-puff.

"Fuck me Margaritte," the shorter brother said, wiping his eyes. "You've always been a funny motherfucker."

"I try," I said, narrowing my eyes at the meth-head. He looked like he weighed all of 120 pounds, but the darkness coming from him was something real, something that made my stomach hurt. Every few minutes, he looked like he was about to leap out of the wooden chair he was sitting on and cause some serious trouble.

I sighed heavily and looked down at the cold cement floor. I had to go to work that night, and I wasn't exactly looking forward to it. I had been waiting tables at the Sugar Plum for about a year and it sucked, hard-core. No one came in hardly, so the tips were terrible. Otherwise, I was paid two bucks an hour. Jake, he made bank from all the weed he sold from his connection in Denver, which is why I had started helping him. All he had to do was put up with crazy fuckers like this occasionally. Mainly we sold to kids at school, like the two brothers, who were cool. They were regulars. Jake worked in the kitchen of the Chinese restaurant, maybe once or twice a week, at most. We kept the jobs so that our parents wouldn't figure out what we were really up to, but I knew Jake's parents at least were beginning to suspect that maybe our money wasn't coming from the restaurant business after all.

Jake shook his head and finished sorting the baggies. "OK, pay up. Much as I enjoy listening to the brilliance coming out of that thing over there," he said, pointing to the meth-head with his lips and his left hand. "I really have shit to do."

"You're a dick," the guy said and Jake looked at him again. The guy looked away, but after a second, he started staring at me again. Staring, grinding his teeth, and picking at his face. I shuddered.

The brothers glanced at each other and then one of them, the older one I think, started digging into the pocket of his ripped up black jeans. He pulled cash, lint, and something that appeared as if it might have once been a grape Jolly Rancher out of his pocket. He plucked the lint and the candy off of the money and slapped it into Jake's palm. "There you go, brother."

Jake frowned.

"You know what I mean," he said, and laughed nervously,

running his hand through his thin black hair. The whole family had that hair, that and black eyes, though as far as I knew, they were white. I had a flash, a memory of either him, his brother, or one of their trillions of cousins, a memory from the school playground when I was maybe five or six. I was trying to climb the rusty-ass jungle gym, my funny yellow arms reaching for the next rung, when I felt hands on my back and turned, afraid. But he was only helping me up. I let him. Later, he ignored me when his friends were around and I remembered the feeling of his warm, pale hands on my back, the familiarity of it, but the strangeness of it too.

"You want a toke, Jake?" the older brother asked. I figured he was the older one because he was taller. Honestly, It was hard to keep any of them straight.

"Sure, one."

He handed the joint over to Jake and he took a hit, handed it to me, and I took a hit, and I handed it back to the brother. I looked over at the meth-head. He had an angry, sullen expression on his face. I began to feel truly nervous. The taller brother handed the joint back over to me but I refused.

I looked at Jake. "Let's be on our merry way, shall we?"

"Merry way," the shorter brother said. "Seriously, you kill me."

"Thanks," I said, thinking that it really hadn't been all that funny.

I stood up, and so did Jake. "Nice doing business with you."

"Yeah, you too, Jake," the older brother said.

We were almost to the stairs when I heard a scuffling sound, like that of a giant, dying roach, and then a weight. And then a piercing pain in my side. Then the weight was lifted off me, and I turned around to see why there was pain. And that's when I saw the blood rapidly expanding on my old, white sweatshirt, right over one of the faded blue unicorns that were scattered all over it. I looked up at Jake and he was already pulling the meth-head up by his neck and slamming him against the cold, cement wall. The dude squirmed. I stood up and lifted my shirt.

"You fuck up!" Jake was yelling, and the brothers were just standing there, stunned. "You idiots," Jake said, turning to them. "Call 911."

"No, Jake, don't. It's not that bad. And they'll find the weed," I said. The blood was flowing, but the guy had barely gotten his knife in so I figured I would be fine. One of the brothers left and the other sat down on the edge of the couch, hard and put his head in his hands. "Shit, shit," he chanted over and over.

"No," Jake said. The guy's face was turning blue. His legs were still kicking at the air, but the kicks were getting weaker.

"Jake, let him go. I'm fine. You're going to fucking kill him," I said. "Serious, hey." I was bunching my shirt over the wound, trying to convince myself that it wasn't that bad. But I had to admit, I was starting to feel weak.

"I gotta sit down," I said. Jake turned back to the guy, let go of his neck. He slid to the floor, coughing. I sat down on the old couch. Jake walked over to me, lifted my shirt. The blood was still flowing, even getting on the couch. The brother who'd left came back with bandages and tape and handed them to Jake. Jake lifted my shirt, my hand, and the blood came even harder. I told myself not to cry. Jake folded the bandages over, and placed them on my wound and taped them.

"I'm driving you to the hospital," he said.

"No, I'm OK." The meth-head had recovered and was staring at me with a grotesque smile on his face. He began picking at a blackened scab on his chin and stood up. "That's what you get for fucking with me, you Mexican cunt," he said, his voice still weak from Jake holding him against the wall by his neck. He laughed, a long, sick, angry sound. Jake turned around and headed over to him.

"Jake! Stop," I said. "We're already in trouble."

Jake stood over the guy and round-housed him, once. The guy fell to the floor, his greasy hair laying over his scarred face.

The brother with his head in his hands looked up. The taller brother looked at Jake. "Jake, he's a piece of trash. We'll toss him where we found him. You take her to the hospital." Jake nodded and helped me up. We walked up the steps and out into a living room that was almost as dank and messy as the basement. A young girl was sitting on another old couch, nursing a baby. She looked up, pursed her lips, closed her faded blue eyes and then went back to nursing.

Jake opened the ancient Subaru's side door, the rusty, creaking noise it'd made ever since I'd whacked into the side of the dirt cliff while driving high one stupid night making me wince. Jake got in on the other side, the engine turning over a few times before it started.

"You OK?" he asked, pulling out of the driveway and onto the road. We were on the west side and had to drive through town to get to the exit for I-70. The closest hospital was in Denver.

"Yeah. Tired though."

"Don't fall asleep Margaritte," he said, biting his lip. I laughed weakly.

"I won't. If you stop speeding. All we need is get stopped by the cops," I said, looking down at the bandages. They were soaked through.

"I just want to get you there," he said. "How are you feeling?"

"Great. I get stabbed all the time," I said, shifting in the seat. There were springs coming through, and they were always poking me in the ass. I planned on getting covers, but I never did. "I can't believe that meth-tard."

"He's a piece of shit."

"Yeah. I guess guys like him are sort of an occupational hazard."

Jake was silent for a few seconds and then said, "This is my fault. I knew not to bring you in on this."

"It's not your fault that those idiots picked up some pile of steaming shit and brought him home. That could have happened if we were just hanging there. And it was my choice. I wanted to help you deal. Fuck, if I didn't, I'd be poor as hell. And our account would be much emptier. No one comes to the Sugar Plum. I make dick in tips."

"I guess," Jake said, and went silent again.

I didn't want him to feel guilty. I had practically begged Jake to let me help, and it had doubled his profits. I looked out the window. It was getting dark and I knew I was supposed to be at work and when I didn't show, Buddy would call my house and Mom would be wondering where I was and what trouble I was getting into. She was always wondering. And I knew when I got to the hospital that they would want me to call my parents because I was only sixteen. I knew that my mom would be making dinner when they called, dealing with the twins clinging to her legs and the TV and when she found out that she would have to come to Denver to pick me up, she would want to punch me in the neck. And my dad would already be halfway to getting motherfucking plastered and when Mom told him what I had done, he *would* punch me in the neck. I sighed. I turned up the volume on the radio. Jake loved Christian metal and I hoped the rough, grating sounds would be enough to keep me awake.

Pulling into the ER at Lutheran's, Jake put the car in park and came around to help me out. I already had the door open and was trying to get out when I fell onto the sidewalk.

"Margaritte! Cut it out! That's why I was coming around," Jake said, picking me up and cradling me into his side.

"I'm fine," I said. "And I'm just going to get blood all over your new fringe jacket."

"Fuck my jacket," Jake said. "It's just a jacket. God Margaritte, sometimes you could just let someone do something for you."

He walked me into the hospital, the wide glass doors opening and shutting like magic, and sat me down on one of the funky ass chairs with geometric designs they had in the waiting room. I looked down at the bandages and pulled up a corner of long, dark hair. It had even gotten into my *hair*. I was beginning to feel sleepy and the white walls and neon lights were pulsing all around me.

"Jake," I said, watching him at the receptionist's desk, "the blood got in my hair." He didn't turn around and the lights and walls became one and I fell forward. I slept.

I woke up to a needle in my arm, my body in a hospital bed.

"Jake," I croaked.

"I'm here."

I felt like vomiting. "I'm definitely never getting stabbed again," I whispered. I opened my eyes. My clothes were folded neatly in the corner on a chair. Jake was sitting in another chair, his long, lanky body far too large for it. He was looking at me, his large slanted black eyes full of pain.

"Stop looking so worried. I'll be fine." I shifted around so that I could sit up.

"I called your mom," he said. "There was a lot of yelling."

"That's her favorite," I said.

A hand appeared at the edge of the pink curtain that surrounded the bed and pulled it open, revealing a nurse in light blue scrubs. She smiled.

"Hi, I'm Karen."

"Hi Karen."

She came over to me, lifted my gown and looked at the bandages. "You're going to need stitches."

"That's OK. I was hoping for a tougher look." Jake laughed and Karen furrowed her brow.

"Well, the doctor's going to be here in a bit and he's going to give you those stitches. I don't think you'll need too many. I took a peek while you were out and though the wound bled a lot, it's not too bad. And we were able to stop the bleeding."

"OK," I said.

Karen took my blood pressure, wrote in her chart, looked at me. "What I'd like to know is how you got that wound. Because to me, it looks like something a knife might do."

I looked over at Jake. Then Karen looked over at Jake. "Do you mind if your boyfriend leaves for a few minutes?"

"He's not my—sure," I said, and Jake got up and walked out.

"Are you and your boyfriend having problems? Maybe he has trouble with his temper," Karen said, sitting down on the chair that Jake had just left. She looked at me softly, sympathetically, her round, white face like a kewpie doll's.

I laughed. "Jake's my cousin. And he doesn't own a knife."

"The thing is," and she looked down at the chart in her lap, "Margaret—"

"Margaritte," I said.

"Margaritta," she continued, "when a minor comes in with something that's clearly a stab wound, we have to call the cops."

"Oh, shit," I said, sitting up and wincing, "no, really, it's not what you think... he's not my, and he didn't... oh, shit... " I said, putting my head in my hands. I wished for a cigarette, badly. "You don't understand. First of all, why would he bring me in if he did it?"

Karen sighed. "Please lie back, Margaritta." She gently pushed me back onto the bed. "Sometimes we do things we don't mean to do and we feel badly about them. And of course I understand why you'd want to protect your boyfriend. Really, I do. But you have to realize that he's only going to hurt you again."

I laughed and looked at the needle in my arm.

"Jake, who is my cousin, is the only person in my life who doesn't hurt me."

Karen shook her head. "I can understand why you'd feel that way. I'm sure it really feels that way, but I really think you should think about you."

"Really?"

I closed my eyes. I wished to God that Jake and I were somewhere else, anywhere else. Maybe up on Mt. Evans, after a long ride on Jake's motorcycle, sitting around the lake and drinking beer. I opened my eyes and Karen was looking at me with her wide, sweet green eyes.

"Karen, if you have to call the cops, I understand. We'll answer their questions. But this has nothing, well, not nothing, but really nothing to do with Jake. He would never hurt me. Some meth-head did this. Some skinny, cracked out white fuck who just didn't like the looks of me. Jake is the one who drove me here from Idaho Springs, who has always protected me. Who has never laid a hand on me. That's my dad's job."

She looked confused again, but then nodded. I had no idea what she believed, but I was sure as shit that she'd already called the cops, and maybe even social services. I couldn't wait till I was eighteen. Jake and me were gonna leave this place with all the money that we were saving up and never, ever look back.

I could hear my mom yelling at Jake outside and I closed my eyes again. "Mom," I said, opening them, "come in here." More yelling.

"Mom!" I yelled and it made my side hurt.

Mom came stomping in through the doorway. "I can't believe you two! I could kill you! Where were you? I know you're dealing, Margaritte, I know it! Don't you know Jake's parents are ready to kick him out?" She yelled, walking over. As soon as she got to the side of the bed she looked down at me and started crying. She never cried. It was Dad who did all the crying. I squirmed in my hospital gown.

"I'm sorry, Mom. It wasn't Jake's fault."

She was silent for a bit, and then pulled her short, dark hands through her tightly curled hair. She had it permed every few months. She closed her eyes, the lines around them crinkling like brown foil. Then she opened them and turned to the nurse.

"I'm her mother," she said. Karen nodded and stood up.

"Please, take this seat," Karen said and Mom sat down.

"How is she?" Mom asked.

"I'm right here, you could ask—"

"Quiet!"

I was quiet.

I could see Jake peeking in around the doorframe. He looked like he'd been spanked, like a little boy. It was actually kind of funny, considering how big he was. He loved my mom and hated it when she was mad at him.

"Can I come in?" he asked timidly.

"I guess," Mom said.

"Mom, can you at least explain to Karen here that Jake is not my boyfriend?"

Mom looked over at Karen. "This is my sister's boy."

Karen looked confused. I rolled my eyes.

"They're going to have to answer some questions for the police," Karen said. "Because your daughter has a stab wound. And when a minor comes in with something like that, the police are called."

"Well, my nephew gets into a lot of trouble, but he wouldn't stab my daughter. He loves her, even if they are both screwing up their lives together."

"I see," Karen said. "Well, I'm going to go. I told Margaret here that she's going to need stitches. The doctor should be in soon to do that. And when you've talked to the police, you can go. But in the meantime, come with me so you can fill out some forms."

Mom looked at the both of us before she left the room. "I'm so angry at you two. And I've called your mother," she said, looking at Jake, "and she is not pleased."

Jake nodded.

We were all silent for a while. Jake leaned against the wall, his head down. Mom walked over to me and ran her hand over my head. I looked up at her. She saw the part of my hair that had matted together with dried blood. She sighed, walked over to the sink, pulled towels out of dispenser, pumped some soap onto the towel and then began cleaning the blood out of my hair. She started crying again. I looked over at Jake, and he was watching us, his full purple lips trembling.

The doctor came in about an hour later. He smiled sadly, asked me questions, told me it wouldn't hurt that much. He sewed into my skin with his delicate freckled hands, reminding me of the time my auntie, Jake's mom, had taught me to peyote stitch beads, before his family had become born again. He used a topical anesthetic. It hurt about as much as the tattoo I'd gotten of a thunderbird on my hip when I was thirteen. Less.

The doctor left. The cops came. They asked questions, nodded, filled out a report, their guns so silver, the walkie talkies attached to their navy uniforms squawking occasionally. They told us that social services would not be called, but since Jake had a record, this was not good. They handed me their cards, said I could call them anytime.

"I'll drive her home," Jake said.

"Fine," Mom said. "But this is not over. And be careful."

"I will," he said. She was sitting on the chair, Jake still against the wall. He had gone to get a pop, had asked my mother if she'd wanted one and she'd nodded that she did. The empty Pepsi cans were sitting by the chairs. The doctor came and signed my paperwork. Jake and Mom left, I got dressed. On my way out, I dropped the cans and the cards into the trash.

In the car I asked Jake if he was going to go home.

"I don't think I should," he said. "They already want to kick me out."

"What are you gonna do? I'd say stay at my place, but I can guarantee Dad's beyond drunk by now, and you know how he feels about you." I looked down at the sweatshirt in my lap. It was one of my favorites and I figured I could try bleaching it, even though it would make the unicorns fade. The tank, who cares. It was from the boys' section at Walmart. I had a million of them.

"I'll just stay with Will."

"Oh God. Well, OK. But don't wake the baby."

"I won't. I called him while I was getting pops for everyone."

Will was a crazy fucker. And totally ridiculous. Pretty though. Long brown fingers and hair like wild horses. Always talking about how different he was from other Indians. He was from the Ogallala rez and living with a cousin of his, Megan, in an apartment complex at the edge of town. He was about to get into some serious shit with her though, on account of the fact the he hardly ever paid the rent, or any of the bills for that matter. I'd met Will one day when I was working at the Sugar Plum. He came in for some coffee and asked me what tribe I was and we got to talking.

We drove the rest of the way quiet. I took the Christian metal out of the deck and replaced it with "Smells Like Teen Spirit." I thought about my dad. I wondered just how drunk he'd be. I hoped he'd be asleep. Mom hated leaving the twins with him.

Jake parked my car in the drive and got out.

"Call Will's if you're in any trouble," he said, putting his hand on my arm. I nodded. Dad hated Jake because he'd defend me and Mom when Dad got mean. Jake got on his bike and it roared to life, and I watched him thunder off into the dark. I walked to the door of our small, shitty white house and stopped. I could hear Mom and Dad arguing inside. I hung my head, ran my hand through my hair. I opened the door.

"Jake's going to get her killed, Christine!"

I closed the door, put my bag down and thought about the fact that my tank was covered in blood.

"Is that you Margaritte?"

"Yeah."

"You come here right now!"

It was midnight. The twins were crying.

Mom was standing in the corner of the living room, glaring at Dad, a glass of scotch in Dad's hand, the bottle nearly empty on the old, wooden end stand next to the couch, the amber glow of it reflecting in the light. It was almost beautiful. He turned to me, his blue eyes red and bloodshot. "What have you done?" he asked, his head wavering slightly. He was sitting on the couch and the light from the TV lit up half of his face as he turned to look up at me. He stumbled over and I flinched.

"I will kill you if I find out that you're dealing drugs, Margaritte. Do you understand me?"

I glanced back at him, and then away. There was no right answer. I said nothing. His hand swung back, hit my face.

"Doug!" Mom said, rushing over to us. She pulled his large, white arm back. He threw her off. "You do not hit her!"

He turned to her with tears in his eyes. "She needs to learn! Your way, Christine, is to let her do anything. Anything! How could you let this happen?"

"Me? What about you? All you do is drink. Why do you think she does it?"

Dad blinked rapidly. "It's not the same," he said, sitting down on the couch and refilling his glass. "This could land her in jail. Or it could kill her. And you need to do something." He ran his hand through his thinning brown hair.

Mom sighed, a long, winding sigh that felt like a blow. "I don't know what to do." Mom turned to me. "You have to stop Margaritte. I can't imagine why you do this."

"Because I want out of here," I said. I was tired. And I was angry and they were so stupid. I just wanted to go into the basement and smoke and sleep and stop thinking.

Mom and Dad looked at me then. I could hear the TV in the silence, the sounds of the late night news filling the room, the voices of the newscasters, who always reminded me of mannequins talking calmly about death, money.

"Here's what's going to happen," Mom said. "You are not going to leave this house except for school. You are going to stay in that room and do your homework. And you," she said, turning to Dad. "You are going to put that goddamn scotch down." Mom grabbed for the glass in Dad's hand.

"Don't you tell me what to do!" Dad said, pulling his hand back, the scotch sloshing over the edge. "I'm fine! This isn't about me."

"The hell it isn't about you! You're an alcoholic Doug, and you need to put that glass down and go to sleep. I'll take care of this because God knows you can't take care of anything."

"You bitch," he said, his breath heavy.

Suddenly, he stood up and almost fell. Mom and I stepped back. He began charging for her. I walked in-between. I could hear the girls from their room as he hit me again, his fist connecting with the side of my face in the same place it had before. I started crying as Mom pushed him. He fell easily, quickly.

"Mommy!" It was Carrie. She sounded scared.

"Don't come out! Everything's fine!"

"Mommy!"

"Quiet, Carrie!" Mom yelled. Dad got up again and started for Mom.

"Stop! Stop!" I said, getting in between them again and holding my hands out to block him but he was huge. As tall as Jake, and 350 pounds. My mom was tiny in comparison, but she fought hard.

"Get out of my way," he growled and kept charging, pushing me to the side and somehow managing to hit my face yet again with his elbow in the process. It was my turn to hit the old, orange shag carpet. Mom and Dad wrestled and I buried my head in my arms and entered the highway, the fog filling my head and turning everything into light, silence. After a few minutes, I came out of my reverie and could see that they had stopped. Dad was heading for his office, where he had an old graphic design style desk and miles and miles of booze.

CHAPTER 2

The next day I woke up to the sounds of *Sesame Street.* It was the twin's favorite show. I sighed, looked at where the needle had been. They had put a Band-Aid over it, but I had pulled it off before I went to sleep, which had come quickly after I had read a few pages of the book I'd just checked out of the library, *Hyperion.* I fucking loved it. But I was too tired to read more than a page or two; there had been too much drama. I coughed and reached under my bed for my pipe and baggie, and sat up. I kept both taped to the bottom of the bed, and Jake and me kept the rest of it under an old plank in my bedroom that Mom and Dad didn't even know was loose.

I smoked. I listened. I wondered why Mom had married Dad. She had told me once that she'd gotten pregnant with me while she was finishing up her teacher's certification in Denver and after that, he proposed. But that she loved him. That she definitely loved him. She told me about watching Mel Brooks movies together and other artsy stuff like that, about dancing with him by the gulf on a pier in Texas, where her family was from, about how shy and quiet he was. How he held her and told her that she was his home on their wedding night. How he drank and though it seemed like he drank a lot, it hadn't seemed like too much until later, much later, when he began to hit her after I was born. I went to the bathroom to look at my face, my side. My face wasn't too bad, just a little bruised up. Nothing a little makeup couldn't cover. And my side was sore but it was nothing bad.

I put on the pink house shoes Mom had given me for Christmas and shuffled upstairs. I knew that Dad, unless he had called in sick, was at Bill's Auto where he worked. He called in sick a lot, and it was getting harder and harder to pay the bills. I tried to help out as much as Mom would let me. She paid most of them with her job at the elementary school, where she taught fifth grade English.

The twins were sitting in front of the TV and eating the brightly colored generic cereal that they loved. They sat too close to the damn thing, but it was old, and you had to turn the channels by hand. I fixed a bowl of cereal and sat down by Mom at the old wooden table that she had inherited from her parents when they died.

Mom was grading. It seemed like she was always grading. She looked up, smiled, her dark eyes full of exhaustion. She touched the bruise on my face with the back of her fingertips and I took her hand. We watched each other like that and then our hands dropped and I ate my cereal.

"Grading?" I asked.

"Yeah," she said.

"Margaritte—"

"Mom, c'mon. Not this early."

She looked at me angrily, straightening one of the many old, oversized t-shirts she used as nightgowns. "You didn't even wait to see what I was going to say."

"I know what you're going to say. Can't I just eat my stupid cereal in peace?"

"No! I… " She closed her eyes, sighed. "I mean, yes. Eat your goddamn cereal. But you are going listen to me."

I was silent.

"Just do your homework, go to school. And I will let Jake come over, of course, but you are not to go out with him or anyone else for a long, long time. Not until I see your report card at the end of this semester, and then I'll let you out only if you have more than passed every class. You're not stupid. I wish you were stupid. Then I could just give up."

I had stuffed half a bowl of cereal into my mouth by the time she was done.

"Are you finished?"

Mom expelled an angry puff of breath. "I guess."

"Look Mom, I do my homework, but with Dad drinking and you two yelling about it all the time—"

"How dare you!" She said, standing up and picking up my bowl. "I do the best that I can!"

I sputtered. "The best? The best? Look, I love Dad. Sometimes when he's not too drunk and not too sober he's pretty cool. We sit around and watch *NOVA* and it's nice, and he's funny and sweet and he asks me questions but that's not enough. I don't know why it's enough for you. And where are you going with my cereal? I'm not finished."

She set the cheap, blue Walmart bowl down—hard. So hard I thought the glass would shatter.

"Mom!"

"What."

"He's too messed up! This is too messed up. We can't live like this forever. Someday he's going to do something really fucked up."

"Don't say 'fucked,' Margaritte. And, well, look—what do

you want? You want to live in a shitty one-room apartment like some of your friends on the edge of town? You want to get on welfare? Is that what you want? And you know what? He was doing better before this little incident of yours."

I looked at her, shoved the rest of the soggy, cheap wheat cereal in my mouth, put the bowl in the sink and started washing dishes. I could feel Mom at my back.

"Mom, you always, always say that."

"Say what?"

"That he's doing better."

She was silent as I finished the dishes and when I turned around, she was sitting at the table with her head in her hands. I looked at her, wiped my hands on the dishtowel and set it down.

"I used to love him, you know," she said. She was looking at the pile of papers in front of her.

"Do you still?"

"Sometimes. Or, I'm not sure. Maybe I love the memory of what he was. Or maybe... I still love him when he's not... you know he does love you, in his way."

"I know."

I sat down and took her hand. "Mom, look, I think Jake and Treena and Julia are coming over. We're gonna do homework, I promise. Let's just forget this for now."

She nodded. She was too tired to fight me. And she liked Julia. She didn't like Treena, but if Julia was around, Treena came. They were a package deal. They always had the same orange home perms and Lee Press-On Nails with flowers and shit all over them, even though they were nothing alike. Julia's a thin, pretty, mixed-blood Choctaw and Chickasaw, Treena a short, round Mexican chick. Julia lives in a foster home and is crazy, parties all the time, but she makes great grades. She'll launch outta this shithole like a fucking rocket. She'd never met her dad, but she thought he was white. Sometimes her mom would come to visit her at the foster home. Her mom's a meth-head though, so most of the time it wasn't exactly a celebration when she came to visit. I mean, one of the last times she came to town, she brought Julia a feral cat as a gift. I mean, Christ. Treena on the other hand could care less about grades, or getting out. Her big thing was dudes. Especially dudes that Julia was into, which killed me. Crazy bitch would go to dances, bars with Julia and just follow her around waiting for one of the guys chasing after her to give up and move onto Treena.

"Just make sure they're gone by the time Dad comes home at five."

"OK."

I walked into the living room and sat down by the twins. They were so cute, their big, amber colored eyes fixed on the TV like it was God. Big Bird was up and he was their favorite.

"I just love Big Bird," Carrie said and Mary nodded.

"He's so friendly even though he's so big!" Carrie said, smiling. She watched in a small, satisfied silence for a few minutes but after a while, she began to frown. She turned to face me. "Margaritte, why were all of you guys yelling last night?" She put one of her small, yellow hands on my face and furrowed her brow.

"Because people are stupid," I said, patting her hand. "Stick to Big Bird."

"I do love him," she said, turning to the TV again. "But he's not real."

"Yeah he is!" Mary said. She usually let Carrie lead the way, but every once in a while she'd disagree.

"Nuh-uh! My teacher told me. He's not. I love him anyway."

I laughed. "You two are silly. You're the silliest six-year-olds I know."

Carrie looked at me incredulously. "No way. Sam's the silliest. He said that he wanted to live on a planet with only Sams on it. *That's* silly," she said, shaking her head.

"That is pretty silly," I said. We watched TV together for a while, *Sesame Street* ending and *Electric Company* coming on. I remembered watching these shows, in this order, when I was their age. I remembered Dad's mom visiting from New York and saying that there were too many ethnic people on the show just loud enough so that everyone could hear. I remembered my mom walking out of the room.

"OK, you two. Be good," I said. They had moved on to playing with their Barbies, Mary whispering in her ratty Beach Barbie's ear. She always did that. The freaking Barbie Whisperer, I swear.

I took a shower, got dressed, walked downstairs and picked up my homework. I knew that when everyone came over, we wouldn't work. I figured I might as well try to get something done. My grades were shitty, which was sad considering that the goddamn place graduated illiterates. But I just hated school. I read Stephen King under my desk in math. I was always getting caught.

A few hours later, Jake came ambling downstairs.

"You OK?" he asked, sitting down on the beat up, frankensteined futon across from my bed.

"Yeah. At least Dad went to work. How's Will?"

"Oh, I didn't see him. He and Megan had a fight over bills and he ran off before I even came in. She was up with the baby anyway, nursing."

"That guy," I said. Will was weird. All I really knew about him was that he was gay, but that he'd never admit it though he brought strange dudes over to spend the night all the time. He'd also said that his mother had been a drunk and his father had never been around. But Megan had it rough too. Single mother. You'd think Will would have a little sympathy for her but all he ever seemed to see in her was another person who owed him something. To look at the world like that seemed vast, empty.

"So... Julia and Treena are coming over. I talked to them Friday, at school," I said.

"Sounds cool," Jake said, trying to not look excited. Jake adored the ever-loving shit outta Julia, though he kept that to himself.

"Jake, are you gonna marry Julia?" I asked and Jake jumped up and put me in a headlock.

"Goddammit, Jake, let me go!"

"Take it back," he said, as my hair got caught under one of his pits and pulled as he twisted me around.

"Jake! Dude! You fucker! Ouch!"

"Take. It. Back!" he said.

"Never!" He gently twisted me around for a little bit more and then let me go. I adjusted my hair and my sweatshirt and gave him the evil eye. He looked at me with a guilty expression on his face then and asked, "I didn't hurt you did I? You've suffered enough physical shit for any kid your age for a while."

"I'm fine, Jake," I said, walking over to him and hugging him. "Now let's call your fiancé to see if she and her life partner are still coming over." Jake's eyes narrowed and he punched my arm.

I walked over to the phone, and made a big production of picking it up, dialing and then making out with it and looking over at Jake and winking before anyone picked up. *I hate you,* he mouthed and I laughed. Julia's foster mother answered on the third ring. Dumb bitch did nothing but sit on the couch, eat

Twinkies and Doritos and watch her five trillion foster kids run around and fend for themselves.

I talked to Julia for a minute or two and hung up.

"She and Treena are gonna come over when the *Real World* is over, which should be soon. They are totally addicted to it."

"What the fuck is the *Real World*?" Jake asked.

"Jealous of a show?"

"No. I just don't know what it is."

"It's some stupid MTV show where they take these people and make them live in a house and film them all the time. They made me watch it once. It's like a soap opera for people our age."

"Huh," Jake said, looking puzzled. All Jake really watched was sports, everything else to him was girlie shit.

Jake sighed and started up the stairs. "I'm gonna go get something to eat."

"Sure." I lifted the remote and stared at it limply.

I looked around and then turned to the old wooden table next to me. There were some magazines Jake had brought with him so I rifled through one of them for about twenty minutes before putting it down and sighing heavily. They were all motorcycle mags. Much as I liked riding the bike with Jake, reading about it interested me about as much as reading about turtles mating.

I leaned back and closed my eyes. After a couple of minutes, I could hear Jake on the stairs.

"Hope you brought something good," I yelled. I could hear Julia laughing, then saying, "I did." An unfamiliar male laugh followed hers. I sat up.

Julia came down first, and she was followed by a boy I'd never seen before, or at least didn't recognize. He was lanky, a little taller than me and quite a bit darker too, with long dark eyes and short, spiky black hair.

"Hi," I said. "I'm Margaritte."

"I'm Mike." He put his hand out and we shook. "You know, I've seen you around."

"Yeah?"

"Yeah. Reading in the stairwells outside."

"I do that," I said.

"Yes, you do," he said and laughed. I laughed too, though I felt like a jackass.

"So what do you like to read?"

"Stephen fucking King."

"Jesus, Margaritte," Julia said, looking at me. I shrugged and started sweating. I never did do that well with guys unless I was related to them or they were gay. Mike looked taken aback for a minute and then started laughing.

"Well, I read too. Though not Stephen fucking King."

"Well, what do you like to read?"

"Well… a lot. Though my favorites are Salinger and Carver," he said, running his hand through his hair.

"Anyway!" Julia said. "I'm in track with Mike and we started talking and so I told him he should hang with us. That is, if you don't drive him away."

"No, no," Mike said, "not at all." And he smiled, and I couldn't help but smile back. A few seconds later, I could hear Jake coming down the stairs, his giant, lanky frame making them creak loudly.

"I found some Doritos," he said, Treena behind him. She was rubbing her stomach, her eyes at horny half-mast, and looking up at him. I rolled my eyes. That girl's a fucking nutcake.

"You guys all met upstairs?" I asked and Jake nodded. He didn't look too happy about Mike, for obvious reasons.

"Mike runs track and just moved here from California," Julia said. She scooted closer to him on the futon they were sharing and Jake narrowed those big black eyes of his, his gaze hovering over Mike like a storm gathering.

I was sitting in an old rocking chair. Jake stopped staring at Mike and sighed, a heavy, wet, male sigh and fell into a shaggy, chewed up green and black La-Z-Boy that looked like it'd been through a meat grinder. We used to have a bunch of dogs, and that chair had been like a giant chew toy, as far as they'd been concerned. There was a ridiculous amount of old furniture downstairs. It was like a warehouse. My dad never got rid of shit, and my mom hated it. It was yet another part of their eternal, pathetic struggle.

Treena tried to wedge her body onto the armrest of the La-Z-Boy and Jake rolled his eyes and tried to scoot as far away from her yawning ass crack as possible. I looked over at Julia and Mike. She was laughing uproariously at something Mike had said. He had an amused, indulgent expression on his face. The thing was, guys loved Julia. She was cute but a lot of it was her charm, you know, that thing some chicks have that dudes just find really fucking irresistible.

"How you liking Idaho Springs?" Jake asked Mike. Jake was leaning back into the La-Z-Boy, trying his goddamndest to look cool. It wasn't working.

"I like it a lot, so far. Colorado's pretty. I like to ski and hike so I'm really glad to see those mountains."

Jake nodded. "You know, I've thought about track, but I've always been really into my bike. That and... other stuff."

"Really?" Mike said. "Actually, I like to bike too, we should bike together sometime."

"Sure." Jake reached into the bag of Doritos with one of his humungous hands, scooped out a huge fistful and then started eating that pile with his other hand. "How many pounds is your bike?"

"I don't know... fifteen?"

"Fifteen?"

Julia broke into amused laughter.

"What?" Jake asked.

"Jake is talking about motorcycles—and Mike about like, you know, bikes—like bicycles."

"Now I feel like a twelve year old," Mike said.

"No, no, bro. It's cool, it's cool. Nothing wrong with that." Jake started stuffing more chips into his mouth from the bag. I could tell he felt bad.

I looked over at Mike again. He was so little and cute compared to my big, burly, motorcycle-riding cousin. Jake finished his pile of chips, wiped his hands on the legs of his ancient looking black jeans and smiled.

Mike laughed again but he looked uneasy. I figured this was probably the last he'd hang with us. He was too... clean.

"Well, I like to bike. I can't afford anything else," Julia said and looked over at Mike meaningfully. I figured they'd set a date right then and there, to bike and fuck to their hearts' content until Mike joined the upper social ranks, but he just looked over at the TV uneasily and ran his hand through his hair.

"Yeah... definitely. Biking is cool. Well, I like it. It gives me time to be alone, away from my friends, my family and just, you know, sift through things," Mike said, looking over at me.

I nodded.

"You know what I mean?"

"I do."

Julia sighed. "I'll be upstairs." She got up. Treena followed her.

Mike looked over at me and shifted a little. "So, ever thought about reading anything other than Stephen fucking King?"

"I sure fucking have."

"Well... I propose a trade."

"A trade?"

"Yes. I'll give you a copy of my favorite book, and you give me a copy of yours."

"OK," I said, and pulled a copy of *Different Seasons* off of my bookshelf. I handed it to him and he looked at it and put it in his backpack, pulling out a copy of a white book with a rainbow on the front. I set it down on the end table and looked at Mike thoughtfully. I'd screwed around with a few guys here and there, but nothing serious. There had been this one guy about a year back that I'd liked but he'd turned out to be lame as fuck. I'd met him at one of Julia's friend's parties. I started talking to him 'cause he was somebody's cousin and he seemed OK. He was this short, lanky Navajo guy who kept saying, "Ya'at'eeh billyganna!" every time a white chick would come up to talk to us, and I would laugh like crazy. But he was also cynical as hell about being Native—didn't buy any of that cheesy new age shit that so many Natives buy into. Also, he said he liked art. So, we sat in a corner drinking and talking and then he asked if he could kiss me. I figured I'd give it a whirl. It was OK. Then he asked for my phone number and I gave it to him. He said he would be around for the week. We hung out a little, but every time we hung with guys, he wouldn't really look at me and wouldn't laugh at my jokes. So I'd pretty much given up on him when he calls this one night, says he thinks I'm a really cool girl and asks if I want to come over. And, because I'm fucking retarded, I say sure. We end up at the house where he's staying, getting drunk and fucking, his wide purple-brown face sweating over me for all of five shitty minutes. Then he fell asleep right after, so I left. And I never heard from him again. And I was totally paranoid that I had gotten pregnant for forever.

"What are you guys up to tonight?" Mike asked, leaning back and putting his slender brown arms behind his head. He looked at me curiously, coolly. It was my turn to look at the TV, although it was off, devoid of any distracting, dreamlike images. There was something different about him. He was mullet-less, for starters. But it was more than that, more than the obvious fact that his family had money. He was like a pool of water at night, reflecting only silver, some kind of mysterious, angry life beneath.

"Well… " I said, looking at Jake. "I'm grounded but that's never stopped me from fucking my life up before."

"Really?" Mike asked, and Jake laughed.

"What are you grounded for?"

"Well, I did get stabbed yesterday." I lifted my sweatshirt and tank enough so that he could see the wound, the stitches. I had taken the bandage off earlier. He looked at it, and though I thought perhaps he would be shocked, would make some sort of pronouncement, he stepped closer and brushed it gently with his fingertips, fascinated. I shivered.

"Hmmm," he said. He had noticed my shiver, and his fingertips had lingered because of it. He looked at me and sat back. I could see that his eyes were even darker and more slanted than my own.

"And how did you get that?"

I looked over at Jake. He looked uneasy.

"Well, there was a meth-head. He didn't like the looks of me so much," I said.

"I'm getting the feeling that you might be the right person to ask this question."

"What question?" I asked.

"I've been meaning to ask someone who I could buy weed from."

I laughed. "You're looking at her."

"I thought as much," he said.

"Now what would make you say that?" I asked playfully, reaching for the bag of Doritos. I scooped a few into my hands and offered him the bag. He shook his head, laughed.

"You know, you should take me with you when you make sales."

I looked at him cynically, assuming for a moment that it was some sort of masculine gesture but realized quickly that it was not.

"Oh yeah? Why should I?"

"Well, it sounds like you lead a hip and dangerous life," he said, and looked at me with his head slightly cocked to the right.

"Indeed I do."

"So, why'd your parents want to move here?" Jake asked.

Mike sighed. "Well, I think they were sick of California, of the suburbs in L.A. And my dad works for this big engineering company, and they said that they would transfer him to Denver, if he wanted. And he said yes, because he knew he could live someplace like here and commute. My dad's from Montana. His parents were ranchers and I think he misses that, though he always talks about how boring it was for him, growing up."

"Well, unless you're into meth or having sex with people you're related to, you'll find shit's pretty boring here. How do you think I got into my hip and dangerous lifestyle in the first place?"

"Well, I'll just have to get into meth. I've heard it's really good for your teeth."

I laughed. "Oh yeah, it's delicious and nutritious. They should put it in cereal."

"I'm just going to stick to good old-fashioned marijuana," Jake said.

"Well, I have to get home, but, tonight?" Mike asked.

I looked at Jake. "Well, we were thinking about doing something fun tonight. Something a little different."

Mike looked interested. "What time?"

"Midnight OK for you?"

Mike stood up and I reached for a pen and paper so that I could write the address down. I finished and handed it to him, his fingers lingering on mine.

He looked down at the piece of paper and then tucked it into his back pocket. "Cool. Well, I wish I could stick around and just go with you but, uh, my mother is a little... well, let's go with, uh, high maintenance?" Mike said, laughing.

"Sure," I said, though I was thinking that was a little weird.

"See you," Jake said and we watched him go up the stairs.

A few minutes later, after Jake and I had turned the TV on again and had flipped through practically all of the channels, Julia came down the stairs with Treena in tow. Treena was looking grumpy, as usual. Jake turned the TV off.

"So, Mike left." Julia said, sitting down on the futon, Treena sitting down next to her, staring at the TV and not saying a word. She thrust her hand into the bag of Doritos, pulled as many chips as she could in one go, and started crunching loudly, staring over at Jake like he was an episode of *The Real World.* Jake looked uncomfortable since Treena was known for getting drunk and aggressive with the dude nearest. Jake had been the nearest dude on multiple occasions. And she was downright fucking creepy about it. She'd always get this look in her eyes, start rubbing her belly and saying shit like, *Yeah, I can fuck the shit out of a guy, if I want to.*

"He said he had to get home."

"Oh." Julia leaned back. "Well, he was kind of weird anyway." She moved the bag of Doritos closer to her and took a few. Treena eyed the bag and as soon as Julia was done, moved it closer to her again and started eating, pulling one handful out of the bag after another.

"What do you mean?" I asked.

"Yeah, he seemed like a pretty cool guy to me," Jake said, looking over at Julia and grabbing one of the bags of chips and sitting down with it.

"Well, like all of that reading, I mean… I read for school, but he reads for fun," she said, looking over in my direction. "Well, I mean, he reads school stuff for fun, not like you, Margaritte. You read Stephen King, that's actually fun."

"Yeah, I guess," I said. "Well, what tribe is he?"

"The hot tribe," Treena said, between crunching.

"You were over at the coffee shop with both of them?" I asked.

"Yeah, I was there when Julia was hitting on him."

"I was not!"

"Yeah, right."

"OK, you're right, I was. Then you up and disappeared," Julia said, running her hands through her thick, chestnut brown hair. She had beautiful hair, highlighted by a friend of hers who used to live in one of the foster homes with her.

"But you met him through track?" I asked Julia. She was looking out the window, her wide, slanted eyes cloudy.

"What? Oh. Yeah. But then we saw him at Java Mountain Roasters today," she said, and I nodded. I pictured it, the one downtown that had been newly renovated. It had been a grungy thrift store, one that smelled of old, wet, moldy wood and suddenly it had become a wooden bar and metal ceiling masterpiece. I was sure the tourists practically came all over themselves when they saw it was there on their way home.

"Well, I figured you wanted to be alone with him," Treena said, sniffing and slouching. I shook my head.

"Like I was gonna fuck him right there!"

"Well, I don't know," Treena said grumpily, shoving more chips in her mouth.

"Anyway, he's some kinda Colombian tribe," Julia said and then sat back, looking thoughtful. She put one of her slender, silver ringed fingers up to her lip and rubbed it thoughtfully. "And he said something odd."

"What?" I asked.

"Well... he said, some people think I'm white," she said, putting her hand in her lap.

"Oh, yeah, I remember that," Treena said, laughing. "That was dumb. I mean, I'm part Indian, but he's like, gotta be almost completely."

"He said some people think he's white?" Jake asked.

"What, blind people?" I said, incredulous.

"No joke. I mean, you and me can pass for Italian, but him, no way," Julia said.

"That's just some dumb shit his parents probably laid on him," I said.

"Yeah. That's what I thought, too. In any case, he likes you, Margaritte."

"Maybe," I said, wiggling my eyebrows.

"He's totally got the hots for you cuz, you betta watch it," Jake said happily, making one of his goofy, faux-sophisticated facial expressions.

Julia looked over at me. "You bitch!"

"What?"

"You stole my man! I should kick you in your ass!"

"Do it," I said, stoically. "Then, like, tear my hair out."

"I will!" she said, laughing. "Watch your back, hooker."

"I could take you. Besides, you have a boyfriend, idn't it?" Julia was crazy that way. She always had one dude signed on for life, or at least a year, and four dudes playing backup, in case player #1 had to be cut.

"Yeah," she said, sighing and looking over at the TV, its blackness and the faint light coming from the windows creating a mirror. She looked at her own reflection cynically, then back over at me.

I shook my head. I admired Julia, I really did. She didn't take any shit seriously; boys, this town, anything. It was all about getting out. But I wasn't like her. I told her about our plans for the night and she and Treena got up and left, Julia telling us that if she was going to party, she needed to study. Jake left soon after. I worried about him.

The thing was, Jake stole cars. He never sold them, but he loved to joyride. He was lucky that he was seventeen, for the next few months anyway, or his ass would already be in jail instead of just the brief stints he did at juvie. The other shit he did was break into buildings at night, sometimes with other guys, sometimes alone, and sometimes with me. In fact, that's what we were thinking about after we'd sold some weed, after I'd crawled out of my window like I always did, once everything was nice and dark and quiet on the streets. Jake had been eyeing an old, abandoned apartment complex that someone had told him was haunted, one that was on the edge of town. He wanted to see what was inside and he'd called a bunch of friends and told them we should party there. Jake always wanted to know what was inside of things, but he was never prepared for the consequences once he found out.

I lay on my bed, thinking about Mike. After a while, I got up, the bedsprings squeaking, and walked upstairs to help Mom with dinner. She was already in the kitchen. I walked in and leaned against the wall, her back to me. She was at the sink.

"Hi Mom."

"Hi."

"Mom! Look! Look!" Carrie was yelling, trying to get Mom to look at her drawing. She was standing at her leg, pulling on her pants urgently.

"Carrie, I told you later!" Mom looked down at her and she stomped her feet angrily. Mom looked over at me. "Dinner's almost done," she said. "Could you take over? I gotta go to the bathroom." Her curls were in a massive state of disarray.

"Sure," I said, walking up to the counter.

By the time she came back, the spaghetti was almost done. Mary ran over and started clinging to her, her Barbie plastered into the hand that was wrapped around her leg. Carrie was sitting on the floor, drawing in the corner of the kitchen, holding her Barbie by her upturned arms and singing something about bears.

Mary was crying. "Margaritte, do something about this," Mom said without turning around. I sighed and walked over to Mary and pulled her off of Mom's leg. She screamed and cried and finally buried her head into my chest. I patted her head and set her down.

"They need a bath. There's just enough time to give them one before I'm finished making dinner."

"Nooooooo!" Carrie wailed. She hated baths.

"You let your sister bathe you!" Mom yelled.

"But I ain't dirty!" Carrie said, and Mary shook her head, walking up to Mom and re-attaching herself to Mom's leg.

"Yes, you are! And no more fussing!"

I plucked Mary off of Mom's leg which was quite a feat, considering that she was doing her damnedest to stay attached to Mom like she had suckers growing out of her dirty little paws, picked Carrie up and dragged them into the bathroom, which kind of made my side hurt. Mary dropped from me halfway there, but as she usually went wherever Carrie was going, she began following me.

I let Carrie down once Mary had gotten past the bathroom door, and then shut and locked it before Carrie could run up to it and out, which she tried anyway.

"No!" I said, and began taking off her clothes while she wailed and screamed. "Stop scratching me!" Once I'd gotten her clothes off, I turned to Mary and got hers off. I went over to the old green tub and started running the water, testing it to make sure it wasn't too hot. I placed Mary in the tub and turned to Carrie, who was sitting on the toilet, crying.

"Carrie, c'mon, not this again, hey?"

"Have to pee, Margaritte! Have to pee!" She did this every time. It killed me.

"No you don't, Carrie. I'm not falling for it this time," I said, laughing a little. I waited a few seconds to make sure she didn't have to pee for real, and then peeled her off of the toilet and set her crying and scratching into the tub. Sometimes she tried bolting, but this time, she just turned her head up to the ceiling and wailed. Mary looked at her curiously for a minute and then turned to her Barbie and started whispering into its ear.

I located Carrie's Barbie, which miraculously had been

dragged in with her and dropped it into the tub. Carrie cried for a few more minutes and then looked over at her Barbie, angrily at me, sniffed a few times, and then started washing her Barbie with bathwater. I washed them while they played with their Barbies, and then pulled them out, dried them and took them over to their bedroom and got them into their pajamas.

I got the twins at the table, their Barbies in front of them, and then set the table with silverware and napkins. I asked Mom if there was anything else I could do.

"Nope. It's almost done."

"Cool," I said, and sat down.

I could hear the door open and close. We tensed.

"Hi girls!" we heard from the living room and we relaxed. He was in a good mood. Dad came into the kitchen, up to Mom and then kissed her on the cheek.

"Smells good. I stopped over at the grocery store for some bread." He set a few paper bags down on the counter. He began pulling items out, including the bread, and a large bottle of scotch. He set the scotch down on the table, opened a cabinet door and pulled a glass out. He poured himself a good amount, and sat down at the table with it.

Carrie looked over at the brown liquid and then up at Dad. "Can I have some?"

"Maybe someday," he said, laughing. I said a silent prayer that that day would never come for either one of the twins. I wondered if he was gonna start in on me about last night, but he just sipped at his scotch and poured himself another once the first was done. I walked over to the bread, pulled it out of the paper sleeve and began cutting it into slices. I buttered the slices and then placed them on a metal tray, turned the oven on and set the tray into it. I went downstairs to read while the bread was baking. When I came back up, Dad was already somehow on his third scotch and looking over at the twins.

"They sure do love those Barbies."

"No joke," I said, "they're freaking in love with them." He laughed loudly, too loudly, and Mary joined in. She loved to laugh, even if she didn't know what anybody was laughing about.

"Your Barbies don't have any hair," Dad said and I closed my eyes.

"That's Mary's fault!" Carrie yelled.

"No, it's Carrie's fault!" Mary yelled back.

"It's both of their faults," I said. "Well, Carrie gave her own Barbie a haircut today, this morning actually, before Mom took them to daycare, and then decided to give Mary's Barbie a haircut too. But only because Mary kept making fun of Carrie's Barbie."

"Nuh-uh!" Mary said. She began whispering in her Barbie's ear.

"Girls," Dad said, slurring, "you have to be good to each other."

"I am good!" Carrie said.

"No, no. You really really have to be good to each other. When I was a kid, my sister wasn't very nice to me and now well, now I hardly see her. Though that's not because I hate her, it's because she's so far away."

I could practically feel Mom rolling her eyes, but the twins just looked at him like he was making sense. They were used to his drunken rambling by now. Most of the time they would stare at him for a few seconds and then return to playing with their Barbies. Their favorite game was Barbie's been captured by a mean guy who wants to kiss her and Ken has to rescue her. Though it was somewhat funky-looking, now that both of their Barbies were completely bald.

"How is Kimberly?" Mom asked, stirring the pot of spaghetti.

"Good, I guess," Dad said, shrugging and pouring himself another scotch.

"Doug... you've had enough, idn't it?" She hadn't even turned around. She had a sixth sense for it.

"No." I could feel his anger rising. "And don't you tell me what to do, Christine."

"You can be a real jerk," she said.

"And you can be a real bitch," he said. She went silent and Dad walked into the living room to turn the TV on, returning quickly to the kitchen to sit down at the table. When the spaghetti was done, Mom poured it into the strainer, back into the pot, took the jar of sauce and poured it into the pot and stirred. She set the whole thing down on the table and I went to retrieve the bread from the oven.

We all sat down and ate in silence, Dad drinking scotch after scotch and finally retiring to the living room, to watch the *MacNeil/Lehrer NewsHour*, which he loved. The TV had already been on all through dinner, and we had learned to be quiet while Dad watched.

After a while, he called the twins to him. He would sit them on his lap almost every night and read them a bedtime story, one apiece. That was the thing about Dad. He occasionally did terrifyingly redeemable things.

After he was done reading to them, I put them to bed and then went into my parent's bedroom to say goodnight to Mom.

"Did you do your homework?" She was flipping through channels, finally settling on *Quincy*.

"Yes," I lied.

"Good."

I got up. "Mom?"

"Yeah?"

"What was it like when you first met Dad?"

Mom muted the TV, put the remote down. "Wonderful. He was always buying me little things. He wanted to know what I thought. We talked all the time."

"Oh."

"Margaritte, come here," she said, opening her arms. I came over, leaned down. She patted me on the back. "I love your Dad. But he drinks. That's what's wrong with him. I can't make him stop. And I got pregnant before I was old enough to understand that."

She held me for a while and then I stood up.

"Goodnight," I said.

"'Night," she said, and turned the sound on again.

I walked downstairs and turned on the TV. I was ready to go out, I had to go. I loved Mom, but I just couldn't be in that house, with Mom and Dad, with the twins, with the stupidity of it, the futility all around me. Futility. I had just learned that word in school.

CHAPTER 3

Around 11:30 I climbed out the window. I drove over to Will's, making sure to keep the headlights off until I was a few minutes away from the house. It was a short drive and a few minutes later, I was parking in the lot outside of the complex Will and Megan called home. I walked up the steps that led to their apartment and I could see Jake outside, smoking, sitting on the balcony of the complex. I sat down next to him. He handed me a smoke.

"How was the old guy tonight?"

"Drunk."

"Yeah," he said. "Will's still gone. Megan's asleep."

"God, Will's such a fuck up," I said.

"I know."

"Man, I don't want to go to school Monday, I really don't," I said. Jake had been drinking a beer and I picked it up and took a long swallow.

"Tell me about it."

I did pretty bad in school, but Jake, he was failing. The whole thing felt like a setup half the time. Most of the kids who went to school in Idaho Springs went on to the Army, or straight into working at Walmart, or waiting tables at the Derby or some career in dental assistantship or some shit like that. And those things were fine, I guess. But it really blew my mind how few went on to much else. I looked into the distance, the lights of the houses dotting the mountainside across from us.

"Fuck it. That's not for a few days," I said, picking Jake's beer up again and drinking the rest of it in one hard swallow that made the back of my throat burn. We smoked for another minute or two, threw the butts over the side and got up, ready to head over to the abandoned complex. Jake went back inside to throw the beer can away and came back out, closing the door softly. We walked down the stairs and at the bottom, Jake stopped. He turned to me and smiled, pulling a bunch of bottles of cheap liquor out of his bag.

"Yeah," I said, and he placed them back in the bag. Jake stole shit from the liquor stores all the time. He was smooth. He knew how to manipulate people into feeling guilty for staring at him. And when they'd look away, he was quick. His hands were nimble, delicate, like when he was drawing his black and whites.

We walked for a few blocks, and when we reached the abandoned complex, we could see that there was faint light inside and noise.

"I guess the party's started without us," I said.

We walked to the side of the building facing the highway, where a window had been propped open with an old plank of wood. Jake stared up at the building thoughtfully, most of the windows and all of the doors boarded up except for the one that had been cleared, the one that was propped open. The windows looked like cartoons with violent Xs for eyes and the entrance had a sign stating, *No Trespassing. By order of the Police.*

"Fuck those guys," Jake muttered, standing straight as an arrow. It wasn't far from a couple of old houses that looked as if they too should've been abandoned years and years ago.

They weren't. I knew, because I went to school with kids who lived in them. In fact, I'd been best friends with a girl who lived in one, in junior high. Her house was filled with faded candy bar and fast food wrappers, commodity food cans, toys and children who were either running around wild or completely ignoring each other. We had sat in her room playing with Barbies from another era, one of them with a button on her back that once depressed, made her faded eye wink. Something about that always made me sad, but it was her favorite, and she used to make it wink, over and over at her Ken doll who was missing a leg.

Jake climbed inside first and then helped me in. There were about fifteen people standing around the living room laughing and drinking. They had lit candles, which gave the place a strange, eerie glow. The walls were covered in old, yellowing wallpaper that was peeling off in large sheets, exposing rotting walls underneath sticky with beige glue. Kids had spray painted everywhere: gang shit, random shit, Betty loves Bob kind of shit. It was as if Idaho Springs had some sort of collective poetry, and it was all over the walls of this abandoned complex. There was a rotting, orange chair in one of the corners of the room, and a couch, and toys and other random objects scattered around. Jake went over to the counter and pulled the bottles of booze out and set them down. He had even brought plastic cups.

"Someone's prepared," I said.

"That's me," he said, pouring vodka into two cups. He handed me one and we clinked our plastic together and drank.

I looked down at the booze and up at Jake. "Tell me I'm not like my dad."

Jake rolled his eyes. "You're not like your dad."

I nodded. We joined a group of guys Jake and me knew from dealing and talked for a while. I got another drink after the first.

I felt a tap at my shoulder and turned around. It was Julia, with Treena and Mike behind her. I smiled at him and he smiled back.

"Hey girl," Julia said. "We were walking over here and ran into this guy," she said, pointing at Mike.

He walked up to me. "Well, I was in my car and saw them walking. So, I stopped and picked them up."

"Drink?" I asked, and we made our way into the kitchen. I poured.

"This place smells like a million bums took a giant fucking dump," Treena said.

"So your gift is subtlety," Mike said, and I laughed.

"What you call me?" Treena said.

"I said you have a way with words."

Treena was silent after that, though I was sure that if I could see her face, it would carry her usual grumpy fucking expression. I wasn't sure if I'd ever seen her smile, though I couldn't blame her. She shared a trailer with her mom, and about four more kids. And it was a small trailer. And she took care of the kids while her mom worked at the gas station down the street.

We left the kitchen and went into the living room.

"What about the rest of this place?" Mike asked.

"I'm sure it's as tastefully decorated as the living room," I said.

"Let's check it out," Mike said and I nodded. I picked up a candle that was sitting in an old cup, and we walked into a bedroom, Julia and Treena following. The only thing left was part of an old wooden bed frame. Something was drawn on the wall above it, some really interesting graffiti. It was intricate, it had dimension. I couldn't quite make out what it was. At first it looked like it was a fancy rendering of a gang name, but there was more to it, I could tell. I walked closer.

"What is this?" I asked. I looked at it for a while, but I couldn't make it out. "I'm getting Jake. He draws," I said, and walked into the living room. He was passing a joint around. "Come and take a look at this."

"OK," he said, and followed me into the bedroom. I pointed to the wall.

"Huh," he said, looking at it as closely as he could.

"It's a couple. A couple having sex... in space," Mike said. I started. I'd been so absorbed in trying to figure out what it was that I hadn't realized that he had walked behind me. I looked again. "Really?"

"Yeah. Well, look—here's her face, here's his. And that's where they're joined," he said, laughing a little sophisticated laugh and putting his hand up to my back in the dark. I shivered. "Ah."

Julia and Treena came over to see.

"Shiiiiit," Treena said, "goddamn, they're fucking."

"Like I said, way with words," Mike said.

"Why waste all this?" Julia asked.

"What do you mean?" Mike said.

"Well, who the hell else is going to see this, besides us and a couple of bums and maybe a few drunken partygoers?"

"No joke," Jake said. "I love to draw, and I'm fucking good at it. But I'd be goddamned if I'd waste my talent on this shithole."

"Don't you get it?" Mike asked, and I could hear him shaking his head, the swish of his neck on his puffy North Face jacket.

"What don't we get?" Treena said.

"They did it for the love of it."

We all stared for a while, and then Jake suggested we sit down and smoke some weed.

"I'll do that for the love of it," Julia said, and Mike and Jake laughed.

I went into the kitchen and grabbed a bottle of vodka and we sat in a circle in the bedroom and passed the joint around and talked, and there was something about all of us sitting there that just seemed temporary, weird. Transitory. That was another word I'd just learned. Yes, transitory. That was how it felt. But I couldn't figure it out. Why I felt that way. The candle was in the middle of our circle, pointing up at the weathered, cracked ceiling and creating all kinds of creepy shadows and I wondered about the people who'd lived there. The lives they'd lived in these terrible, rotting apartments. Their children. Where they were now. It didn't matter. The joint came around to me, and I took a hit, and held it in, and blew the smoke out into the cold air, not knowing where the smoke ended and my breath began.

"So Mike, what do you think about our all-star track team?" Julia asked.

"It's not bad."

Julia looked at him thoughtfully and Treena began rubbing her stomach. "Not bad for a hick little mountain town," Julia said.

"Well, it's harder to run when you're pregnant," I said, and Mike laughed.

"Yes, especially when it comes to the hurdles. Even getting one person over them is a challenge. When you're jumping for two, well, that's a real challenge."

"Maybe they should have a special category for that."

"Oh, totally," I said, the bottle of vodka coming around. "It could give new meaning to the term endurance."

"What are you two fucking even talking about?" Treena said, mid-rub. "Who's pregnant?"

Mike and I looked at each other and laughed. "No one Treena," Julia said. "Have some vodka." Treena looked at Mike and then at Julia and then pulled the bottle out of Julia's hand roughly, and took a long swig, staring at Mike the whole time.

"It's something to do here," Julia said. "Track, I mean—not getting pregnant. Although that's something to do here too."

"Well, I want a baby," Treena said. "Not that I'm pregnant right now or anything."

"Not drinking for two?" I asked her.

"Fuck you Margaritte. You think you're so funny," she said.

"Sorry," I said, not meaning it.

"Why aren't you in track?" Mike asked me.

"I'm not exactly the sporty type."

"Well, but it keeps you in shape," Julia said, looking at me and rubbing her lean, muscular leg. "And it's not like it's football, Margaritte. I don't consider myself a jock of any sort. It's a totally different thing. It's more like tennis, or skiing. But it's just your body. And time. And well, I can afford it, because it is just your body, there really isn't much in the way of equipment to buy."

"Yeah," Mike said. It was my turn to swig moodily at the bottle of vodka as they talked about running, and how fucking awesome it was. I looked over at Jake and he was rolling his eyes.

"Julia, where's your boyfriend?" I asked.

"I don't know. Probably hanging with all of his football buddies," she said, drinking from the bottle. I'd met her boyfriend a few times at different parties. He was a football player, and a real moron in my opinion. But that meant that it was easier for Julia to screw around on the side. The poor meaty fucker seemed to adore her.

One of Jake's friends came in and asked what we were doing in there and Jake told him about the drawing. A handful of people came in to look at it, and we cleared out.

I noticed that the party had gotten bigger, much bigger.

"Hey," Mike said, catching my hand.

"Yeah?"

"Want to take a bottle of something and a candle and check out more of the rooms?" He asked, smiling.

"Sure." I walked into the kitchen, grabbed a half-empty bottle of vodka and went back over to Mike. As we walked away, I looked over at Julia. She had joined a group of people after we'd left the bedroom. She was watching us. I smiled uneasily at her. She smiled back.

We walked into the second bedroom, but there was nothing in there. No old furniture or toys, so we walked out again and into the living room, where things were thundering.

"Let's try another apartment," Mike said.

"OK," I answered and we walked through the growing throng of people and out the door. In the hallway, we could see that the door to the apartment beside the one where we were partying was wide open. I shrugged and Mike took my hand, leading me inside. There was an old couch in there, by a window. We walked over to it; putting our jackets down onto the couch, dust billowing up and into the air as we sat. I looked around. The windows in this apartment were all broken out, pieces of glass on the floor everywhere, including the window above us. Cold air was rushing in and I shivered.

"Don't these kinds of places make you feel lonely?" Mike asked.

"Yeah," I said, taking a swig from the bottle we'd brought and grimacing. I handed it to Mike and he did the same and then set the bottle down on the floor.

"This whole town makes me feel lonely."

"Hmmm."

He stood up and looked out of the window. "I feel like that a lot, though."

"Me too."

"I've never said that to anyone," he said, looking at me with a puzzled expression on his face.

"What?"

"That things make me feel lonely," he said, sitting back down.

We were silent for a while, trading the bottle back and forth.

"I think we think too much," I said and he laughed. "You know what I think about? The toys."

"Toys?"

"Yeah, look at all of the toys in the apartment we were just in. How many kids lived in these awful apartments. You know, this wasn't abandoned when I was a kid. There were people living here. And it wasn't in much better shape than it is now."

Mike nodded. "I guess I forget how lucky I have it," he said, looking down at his shoes.

"Me too. Well, at least better than these people had it."

"Yeah?"

"My parents struggle. But my mom teaches at the elementary school and my dad, he's a mechanic. But he drinks."

"Don't we all," he said. "My parents drink. My mom drinks merlot. Only merlot. A lot of merlot. My dad drinks only single malt scotch. Alone. In his office. Which is maybe why my mother drinks."

I looked at him curiously. “What does your mom do?”

“My dad makes enough, so she doesn’t have to work. She goes to church. That’s her thing. Not mine. I told her a few years back that I wasn’t going to go with her anymore. My dad doesn’t. Why should I have to?”

“And you’re an only child?”

“Yeah… I was adopted when I was two months old. From Colombia.” He picked the bottle up from the floor, looked at it thoughtfully and took a quick drink, wiping his mouth after.

“Ah. Yes. I think Julia said something about that.”

Mike looked uneasy.

“What?”

“She asked what tribe I was.”

“Well, you look Indian,” I said.

“Huh. I guess I’ve… never given it much thought,” he said, drinking and shifting uncomfortably on the couch, particles of dust coming up and reflecting in the candlelight.

“You know, Jake was adopted.”

“Ohhh,” Mike said, “that makes sense.”

“People are always curious about him. They never believe he’s my cousin. They always think he’s my boyfriend. Then they get worried for me.”

“Nice,” Mike said sarcastically.

“Yeah.”

“People are fucking stupid sometimes.”

“They really are.”

“So, Jake said something about Native American Church. That his parents and your mom used to go there, but they don’t anymore. In California, I remember meeting a couple of Indians at a party once that talked about it. Do you go?”

“When I can. There’s one in Denver and I took Julia to it

once. She seemed to like it. I don't know. It's not like other churches. At least not to me."

"How's that?"

"Well, it's not so much about some God in the sky, looking to punish you and shit. More about this life."

Mike looked thoughtful. "I like that."

"Me too."

"But my dad doesn't like it when we go, or when we go to powwow." I looked down at the bottle and picked up it up, drank. Set it back down again.

"Why?"

"Don't know for sure. I guess he feels threatened or something."

Mike looked confused. "Your dad is white?"

"Yeah."

Mike looked at me thoughtfully. "Is that how you got that?" he asked, brushing my bruise lightly with his hand.

"Yeah. Sometimes he gets mean when he gets drunk. But to be fair, I had just come back from the hospital after a deal gone wrong. You know, the thing with the meth-head. My parents know Jake and me deal. I can understand why they don't want me to do that. But we want to get out of here when I turn eighteen, and we make pretty good money dealing. I've got a savings account." I laughed cynically, the sound of it echoing a bit in the dark, nearly empty room.

"What?"

"My mom set it up for me. When I was twelve. For college."

"College," he said in a funny, bitter way.

"You don't want to go?"

He sighed heavily and looked out into the room, his eyes cloudy. "Well, I know my parents want me to go. They think college is the answer to everything. They want me to be like them."

"What do you want?"

He was silent for a while, drinking from the bottle. "Do you have a cigarette?" he asked, and I pulled one out of my pack. He lit it.

"I'm surprised you smoke, track guy," I said, lighting one for myself.

"Sometimes."

"What do you want?" he asked me.

"You first."

"Well, maybe to travel. Maybe to South America. To... not be like them. My parents I mean."

"Yeah. That's what I want too. My mom got pregnant with me and well, then she had to stay with my dad. Fuck, that's what half the dumb broads in this town did. Now they're like, in prison. Serving life sentences."

"Jesus."

"Yeah."

He was silent again for a while, smoking.

"Well, I want to have kids. I mean, I don't have really anything of my own. Not that I don't love my parents, I do." He stopped again. "Well, I think I do." He shook his head and smiled at me uneasily. "I don't know. I don't know what I want."

"You know what I want?"

"What's that?"

"Rainbows and ponies."

He laughed.

"That may not be a reasonable goal. That's how my dad would put it."

“Yeah, I’m sure my dad would put it the same way.”

He put his cigarette out on the floor. He had only taken a few puffs, so it was long, crooked. He brushed it out of the way with his foot, dirtying what was clearly one hell of an expensive sneaker.

“Well, I’m sorry your dad does that. Hits you. If you ever need help...”

“Are you going to beat my daddy up for me?” I asked. I wanted it to sound playful but I could tell that what I felt underneath was bubbling up. A vulnerability.

“Maybe,” he said, taking my cigarette from my hand and putting it out next to where he’d put his out on the floor. He brushed it out of the way the same way he had his own. He looked at me and I resisted the urge to look away, down. He pulled my hair back from my face.

“No one should hit someone with a face like yours.”

“No one should hit someone with a face.”

“You’re funny,” he said, “and beautiful.”

“Just kiss my face,” I said and he leaned over carefully, slowly and kissed me. He was soft, gentle, and yet I could feel my heart hammering hard against his and his hand snaking up and around my waist.

“Where have you guys been?” It was Julia, with Treena right behind her. “Oh, sorry,” she said, watching us as we broke. “But someone brought a stereo. And they’re playing music. And dancing. And I thought you might want to dance.”

I shrugged. “Sure,” I said. “Dance?”

“Dance,” Mike said, and we got up and followed Julia and Treena back. Folks were dancing in the middle of the floor, Prince’s “Purple Rain” blasting. I stood at the edge and looked at Mike.

"Come *on*," Julia said, dragging me by the arm. I looked over at Mike.

"I don't really dance," he said, running his hand through his hair. "But you can if you want to."

"Come on! Dance with us!" Julia said, pulling me away. I smiled and followed her onto the floor, not that I had much choice. I danced to "Purple Rain" with Julia and Treena. Julia was a good dancer, but Treena just scanned the crowd for boys whenever she danced, which caused her to bump into people. I felt awkward and weird dancing in front of Mike, even though by that time I was starting to feel pretty drunk. I danced for a few songs and then leaned over to Julia and told her that I was going to sit down.

"No! Keep dancing with us!"

I shook my head and told her that I would later. I walked back over to where I'd last seen Mike, but he wasn't there, so I went around and found Jake. It took a while to get to him, as the place was now full to busting with drunk partygoers. When I finally got to him, he was standing with a bunch of guys and they were passing a joint around.

"Hey. Did you see where Mike went?"

"I've made serious bank tonight," Jake said.

"Awesome. But, have you seen Mike? I was with him a second ago and then Julia came around and wanted me to dance with her."

Jake squinted thoughtfully. "Come to think of it, I thought I saw him running off with some of the other guys from track. They just showed up. I didn't invite them. They went off somewhere."

One of the dudes standing around looked at me. "Yo? You mean that little Mexican dude? The one with the North Face jacket, orange?"

"He's not... yeah. That one."

"Oh, yeah, he went off with some guys. Those guys are fucking cokeheads man. I mean, I like coke and shit, but they're like, rich and shit, and all they ever do is coke. I think that's how they run so fucking fast," he said, cracking himself up.

"Oh," I said, looking at Jake, who shrugged.

I wasn't going to go running after him like a freak, so I figured I'd just hang out until he reappeared. I felt bad then about abandoning him to go dance with Julia, but she'd been so insistent that I felt like I couldn't say no. I went to the kitchen to get another drink. It was crowded and I had to fight my way to the counter. There wasn't much left, and so I pulled my flask out of my pocket and filled it. As I walked back over to Jake, I started to worry about the police coming, but on this side of town, it was kinda wild anyway and I figured the neighbors probably wouldn't complain. The problem was that the cops drove through this section a lot and if they spotted the lights and heard the noise, they might decide to check it out.

I stood around with Jake and his pals listening to them talk about heavy metal bands. Dudes killed me. Whenever they got together, they always had to talk about shit they knew about and compete over who knew more.

"Jake. You think Mike left?" I asked, turning to him.

"Oh! Look at my little cousin! She's so cute!" He said, pulling me into a headlock. "She's so cute and all in love. You got yourself a little boyfriend," he said, twisting me around.

"Jake! You drunk, cut it out. He's not my boyfriend, for fuck's sake. You suck. Let me go," I said, trying to get out of his grip, but the fucker was crazy strong, and it was impossible.

"Admit you loooooove him and I will."

"No!"

"C'mon. You looooooove him. You want to have pretty Colombian babies all day long."

"Oh, God, let me go! You're catching my hair again, Jake!" He was drunk though, and I forgave him, though he was embarrassing the ever-loving hell outta me with the Mike stuff.

"This is revenge!" He said, but he quit when I told him it was hurting my side.

I straightened myself out while his friends laughed, one of them even snorting vodka out of his nose. "She's like a pissed off cat, man!" The guy who'd told me he'd seen Mike said.

"Yes. I'm a pissed off cat," I said in monotone and this only made them laugh even more.

"Hey," I heard at my back. It was Mike.

Jake's guys started laughing like mad, and I worried like hell that he'd overheard them teasing me about him.

"Let's go over here," I said, leading him away.

"Like a cat, reow!" I heard one of them say as we left.

"What was that all about?" Mike asked.

"I have no idea. Those are Jake's friends. Some of them are fucking idiots."

"I gathered that," he said. We went over to a semi-empty corner and he looked at me. I smiled, looked down.

"Hey," he said, "I'm gonna head home soon. But my parents are out of town next weekend. You want to come up?"

"Sure."

We exchanged phone numbers and before he left, he hesitated, leaned in and kissed me. He squeezed my arm. "Talk to you soon. I'm going to have to visit you in your office."

"My office?"

"The stairs. Outside."

"Oh, that office."

"Bye," he said, walking away.

I walked back over to Jake and once I could see that Mike was definitely gone, I punched him as hard as I could in the arm.

"Cálmate, Kitty!" Jake said.

"You calm down. You asshole," I said.

"I'm sorry little cousin, I couldn't help it. It really is cute, really."

"Cute hell, you're just happy he isn't going after Julia."

"Julia who?"

"Hilarious, really." I looked at my watch. It was 4:00 in the morning.

"Man, I—" Jake said, and stopped. People were yelling.

"What's going on?" I asked.

"Cops!" Someone yelled.

"Oh fuck," Jake said.

Jake pointed with this lips and his hand at the window. "Someone must have seen us in here," he said. We looked over at the window we'd come in through and it was crammed with people trying to get out of it. Jake took my hand.

"This way," he said, "let's head towards another apartment. Another window."

"What's happening?" Julia asked.

"Cops," Jake said. "Get your shit and move."

"Fuck!" she said. "What are we going to do?"

"Follow me," Jake said, leading the way out of the apartment. We followed him, my breath caught in my throat. Jake led us out into the hallway, but we could hear the cops breaking in through the doorway at the entrance and so he turned into another apartment, one that was different than the one Mike and me had just been in, the door off the frame and lying in the corner like an abandoned child.

"Fuck, fuck!" Treena said.

"Shhh," Julia said and we all walked into the apartment and stopped. Toys were everywhere; it was as if someone had had to move out on a minute's notice. It was awful to look at: the kinds of things that very young children played with, dolls with missing eyes and legs, covered in years of dust. Jake ran over to a window and kicked at the wood criss-crossing it.

"Hey!" We heard behind us. We could hear footsteps in the hallway.

"Shit!" Treena yelled.

The wood was coming loose and Jake continued to kick, hard. Finally both boards came loose with a crack. Jake kicked quickly at the remaining wood and glass and then got out of the way.

"Go!" He yelled and I hesitated. He pushed me forward and I began to scramble out the window.

"Jake!" I said, looking back.

"Go!" He repeated. Outside, I could see that we were by the highway, and a few seconds later, Julia and Treena got out behind me.

"Stop!" I heard right behind us.

"Go!" Jake yelled. We ran.

CHAPTER 4

The next day, I woke up to a hangover. And guilt. I turned to the phone and dialed Megan's number.

"Hello?" It was Will. Guess the fucker was back.

"Hey, so, uh, did Jake come in last night?'

"No," he said. I closed my eyes.

"Oh, God."

"What he do now?"

"I... we... had a party in this old, empty complex and the cops came. And most of us got out, but Jake didn't."

"That crazy fucker," he said.

"Yeah," I said, rolling my eyes. At least Jake was a non-dickface crazy fucker, which was more than I could say for Will.

"So where you been?" I asked.

"Nowhere."

"Will, Megan's gonna kill you, man."

"Whatever. Bitch'll have to deal."

"You, my little friend, are going to die."

"Not by that fat bitch's hands."

"Man, you're rough on her."

"Well, she's a fucking bitch."

"A fucking bitch who took you in."

"Why don't you shut the fuck up?"

"Whoa, whoa cowboy. Calm down," I said. I

could hear the click sound of Will's lighter and then an exhale. "Look. Jake's probably in trouble. My guess is that his parents were called."

"What do you want me to do about it?"

"Nothing, Will. Jesus. Look, I have to work today and I'm grounded but I'll come by tonight. Jake might need some of his stuff."

Jake had just gotten a shipment from Denver, and the plan had been to get the rest of it after the party so that I could transfer it to my place.

"OK, laters."

"Bye," I said, and hung up.

I grabbed for the baggie and pipe under my bed. Smoked. Laid back down. Eventually, I trudged up the steps and saw Mom sitting at the table, grading. I went and fixed a bowl of cereal and sat down.

"So, your auntie called this morning. Jake didn't show up at home last night, and he just got caught by the police. Turns out he and some other kids were partying last night somewhere they shouldn't have been. You know anything about that?"

"Uh... no."

"Margaritte, if I find out that you were there, I am really going to be angry. And so is your dad."

"Dad," I repeated, rolling my eyes.

"Your dad has every right to be angry at you."

"I guess."

"I don't know what we're going to do with you, Margaritte. You just keep doing things that are going to destroy your life. Do you know where your cousin is? Again? Juvie. And your Auntie told me that if he is caught doing one more illegal thing, he will be tried as an adult. Did you know that?"

I was silent. I hadn't known that. But I'd wondered. I was just glad that he'd sold out of the weed that he'd brought to the party.

"And do you want to end up in juvie?"

I shuddered. Jake wasn't the only kid I knew who'd done time there. And Jake did OK, because he was big. But not everyone did so well. There were fights, and people molesting people. One girl I knew had a scar on her face, a big, angry pink pucker from the right side above her eye to just above the left side of her mouth. From a knife. Because she'd refused to let some other girl fuck around with her in the middle of the night.

"No," I said, my voice flat, moody. I went up to the counter and poured myself some coffee, put cream and sugar in the cup and looked out the open window, the dingy curtains flapping in the breeze. The window faced the street. It was sunny, and watching the cars pass by, the people on their way to work, something came over me, into my stomach.

"Where is Dad?" I asked, still looking out. There was a robin that came every spring. It would sit in the tree outside of the window, cock its head at the reflection of the branches and fly into the window. It did it over and over again. I was wondering when it would make its annual appearance and start knocking its head on the glass.

"Work."

I turned around and she was grading again. I suppose she'd given up on trying to change me for the better for the moment. I finished my cereal and went into the living room to watch TV with the twins, who clapped their hands at the images every few minutes and then went silent, staring into the box.

I'd watched about an hour's worth of kiddie shows with them when Mom asked me if I could give them a bath.

I hung my head. "Sure."

"No!" Carrie yelled.

I spent the morning taking care of the twins and actually doing some of my homework. Afternoon, I drove over for my shift at the Sugar Plum. It was slow as hell and I only came home with five dollars in tips. There had been two tables the whole time. A townie family, who gave me five bucks. And a yuppie family, on their way to something else, probably a ski resort, probably Vail or some shit. They hadn't tipped at all. I drove home in a funk and ate dinner with Mom, the twins, and a silent, drunken Dad. By the time night hit, I was more than ready to make my escape.

I waited until everyone had settled down for the night, the sounds of television from the living room and Mom's bedroom drifting downstairs before I opened the window and crawled out. I drove over to Megan's, the evening growing cold and the streets empty. When I got there, Megan was just getting home, slowly coming up the steps a little ahead of me, her baby on her back. She always complained that the cost of daycare barely made working worth it. I called her name and she looked over her shoulder at me, sweat pouring off her brow even though it was dark and cool. She said nothing as I helped her carry her groceries in, her large, yellow arms unloading into my wiry yellow ones. We put the groceries away, Megan glancing over at Will like she could rip his head off and shit down his throat. He was sitting on the couch, watching us, a fucking petulant ass expression on his face. I figured they had been fighting about bills, again. I don't know how Will wasn't afraid for his life. Megan was a tough broad. Talked all the time about the fights she used to get in on her rez when she was a teenager. Like jumping on chick's heads and scratching at their eyes kinda stories. I made sure to never get on her bad side.

She breastfed the baby and went into her room to put her down for the night. I watched them go, the baby's dark, fuzzy head peeking sleepily over Megan's shoulder. It was cute as hell but cried all the time. When I first started hanging at Will's, just watching the baby sleep made me want to pop one out. But after a while, I started calling it birth control 'cause just seeing how much you had to do to be a parent was exhausting, especially when you were alone. It was hard enough being a part-time parent for the twins, who were at least old enough to shit on their own. I couldn't imagine how Megan did it. Her husband is this Ute guy who had ended up in prison and because it was cheap to live here, she had asked Will, who was living with a bunch of deadbeats in Denver at the time, if he wanted to live with her. She had gotten a job waitressing at the Derby. Will had gotten lots of jobs, and been fired from, or quit, all of them.

The weird thing about Will was though he could be a giant shithead, he could be real sweet with the baby. He would even change her diapers. Sometimes, Megan would get so tired from her job and the baby that she'd fall asleep in front of the TV while she was breastfeeding. Her head just would roll back into the couch and the baby would wake up and cry and Will would come. He'd gather her up in his arms and sing to her in Lakota, which impressed the hell outta me. I mean, the last person in our family who'd spoken Indian was my grandma, though my mom and auntie know a few words.

Megan came out of her room and fell into the couch like it was her final resting place. She took her sneaks off and started rubbing her feet, her eyes closed and her mouth in a tight, angry line.

"My feet feel like they're falling off every time I get home. And the people, goddamn, they're so fucking annoying. It's like, this isn't good, give me a side of some shit, could I get more ice tea. Jesus. Spoiled fucking wasichus never had to worry about a thing besides getting more ice tea."

"So you don't feel like it's a calling?" I asked. She looked over at me like now it was my throat that was in danger of being ripped off and shit down. Megan was just real serious and sometimes didn't get when I was kidding.

"Like it's spiritually fulfilling," I said.

"You're an asshole," she said, cracking a smile.

"So, you're gonna stay with it. For the spiritual fulfillment."

"Right," she said, rolling her eyes. "I should get a goddamn eagle feather for coming in every day. No joke. It just gets harder and harder to give a fuck." I nodded. I mean, I wasn't sure what I was gonna do with my life, but if I was still waitressing in my thirties, I'd want to fucking lose my shit too.

Will was silent during this conversation. And even though I'd gotten Megan to laugh a little bit to distract her from the fact that a big, stupid leech was sitting on her couch, I could feel the tension rising.

"Who wants to have a smoke?" I asked, and Will got up and followed me outside.

"So, how's it?" I asked, handing him a cigarette.

"It's cool. Just trying to think about how I'm going to get out of here. This town is just not for me."

"Tell me about it," I said, looking at my watch. I had to go soon, do a couple deals.

"Once I save up, I'm gonna get my ass back to Denver," Will said. "Get a real job, one that pays, and never look at trash again. I had a good job for a while there, on my rez. I was a manager for a construction company and told all of these wasichus running the show that they could hire Lakotas to do the work a lot cheaper than their regulars. So, they did, and then they promoted me. Had this kick-ass car with Navajo rug type car seats."

"Wow," I said. But what I was thinking was, what the fuck ever man. You ain't no reincarnated Geronimo. I used to believe him when he talked about getting things he said he wanted, cars and houses and that, but after a while I realized he wasn't never gonna get that stuff. He's thirty-five and has never held a job for more than a month or two and he doesn't even have a degree. And he hangs with high school kids and losers. And I'm not exactly a debutante, but goddamn if Will isn't one of the crudest guys I've ever met, and that's saying a lot, unfortunately. He just isn't the kind of guy that's gonna make money, it doesn't matter how much he wants it. Stupid fucker can't even pay the rent or the bills and keeps charging the phone bill up with sex numbers.

We were high enough up that in the far distance I could almost see the 7-11, the dirty, faded neon lights glowing faintly, and I imagined the kids hanging out in front of it who were always hanging out in front of some convenience store somewhere, smoking, angry, young; their dirty black t-shirts and jeans covered in years of working shitty jobs too early in life, the skin of their hands cracked open with the soap that they make us use to clean things that will never be clean.

I sighed heavily and looked over at Will. "There's this crazy girl who hangs out at the 7-11 until dawn and asks anybody who'll listen if they want to see a picture of her baby. So one day I was crazy drunk and it was about two in the morning and there she was. I marched up to her and said, *Yeah, I wanna see it.* She pulled out a picture of a dead baby. I guess maybe I know Indians that crazy but she was one fucked up white girl, I tell you what."

Will laughed and said, "Well, that's not the kind of people I wanna to hang out with."

"Oh, yeah?"

"Yeah. The kind of people I want to hang out with have class."

"Class?"

"You know, the kind of people who want good, tasteful things, not trash."

I rolled my eyes at him and then said, "Will. Nobody wants trash. Nobody."

"I guess," he said.

We finished our smokes and I went back inside to tell Megan I was leaving, and to thank her for letting Jake stay with her but she was asleep. Will sat down on the couch as far away from her as he could. I sighed, picked Jake's stash up, and left.

Thursday, I was sitting on the stairwell, eating lunch and reading. I'd come out through the large metal doors, a part of the endless stream of bodies, the smell of people everywhere, and into the sun, happy to no be in a classroom for awhile. I'd been able to talk to Jake once on the phone. He'd told me he was going to be in for a month. That maybe that was best, as his parents didn't want to talk to him, wouldn't take his calls. I figured I could do our deals by myself, though I missed him. And I hated going to the house in Denver where we got our supply. It was full of creepy guys who always eyed me hard, with paranoia or interest or both.

I'd been trying to do my homework, too. I was just bad at it. I'd get home from school, and I was just so tired, and then Mom would need help with dinner and the twins, and you never knew what kind of mood Dad was gonna be in, which was draining. So by the time I got to my homework, if I'd avoided once of Dad's drunken monologues, or him trying to bond with me by pushing me to watch the *MacNeil/Lehrer NewsHour* with him or *NOVA* or some shit, it was 10:00. So most times I rushed through it, if I even did it at all.

A dude came up looking for weed and we exchanged money for baggie in a quick, intricate handshake. I looked back down at my book. I knew I should be doing homework, but I was reading the book Mike gave me. It was weird but I liked it. It was about loneliness. A few minutes later, I saw Mike making his way up the cement stairway. I smiled. Patted the cement next to me.

"Step into my office."

"I thought I might find you out here." He sat next to me, put his hand on my leg. He saw what I was reading and picked the book up. "You know, I can't get on an airplane without a copy of this."

"It sounds like you and this book are getting pretty serious."

"Oh, yes. It's been on and off again for years. But I think we're stuck together."

"Isn't that always the way."

"Hey, so, I heard about what happened after I left. What happened to Jake," Mike said sympathetically. "I'm sorry."

I sighed. "Thanks. I suppose we should have known better. But he's been in there before. And he'll get out."

Mike looked at me kindly and brushed my arm with his hand. I took it and squeezed it. He smiled.

"So, what's the plan for this weekend?" Mike asked, rubbing my leg. "I think maybe you need a distraction. I think perhaps you and I should do something together."

"This could be arranged."

"Yeah?"

"Well, since my parents aren't exactly happy about my leaving the premises, I have to have a plan. Then again, they're never really happy about my leaving the premises, and I often have a plan. Or, variations on the same basic plans."

"Ah. Clever," Mike said.

"Often, I just climb out my window. But this is risky. And time sensitive. So my other plan is to tell my mom that I'm studying with Julia. My mom loves Julia, because she makes straight As. So I figured she might suspend my grounding if I told her I was going to hang with Julia. If that fails, I can always just climb out the window."

"I'm what?" It was Julia, walking down the stairs behind me.

"Hey," I said, and she sat down. "Where's Treena?"

"Oh, rubbing her belly at some poor, unsuspecting victim."

"Ah. Well, can I tell my mom that I'm coming over to your place this weekend? Mike and me want to hang out, and well, you know I'm grounded, but she might let me out of jail if she thinks I'm coming over to your place."

Julia looked at Mike, his hand on my leg.

"I don't know Margaritte, I really don't want to get in trouble. I mean, what if your mom calls?"

I looked at her incredulously. "Julia! You were always fine with this before. Besides, if my mom calls, your foster mother never comes to the phone. One of her billion foster kids always answers, and half the time they just hang up."

"Let me think about it. I mean... "

"Look. You don't even have to be involved. If my mom calls, you don't have to talk to her. And you can just tell her you don't know where I am."

"Let me think about it," she said. "And there's a party. I thought you... two might want to come."

"So, you'll let me use you as an excuse for a party, but—"

"Fine! Whatever. Really, Margaritte, you should study."

"OK, Mom."

"I should go. I need to look something up in the library before history. See you at track, Mike?"

"Yeah, sure," he said, and we watched her walk down the steps, her long, slender, athletic legs taking the stairs slowly, elegantly. I didn't know what had gotten into her. Though she was used to getting the attention of any dudes she wanted, she had a ton of them, so I really didn't know why she was being so weird about Mike.

"Huh," I said.

"What?"

"Well, Julia."

"Yeah," he said. "She's alright. How long have you known her?"

"Since junior high. She lives in a foster home. She'd come in from another, a really bad situation. She's good to me though. Always tries to help me with homework, and I admire her."

"Why?"

"She has a lot less going for her than I do, but she works hard. I don't know what my problem is," I said, picking at the beige dust on the edges of the stairs.

Mike laughed. "I have it better than you. But I have the same problem. I hate school. It's just like a job. Like my dad's job, which he hates. It's do what they want, hit the pellet, get the reward. Repeat. It's repugnant. I don't want to ever do what people tell me to do. In fact, most of the time, I'll do whatever the opposite is."

I made a mental note to look repugnant up in my mom's old dictionary. "Yeah. I see that. I don't know. Maybe Julia has it right though. She says she wants to be a lawyer. To help people."

"She won't."

"Why do you say that?"

"She's just saying that to herself. She wants money. I'll bet that she ends up a corporate lawyer. Screwing people over."

"I hope you're wrong."

Mike looked over at me. "You're too good to people. You know Margaritte, she's asked me out. Well, she's asked if I wanted to hang out a couple of times."

I felt my heart race. "Yeah?"

"I said no."

"Oh," I said, and he reached over and kissed me.

He rubbed my leg and got up. "See you very soon."

"OK."

A few minutes later the bell rang and I sighed, picked my things up and went to class. Instead of reading Stephen King under my desk, I was reading Mike's book. The teacher didn't catch me.

That weekend, I was practically peeing myself. Mom had looked at me suspiciously, my most faux-sincere expression on my face when I'd asked her if I could spend the night at Julia's, and said yes. I'd also told Julia that I'd come to the party, though it sounded awful. It was at George's house. He was this crazy fucker who lived way up on Fall River Road. His parents were never home.

Mike had called me and given me directions to his house. He lived up on Highway 103, in between Evergreen and Idaho Springs. I took the twists and turns on narrow mountain roads to the sound of Biggie and almost drove past Mike's house because I was so busy nervously jamming.

I pulled to a stop when I realized I'd missed the turn and threw my car into reverse, my tires kicking up dirt and rocks as I drove backwards until I saw what I was looking for, a long, grassy driveway with a sign that said *The Walkers*. I drove up slowly. As his house came into view, I could see that it was huge, much larger than most of the houses in town. It was a log house and it looked like the kind of house that a Californian would think was really authentically Colorado. I parked behind his SUV and got out, pulling my backpack out of the passenger seat. I walked up the stone steps to his front door and hit the doorbell and the sound of some kind of classical tune echoed distantly into the house. I could see him inside, walking towards me through the large glass windows that surrounded the door.

"Hey. Come on in." He stepped back and gestured with his hand and I walked inside. The living room was covered in sculptures made of wood or stone, in the shapes of animals and trees and other stuff that was nature-themed. The couches were white leather and expensive looking.

"Have a seat," he said, hugging me. I hugged him back and walked over to one of the giant couches and plopped down, putting my arms wide. "Nice digs," I said, and he laughed.

"Want something to drink?"

"Sure."

"Gin and tonic OK?"

"Hell yah. Or as they would say where you come from, hells ya."

He cocked his head and smiled sarcastically. "Thanks for appreciating my culture. That's super culturally sensitive of you," he said, disappearing around the corner. I looked around again, staring at the gigantic TV, even though it was off.

"I'm really sensitive. Culturally so," I said, and I could hear the faint sound of his laughter in the kitchen and then, "Good to know, Margaritte."

There was a ridiculously large, technologically impenetrable-looking cable box on top of the TV. I had loads of friends with fancy cable, even the ones who lived in tinderbox trailers. I shook my head. I thought about Treena's place, where they had so many channels that I could never flip through all of them in one sitting. The kids just sat in front of the TV at her house, eating corn chips and staring. A few minutes later Mike returned with two glasses and handed one to me. I drank and asked him about the nature-themed shit all over the place. He told me his parents were really into it, that they'd gone to a ton of galleries when they'd first gotten there and bought a load of it.

"It's kind of funny, because you know, well. Nature's all around you."

"I know. Whatever. That's their thing right now."

"Where's the bathroom?" I asked, and he pointed me in the right direction. I went down a hallway, with pictures of Mike and his parents and professional looking prints and pictures of more nature scenes covering the walls. I opened the door and walked in. The bathroom was all white. Not mostly white, like the living room, but *white*: from the walls to the curtains to the soap. "Christ," I whispered to myself, closing the door softly. It felt like me just being in there would somehow taint it.

When I returned to the living room, Mike was looking out the window. He turned around and smiled. "In the interest of all things natural, let's get high," he said.

"Sure," I said, pulling a baggie and a pipe out of my bag. "Should we do it in the nature?"

"That sounds exciting," he said and I laughed. We walked outside and sat down on some incredibly expensive-looking beige patio furniture.

I stuffed the pipe and handed it to him, after I'd dug a lighter out of the pocket of my jeans. He took it, and hit it, hard. He held the smoke in for a while, and then let out a long stream of it from in-between his lips.

"You make this shit look refined," I said, and he handed the pipe back to me, shaking his head gently.

"By the way, the weed, good stuff."

"Only the best for you."

We took a few more hits and then he picked our glasses off of the table and went back into the house. I could see through the windows that he was walking over to a large stereo system. He pulled a CD out of a standing CD rack and slid it in. Strange music I didn't recognize at all started playing, and he disappeared into the kitchen. He walked back, handed me my glass and sat back down. We were both silent for a few minutes and I listened to the music. Most of what I listened to was rap. This music was different, it moved through the air in the most disjointed, painful way. There was something angry about it that was completely different from the violence that came out of rap. Something beautiful, but kind of rotten, underground, like it was coming from a distance. I couldn't find the origin of the pain inside of it.

I downed my drink in one swallow, threw my thumb in the air and said, "One, two, three, four, let's have a thumb war!" I was feeling good, the booze and the weed beginning to dance through my blood in a violent ballet.

Mike looked at me, put his glass down and we locked hands.

Our thumbs struggled and he stood up. "Cheater!" I said, and he wrestled my thumb down.

"OK, since you cheated, we have to go again."

We locked hands and wrestled, and this time I stood up and wrestled his thumb down.

"Now who's the cheater?" He asked, and threw his thumb out again.

"Me," I said. I was feeling nervous though, because my hands were sweaty. I wiped them on my jeans, smiled, and threw my thumb up. He threw his up and we locked hands, both of us standing up and laughing. He won.

"Now you're the cheater and the winner," I said. We sat down. Mike looked at me.

"What?"

"You're a silly girl."

"Yes, yes I am."

"How's home?" He asked, brushing my arm lightly, tenderly with his hand.

"It's what it is. Yeah, it really does blow that Jake's in juvie for a month."

"What is juvie exactly?"

"Jail for kids. It's probably better, though. His parents weren't exactly wanting him to come home."

"Really?"

"Really."

Mike sat back, shook his head. "That's terrible. Pretty much no matter what I do, I know my parents will always let me come home," he said, touching the rim of the glass thoughtfully. "And I've really put them through it."

I thought about asking him about this. What he'd put them through, but before I could he asked if I wanted to take a walk.

We went down his driveway and onto the side street I'd turned in on and started down the road. "Ha," I said, pointing to the street sign. "That always kills me."

Mike looked up. The sign said *Squaw Pass.*

"Wow, isn't that… I mean, doesn't it mean 'cunt' or something like that?"

"Yeah, I heard it was insulting, like it means slut or cunt, but then I heard it's an old Iroquois word for you know, vagina."

"Say vagina again," he said, laughing and poking me in the arm with his elbow.

"Yeah. That word is hot. 'Let me touch your vagina' will get you in every time," I said, my stomach twisting pleasantly.

"Will it?" He asked.

"About as much as 'let me touch your squaw' will," I said and he elbowed me again and I pushed him a little. He laughed and put his arms around me, sideways, hugged me and then pulled back and took my hand.

"Let me touch your vagina," he said thoughtfully, shaking his head.

"Just keep saying it, Mike, just keep saying it… " I said.

"You know," he said, kicking a stone, "you're the only Indian I've ever been friends with."

"I thought you said you hung with a few, back at home."

"I mean, I saw them around, but I lived in a really white neighborhood. All my life. My friends were white. My girlfriend is, well she was white."

"She isn't anymore, huh?"

He looked at me, a sarcastic expression on his face. "Yes, she's still white, but I don't think she's still my girlfriend."

"You don't think so, huh?"

He unclasped hands with me and punched me on the arm, gently. "No."

"How did you leave things?"

He sighed hard and ran his long fingers through his hair.

"We didn't really, I mean, we didn't talk after, well, after she cheated, and then I found out, and then I cheated."

"Yikes."

"Yes. I suppose that wasn't very smart of us."

"Well, no, but... did you try to work it out?"

"What was to work out? I mean, I loved her, I think I loved her, but we were young, and stupid and probably very bad for each other in a lot of ways," he said, looking off into the distance. "And then my dad moved and it was probably for the best."

We walked in silence for a while, and he took my hand again. It was nice, late March, and things were beginning to really warm up, and become green. The road twisted up, and we followed it, walking into the woods when we saw a path. It was rocky, and we could hear birds in the pine trees, squirrels and chipmunks yelling at one another. We walked for a while, and then sat down by a creek where there was a series of large, moss covered rocks by the edge. I picked a small rock up and threw it into the creek, watching the water ripple.

"So, have you ever tried meth?" he asked. I was surprised by his question.

"You mean the delicious and nutritious drug? Well, once. I didn't like it," I said, running my hands over the bluebells growing beside the rock.

"Why not?"

"It rots your body and soul, eventually. So there's that. But it makes you feel, or no—it makes you not feel," I said, sitting down on a fallen tree. I took my sweatshirt off. I had on one of my millions of wife-beaters.

"That can be good though, sometimes, don't you think?" He asked, peering at me intently, as if I was under glass, or underwater. "Well, not the rotting your soul part, but the not feeling part."

"I don't know... "

"Well, sometimes it's good to not care," Mike said.

"I can understand that. Sometimes I feel like that, especially at home. I think that's why I smoke weed so much. Otherwise I'd have to really deal with shit my parents are always spewing."

I pulled a stick out of the dirt and threw it in the water. I watched it float down the creek, the small bubbling sound it made comforting. The aspens shook in the wind, the sound of it like coins rattling. The sun was beginning to fade. I turned to Mike. "So, where are your parents? You said they were gone for a bit."

"Bahamas."

"Wow. For how long?"

"Only a few days," he said.

"Do they travel a lot?" I asked, and Mike looked strange, pensive.

"Well, my dad does. He used to travel alone. I think he liked it. He doesn't talk much." He paused, threw a stick of his own into the creek. "But now my mom insists on going with him."

"I see."

I had wondered if my dad had cheated on my mom. In fact, I assumed he had, considering the way he was. Once, I had come home to my mom crying, my auntie in the kitchen with her, her hand on the small of her back. *Just come to church with me, you'll feel better*, my auntie kept saying, but I didn't think church made *her* feel any better about anything. Jake's dad was a quiet Cherokee guy, a preacher, and he took his conversion, and everything else, extremely seriously. Every time I went over there, the house was silent. No TV. Jake's older siblings, the ones that his parents had had naturally, had already gone. I remembered their braids though, Jake's dad's eagle fan. My auntie's beading. Now all of that was packed away into boxes, all of it in their dusty, quiet attic, as if it were evidence of a secret life. Though sometimes my auntie would come over and try to teach me to bead, ask me about Native American Church. My mom had never gone. And had stopped going to Church with my auntie years ago. There was so much I didn't understand about them.

I leaned over and kissed Mike, gently, and he kissed me back. He had come to sit down next to me on the tree and he leaned towards me, his hands sliding down the backs of my arms. He pulled back, brushed my face with the back of his hands. Looked into my eyes. I looked back, the black of our gaze reflecting something that was the same: the same pain, the same anger, and the same strange, dangerous hunger. He put his hand on my shoulder, slid it to my back, put his lips on my neck. I leaned into it.

"Oh God," I whispered, and then I jumped up suddenly, pain radiating out from my ass.

"What?" Mike asked, looking offended.

"I-I think something bit me!" We looked down at the log and saw that there were fire ants beginning to crawl to the surface, their little red bodies busy running the various worn-in crevasses. We both brushed our pants, and started back, holding hands as the light died, the mountains golden, the trees making their deep, mysterious noises.

Back at Mike's house I sat down on the couch and looked up at him. He looked down at me. "Do you... want to stay?" He asked, and I nodded. He looked happy, almost goofy, and he tripped on his way to the kitchen to get us drinks. I'd never been around someone like Mike before. The boys in town were so tough; they didn't want to know what I thought.

"You like Woody Allen?" he asked.

"Yeah. He's funny. My parents have some of his movies. I think that's why I have different taste in movies than some of my friends. We always watched Woody Allen. And Mel Brooks. You ever seen *History of the World Part I*?"

He handed me a thick wool blanket and I folded into it while he lit a fire.

"Yes. I love that movie. Oh, my God, the opening? With the cavemen?" He put a movie into the VCR and settled on the couch next to me, laughing as he fit his body into mine.

"Totally. That always killed me."

"Yeah," he said, kissing me and then picking up the remote. "You ever seen *Annie Hall*?" he asked.

"Nope."

"Well, you're in for a treat. The woman in the film—Annie—she kind reminds me of you. Though you have more, ah, bravado I'd say."

"Bravado?"

"Balls, Margaritte, balls," he said, and I laughed.

"My balls are totally giant. It's actually a problem."

"You should get it checked out," he said.

"I don't really see myself coughing and bending over for someone in the near future."

Mike looked at me, his eyebrows coming together and his eyes lighting up. "You don't?"

"Not if it's to check my giant balls out."

"I'll keep that in mind."

We sat and watched the movie, and it killed me, it really did. Though I didn't know why Mike thought I was like that

Annie. She was skinny, and insecure and said stuff like la-dee-dah. I wouldn't be caught dead saying shit like that. Though I liked the part about the eggs. Me, I felt like I was more like that Alvy guy, always saying the wrong thing and enjoying it a little too much.

Leaning into Mike felt good, like we'd been doing it forever. And yet it was exciting too, because we were so new. After the movie he asked me if I wanted another drink and I asked him if he was trying to get me drunk.

"Yes," he said, and disappeared into the kitchen to get us yet another gin and tonic. He sat down next to me, handed me a drink. He looked up at me, his long eyelashes pointing down, just like my mom and auntie's did. It made Indians look shy, even when they weren't, like in the case of my auntie. But Mike, he did seem shy. But there was a funny kind of boldness to him too. I liked that combination.

"Margaritte… I like you but, you don't have to—have to—*you know*, unless you want to."

"I don't have to bend over and cough for you?"

"Stop teasing me," he said, running his hand down my arm.

"But it's fun. And it's all I got."

"Like I said, you are a very silly, silly girl."

"Yeah," I said, and he began to kiss my neck. His hands moved to my breasts, hesitantly. And then away. He looked at me.

"It's OK," I said.

He smiled. "Maybe I should touch parts of you and stop. And ask if it's OK. Like a game."

"Yes, just like bingo. Or Monopoly. Except with my vagina."

He practically roared and then stopped. "You're trying to distract me."

"Maybe."

"You're not… "

"A total vagina? No, but my balls are huge."

"Margaritte… "

"No, I'm not a virgin. I'm a total whore. Actually, I need fifty dollars to make you holler, heyyyy."

"I don't know what to do with you," he said.

"I have a thought."

"A sexy one? A sexy thought?"

"Pretty sexy."

"What?"

"What if like, we don't really exist. What if we're something… "

"Cruel, Margaritte, cruel."

I laughed a large, maniacal laugh and then leaned over and kissed him. I broke. "I'm sorry. I guess you just make me nervous. In a good way."

"Don't worry. I like you too."

I looked into his eyes and wondered. I had to admit, I didn't know him. Not really. But he seemed kind. "What the hell," I said, and stood up.

"Where are you going?"

I reached down, took his hand. "To your bedroom, you naughty thing you."

He smiled and stood up. He led me down the hallway, and into his room.

I got up the next morning and Mike was wrapped around me, still sleeping. I'd remembered waking up in the middle of the night because he'd kept mumbling "hmm," in his sleep, which struck me as pretty funny. Every time he'd done it, I would wake up, giggle, and try to cover my mouth so I wouldn't wake him up. I'd look over and his face was all scrunched up, and even that was so funny that I'd have to work even harder not to laugh, which would almost wake him up.

I disentangled myself and went to the bathroom, then into the kitchen and drank a glass of water. I couldn't get over his house. The kitchen was full of marble and everything that wasn't marble was brass. I looked around for a coffee maker and found one, and then opened cabinet after cabinet looking for coffee. I was trying to figure out how to work the coffee maker when I heard Mike behind me, and jumped.

"You scared me!"

"Sorry," he said, wrapping his arms around me from behind and kissing my cheek. He looked at the coffee maker.

"Trying to figure it out?"

"Yeah. It's... smarter than me."

"Nah. Just more complicated."

I didn't know what that meant, but I let him take the coffee out of my hands and work the tall silver machine until it was singing along. I sat down at the table.

"What have you got planned for today?" He asked.

"Well, I'm gonna go back home. Not 'cause I want to but because I'm due to be back from Juila's. And you know, I'm grounded."

He nodded and got up. He poured us coffee, set a mug down in front of me and went back up to the counter, the morning light coming in from the windows and hitting his black, black hair. He stood there for a while, looking out the window, his long, brown body leaning, his mug by his hand on the counter. I looked at him and a surge of something come up inside of me.

"You're really a beautiful guy, you know that?"

He turned to me, his blue boxers and white v-neck t-shirt

wrinkled from nights of sleep. We'd slept naked but clearly this was what he regularly slept in. I could see he was embarrassed.

"I always thought I was kinda tiny for a dude. And strangely hairless. But I figure maybe when I get a little older, that'll come in. Well. Not the height maybe. But the hair."

I laughed, hard.

"What?" He said, sitting down.

"Oh, Mike. You're *not* tiny. You're muscular and tight and I don't know... that's how Indian guys look. And it's plenty manly. And very hot. And I'm afraid you're not going to grow any more hair."

He looked at me, confused. "Sure I will."

"No—no, Mike. Indians don't really have a lot of body hair. I mean, I have some, 'cause I'm part white. But you... no."

He looked down at his arms and back at me, his eyes wide. "Oh... oh."

I leaned over and stroked his hair. "Oh, you're funny."

"You're the funny one."

"I am pretty fucking funny," I said and wiggled my eyebrows. I tapped my feet under the table in a funky little pow-wow rhythm.

"You're also very weird."

"Now I'm very offended."

"How offended?"

I adjusted the long, white t-shirt I'd pulled out of his dresser that morning and looked at him.

"Enough to kick your hairless ass."

"You think you can take me?"

"Bring it on," I said, and he drank from his coffee and then sprung up, surprising me and wrestling me to the ground.

"You've been very bad," he said, and kissed me.

"You should punish me."

He looked at me playfully, hesitantly, and gave me a spank. I squealed and ran strategically over to his bedroom. He ran after me.

Pulling out of his driveway, after having to turn the engine over several times before it would start, I thought about how happy I was. It frightened me, but looking up, I could see that the sun was strong. I heaved a heavy sigh and turned the radio up. The drive down was a little rocky and steep, and I had to hit the brakes a ton to keep from speeding like hell around the corners that led into town.

After driving for about twenty minutes, I could see the school on my left. I'd be hitting town in a few. For some reason, this triggered something. I squinted, thinking. I searched my mind and realized after a few seconds what it was I was trying to remember.

"Oh, fuck," I said, turning the radio down and then slapping my hand to my forehead. I realized that Mike and I had forgotten all about the party.

"I'll just call Julia later," I muttered to myself. I hoped she wouldn't be too mad at me; fuck she'd dumped me about a billion times for some dude, and I'd always been fine with it. I stopped at the gas station as I pulled into town and filled up. I remembered that I had to work that day and had to do some deals that night. I thought about Jake as I pumped the gas, hoped that he was OK. He had called me a day ago to tell me that he was but I didn't believe him. Those places were shit.

I got out, hoping Mom wouldn't be able to sniff dude on me. Inside, things were peaceful. Dad was nowhere to be seen, which meant that he was more than likely sitting in his office, drinking and doing whateverthefuck he did in there and Mom and Auntie Justine were sitting in the kitchen, laughing up a goddamn storm, and the twins were sitting by the TV.

"Hey guys," I said, walking into the kitchen. They looked at me suspiciously, turning towards one another and then back at me as I maneuvered around the kitchen, putting a bologna sandwich together.

"Did you get your work done at Julia's?" Mom asked and Justine snorted.

"Yeah."

Mom was silent for a few minutes, and I leaned against the counter, eating my sandwich and sweating.

"I just don't know how you concentrate with all of those kids running around," Mom said and Auntie Justine looked at me, hard.

"Heard from Jake?" I asked.

Justine picked up her mug of coffee and drank. "Yes. He called. Though his father won't talk to him. Those two are stubborn. But Jake. He just won't do right," she said, her mouth in a thin, angry line. She was lighter than my mom, shorter too. And tough. Real tough. She was the only person under 5'2" I truly feared.

"I'm sorry Auntie," I said, finishing my sandwich and washing my hands.

"You better be studying up there," she said. "You need to work hard if you want to do something with your life and you know it."

"I know... it," I said, finishing lamely.

"Don't you get saucy with me, hey," she said.

"I'm not. I want to do well, I do."

"I worry about you Margaritte. You're just like your great-grandma. Crazy and wild and full of it."

"I'm nerdy," I said.

"Nerdy, hell. Just 'cause you read those damn demon books doesn't mean you're a nerd. It means you're bored. Nerds get good grades," she said and Mom got up and started making a fresh batch of coffee.

"I… I gotta go to work," I said. I could feel my pits becoming a swamp. Auntie Justine didn't pull any punches. Mom sat down and looked at me.

"Dammit, Margaritte, just don't screw your life up. You're smart. Don't be stupid."

"I really gotta get ready for work," I said. "Later you two."

Both of them sighed, hard and in unison, and just the damn sound of it stressed me out. I probably smelled like boy and I'm sure the both of them knew exactly what I'd been up to. But they probably didn't know where. The thing was, if I had gone to Julia's, I probably would have ended up going to her party, where trouble of all kinds would have been much more possible than it had been at Mike's. We'd watched a goddamn Woody Allen movie for fuck's sake. 'Course I hadn't done a bit of homework.

The hallway felt long and white and endless and I put both of my hands on either side of it, moving them forward as I walked towards the bathroom, sliding them down as the pictures we had put up came into view. I opened the bathroom door, closed it and sat down on the toilet before I took my clothes off. I shared the bathroom with the twins and their shit was everywhere: little yellow bathtub duckies, tiny toothbrushes in the shapes of animals, pink matching pajamas from Dad's mom in Jersey, all of the stuff that it took to wash and brush *and* entertain two children while doing so. I could hear them yelling at their toys in the living room, the sound of the TV overwhelming. Mom and Justine were laughing about something. Justine told the dirtiest jokes, which killed me considering how Christian she was.

I turned the shower on and got into the stall, shutting the water-stained and rusted sliding doors behind me. I closed my eyes and stepped into the water, the sounds of the house fading. I thought about Mike, his hands on me, and smiled as I washed my hair with the cheap shampoo that I bought from Safeway. It smelled good though, like the way lilacs and candy would smell if there was a way to naturally combine them. I put conditioner in the long ropes of my hair, pulled it up in a thick black rubber band, washed my body, shaved, rinsed. I got out and dried myself off with a towel, wrapping it around me when I was done and walking downstairs to get dressed. I hated what my boss liked for us to wear: khaki pants and a white collared shirt. I looked like a fucktard.

I tied my hair back, walked up the stairs and outside, passing the twins who were still watching TV, and Mom and Justine, who were still laughing in the kitchen. The day was beautiful and the car only needed a few turns this time to start. I'd had a lot of luck with it lately, but it looked like it was back to its usual behavior. I pulled out of the driveway with a noisy, rusty squeak and into the road, which was busy with tourists. I could see as I came into town that they had descended like locusts and were running in and out of the stores, buying ice cream, weird wooden birdhouses and carved ducks, bullshit Indian dream catchers and the like, and were probably loving the hell out of it.

I pulled into the short, dirt driveway and parked and got out, walking past the large, dormant cherry tree that stood outside of the restaurant and into the dark wooden smell of the place.

I worked hard and the first couple of hours went quickly. The place was actually packed for once. But the last hours passed slowly; it was like I was living in someone else's body, the body of a stranger that was moving through fog. I was thinking about Mike but mainly that was always the way I felt around people, especially at work or at school. There was no way to be myself. I was talking, taking orders, cleaning, getting high in the bathroom, looking at myself in the mirror and fixing the long black lines of my eyeliner as slowly as possible. The mirror in the bathroom always made me feel foreign to myself. It always left me wondering if I was still in there.

I walked out of the bathroom and into the kitchen to get the order that was up. It smelled of meat, spices, cleaners of various kinds.

Buddy looked at me, her medium-length grey hair tied back in a short ponytail.

"You better not be getting high in there. I know that smell. I was a teenager in the '60s," she said. She was a weird lady, always giving me and half her patrons advice even when it was clear they didn't want it. I remember her trying to convince an obese white lady about a year ago to order light ice cream instead of the regular. The woman wasn't having it and just kept saying *I want my treat.* Buddy continued to try until the woman got furious and left.

"I was burning sage."

"Yeah. Sage. Don't you try to fool an old lady with that Indian shit."

"Never," I said, smiling and picking the tray up. I walked into the wood paneled dining room and over to the couple sitting over in the corner. They had two kids, and the whole damn family was dressed in North Face jackets. The parents were wearing dark colors and the kids, bright. I could see the white stitching on the front of all of their jackets, which none of them had taken off. The kids were yelling like hell, launching bright pieces of silverware into the air every few minutes. I just picked the forks up from the old, slightly yeasty smelling carpet and slid them into the pockets of my apron. Both parents were clearly depressed, exhausted. They weren't talking to each other. In fact, they weren't even looking at one another. I could only imagine that they hadn't realized that this was all part of the deal.

I set the tray down and served them their dishes. I asked them if I could get them anything else. The woman turned to me, her little blue eyes empty, worn.

"No, just the check when you get the chance," she said, smiling weakly.

"Cool. 'Cause I never remember what we got for dessert anyway," I said, and she laughed.

"We just got back from skiing," she said, "and we're beat."

"You took them skiing?" I asked.

"Yeah, they take lessons. And we love to ski. Do you?"

"No, I don't ski. Lots of people from here don't ski."

She laughed, and it was a tiny metallic sound. "Well, we're from California. We moved to Evergreen a few months ago. Try not to hold that against us."

"Oh, I'm dating a guy from there," I said. "Well, he's closer to Evergreen than Idaho Springs. So I guess he's from Evergreen. And originally from California too."

"Oh, really?" she said, smiling.

"Yeah," I said and felt silly. The woman smiled. Her husband hadn't looked up at me, once. He was already eating. The kids were looking at their piles of cheesesticks as if to figure out how quickly they could make them airborne.

"Well, enjoy your meal," I said, walking away. I returned a

few minutes later to ask them if they needed anything else, fill their drinks, see if they were enjoying their meal. A while later I came back with their check, and watched their kids throw their piles of untouched cheesesticks at each other as I picked the bill up. In the kitchen, I looked at my watch. I could go soon.

I cashed the couple out, folded my apron into my backpack and told Buddy that I was leaving. I had already done all of the prep I needed to do so I was really free to go. I walked into the slowly darkening night, the wind blowing stiffly against me. I got into my car, turned the engine over a few times and got it started. I'd told Mom that my shift ended later than it did so that I could go over to Megan's and hang after I'd done my deals. I just wanted to sit and have a couple drinks without having to deal with my family. Plus, Megan smoked a little and had asked me if she could get a dime bag.

I did a couple of deals and then drove over to Megan's. I walked up the stairs, knocked, and Megan answered, the baby in her arms, an *I'm going to ram a fist down Will's mouth* expression on her face. I handed her the dime bag and when she went to her bag, I said no. I told her that I hung there all the time and that she'd taken Jake in when we needed it.

"Thanks," she said. "I'm going to go put the baby down." I quietly followed her so I could watch her and that's when we heard the door slam. I looked over at Megan anxiously, and she said nothing. She put the baby in the crib and tucked her old, fuzzy blankets around her. I walked out into the living room.

"Hey, Will," I said, sitting down on the couch.

He had turned the TV on. He kind of nodded in my direction and then went to the kitchen, opened the door of the refrigerator, stared in for a time and then shut it when he heard a door opening and Megan come down the hallway.

"So, Will, where you been?" Megan asked, standing in the living room, her green-brown eyes flat and full of anger. Will didn't respond. He walked over to the couch, plopped down, picked the remote up and started changing the channels, his eyes on the TV.

"Will?"

"Hanging out."

"Really?" Megan said, the channels still changing.

"Yeah, really, Megan. Why you all in auntie mode? I know you ain't getting laid with your man in jail and all, but why you gotta take it out on me."

"You asshole. You fucking jerk."

"So," he said flatly.

"You know what Will?"

"What."

"I think I'm gonna give your dad a call."

"What the hell does that mean?"

"It means I could talk to your dad about who you like to hang with."

Then, silence. The channels not turning.

"You never got it, Megan. I never brought home women 'cause of Mom."

Megan laughed.

"What's so funny?"

"Your mom is dead," she said.

"You fucking *bitch*."

Will yelled some word I think means half-breed in Lakota, scrambled off the couch, tore his jacket off the coat hanger and started walking towards the door. I looked sharply over at Megan.

"Where you going Will? To hang with your friends?" Megan asked, her hands on her hips.

"Fuck you!" Will yelled. He pulled the door open and then slammed it after him.

"NO! Fuck you, you winkte motherfucker!" she screamed at the front door. "I fucking hate him!" She walked over to her room, opened her door roughly and slammed it shut. I let her alone for a few minutes and then I went over and knocked on her door.

"Are you OK?" I asked, trying to sound as gentle as possible.

"Yeah... " Megan said behind the door, the baby crying. "Oh, God." I could hear her walking over to the crib. After a minute, she opened the door with the baby in her hands, its head all sweaty from crying and Megan's face puffy with tears.

"I just fucking hate him," she said. She sat down on the couch with the baby in her arms, her eyes looking so empty, it scared me.

"Wanna order some pizza?" I asked and Megan nodded mechanically. I went over to the phone and ordered a couple large pizzas. We sat in front of the TV for hours, eating, watching one stupid meaningless movie after another until I fell asleep, the noise of the television becoming like the sound of a buzz saw in the distance.

I woke up to the TV on, Will stumbling through the door late, stinking of whiskey and sex, his eyes two blackened bulbs. He shuffled to his room without even looking at me, not saying a word, the door opening and closing with barely a sound.

"Crazy bastard," I whispered to myself.

This shit happened like clockwork. Will wouldn't pay the bills, he'd stop talking to Megan. And then the guys would appear. A steady stream of them who spent the night and always left in the morning. They'd shuffle past me and out the front door and if I happened to be on the couch they'd smile all funny and walk out looking confused.

I shook my head, trying to clear it enough to wake up fully and go home. I hadn't meant to fall asleep there, knew if I didn't go home at some point I'd only get in trouble, but I just couldn't leave Megan like that. I thought about a conversation me and Megan had once had.

He always wakes the baby up with his music.

Really?

Yeah... and once I heard him say to one of those guys that he had a wife.

You're shitting me.

Nope. And another time I heard one of them crying.

Holy shit, either he's a fucking stud or a total dickhead or both.

What's up with all of these fucked up guys?

I scrambled up from the couch and looked at my white plastic watch, large on my small wrist. It was a digital that Dad had given me for my birthday. It was only midnight. I sighed with relief. I walked out and shut the door as quietly as possible. I went down the steps, my shoes making a clang-clang sound I hoped wasn't waking anyone up. There were a few people sitting outside their apartments, getting trashed and talking on the second floor. A light brown boy in a long, black tank top yelled, "Hey girl," but I kept going until I was all the way down and into the parking lot. I got in my car, turned the keys and after the engine turned over a few times it started. The streetlights were on and the town empty as I drove. I was thirsty and I decided to stop over at the 7-11 before heading home. There were cars parked in front and kids sitting on their cars, smoking and exhaling long streams out into the dark beside the neon lights. I bought a pop and got back into my car, which started without a hitch. I unscrewed the bottle and drank, driving past the park, through town and into the neighborhood where I lived. Pulling closer to the house, I could see that the lights were off. I parked and opened the front door, peering in to see if Dad was still watching something on TV and I'd have to talk to him as I tried to make my to the bathroom and then downstairs. He wasn't. Downstairs, I got into my pajamas, set the alarm and picked the book up Mike had given me to read before I fell asleep. I lay down and thought. I could just tell Mom that it had been a late night, that tourists had kept me forever. She was used to my excuses by now, knew I was full of shit. But she took it because I knew she didn't know what to do with me, how to make me stop. I wished that I was like Julia, making great grades, not giving a shit, doing what was right. But I just wasn't.

CHAPTER 5

Mike and I started hanging out almost every day. I'd go up any weekend his parents were somewhere stupidly exotic. Mom was relenting on the me being grounded thing, mainly 'cause she was too busy with Dad's shit and the twins to really come down. The key was to stay out of her way, not make it obvious that I was fucking up. You know, not end up in the back of a police cruiser. And Jake was talking to his parents again, his month almost up. We were going to party at Megan's when they let him out. I was also excited, 'cause the coming weekend Mike's parents were in Philadelphia and we were going to run up to Mt. Evans and camp.

I had fallen asleep on Megan's couch again after doing a couple deals and celebrating my success as a small town drug dealer with a few beers. Around 6:00 I guess, I woke up to the sound of one of Will's dudes leaving the premises. I rolled over and cracked my eyes open just a little, hoping whoever it was wouldn't realize that I was awake and trying to get a look at him. He was young, real young, and black. He was wearing a white t-shirt and jeans and he looked, I don't know, nervous. I rolled over again as the door opened and then shut, letting some of the cold in. I rubbed my nose and closed my eyes. I heard a door open and footsteps and then the fridge door opening. I sighed quietly. I knew he wasn't paying any of the bills, including the grocery bill. Megan had wondered if he wasn't doing exactly what I could hear him doing five feet from me. I rolled over and went to back to sleep. The Friday before had been bad.

I'd just come back from hanging in Denver. There were Skins who liked to play ball by the lake on Colfax and sometimes I went and if there were any chicks, I'd join them. There'd been a few girls, some I recognized from the Indian Center and we'd shot the shit and played. I felt tired after, and like not going home. Dad seemed to be drunk all the time lately, crying and waking the twins up and driving Mom crazy. I'd done a couple deals and called Megan. Told her I'd buy her some groceries. When I got there, I could see Will sitting in the dark, watching TV.

"Hey Will," I said, closing the door behind me and setting the groceries on the counter. Will grunted and I put the groceries away. I took a shower, changed, and then sat on the couch to watch TV and wait for Megan. When the door opened about thirty minutes later, my heart started thumping in my chest. She took one look at him then walked past him and threw on all the lights. He just blinked and looked up at her, like he'd been sitting there for years with the lights out and the TV on.

We had talked about making frybread and chili, so I went to the kitchen without a word. I started on the bread. I looked over at Will and Megan as I pulled a bowl out of an old, wooden cabinet. Megan was standing over Will and staring at him and he was staring back.

Finally Will licked his lips and coughed and was like, "What?" He had on this old grey t-shirt and jeans that looked like they'd been through the gutter about fifty times and never washed once but the guy looked good. He was usually the kinda guy who could sleep in a paper sack for four days, never shower and come out looking like some kinda model unless he had gone on a super-bender. He almost always smelled nice too, like sweetgrass and frybread and some hot-ass cologne.

"Oh, shit," I whispered, my eyes sliding over to see what was happening in the living room. Megan was still standing over Will, staring at him silently.

Finally, Will said, "Megan! What the fuck!"

"Where you been?"

Will looked back at her all innocent. "I'm so sick of you asking me that. Right here is where I been."

Megan snorted. "You're always gone, Will and you know it. And you never pay the fucking bills."

Will crossed his arms and said, "Look Megan, I never ask you where you and the intertribal posse been. So why you asking me?"

Megan's lips tightened. "I don't really give a shit where you been, though I don't disappear for days at a time. But like I said, you ain't paying the bills and to top it all off, your goddamn dad's been calling."

Will flinched.

"What do you want me to tell the only uncle who's ever given a shit about me where his son is?"

Will's mouth opened and then closed and Megan stopped talking and crossed her arms over her large stomach and looked real hard at him. "'Cause I could tell him something." Will looked like he was choking. He raised his hand to his mouth and coughed. "Yeah... " she said real slow and almost lazy. "I could tell him about who you spend your time with."

Will was staring at the floor and pulling his hands through

that thick black hair of his, though he stopped for a second when she said that.

Megan stared at him.

After a couple of minutes Will sighed real heavy and pulled his hands out of his hair. He stared at them and then set them on his lap. Just then, the baby started crying. Megan had put her on her blanket in the corner, the one with all the toys.

"What you wanna tell him Megan?" he said all soft, his eyes slowly raising from his hands to her eyes. I held my breath as Megan went over to the baby and picked her up. Megan brought her to her chest and patted her on the head and then bent over and picked up a toy from the blanket, a fuzzy white elephant, and thrust it into the baby's hands. She stopped crying and giggled at the elephant and crushed it to her mouth. Megan handed the baby over to me. I set her on my hip and started on the chili.

"You know."

Will watched her and licked his lips, over and over. "Why don't you go ahead and do that, Megan. You always did talk better with him than I did."

Megan shook her head, looking like she'd just run right outta steam. "Look Will, just gimme the money for rent, alright?"

He looked down again at his hands. "I will when I get a job, OK?"

"Oh, Jesus, Will. Jesus fucking Christ!" Will flinched again.

"I just—just—lost this last one OK? My boss was a jerk... ." and when he looked up, he looked so, I don't know, *open* there for a second, but he closed back down real fast.

"Jesus!" Megan said again.

"What about Him?"

"What?" Megan asked. I had put the baby in her highchair

and cut up chunks of cheese and fruit for her. The dough was ready, and I stuck a piece into the pan of oil, silent.

"Why don't you ask Jesus for the rent?" he said.

Megan was silent for a long time then, watching Will, his hair all rumpled and his face so beautiful all twisted up like that, and she started to cry, just a little. Then she said, "Oh… Will."

Will sat there with that look on his face, that mean ass smile that wasn't really a smile at all, and then he kind of slumped a little and picked up the remote and lifted it, all slow, and turned the volume up. I handed the baby more cheese and fruit and she laughed and clapped her hands.

I walked over to Megan and put my hand on her shoulder.

"Wanna help?" I asked.

"Yeah," Megan said and followed me meekly into kitchen.

I went into the living room and set the table. Will switched channels a few more times and then stood up, got his jacket and walked out. We sighed and finished making dinner.

We sat down. I looked over at Megan. "What are you going to do?"

"I'm probably going to have to move home. Because that fucker," she said, pointing with her lips to the door, "is not going to pay the bills. I hate this shit."

I nodded. Megan's mom lived in a tiny HUD house on the Ogalala rez, and there were no jobs there. Megan had been doing OK when the shit with her husband went down and everything fell apart. That's when she decided to move to the Springs.

"What the fuck is wrong with Will?" I asked Megan.

"I don't know. He's always been like that. Selfish and mean and bitchy. 'Course, his parents weren't around much. Always off drinking and riding motorcycles and letting the kids to themselves."

"Jesus," I said.

"Yeah. I mean, that sucks. But, I didn't exactly have it easy either, growing up. But I go to work, I take care of my baby. I don't put my shit on other people. Will's a dick."

I nodded. I knew what she was saying. We'd sat down to eat and watched TV until I had to go.

After that, I'd been trying to spend even more time at Megan's because I was worried for her. I was worried she would fully lose it on Will and shit would go down that would fuck everything up for her. I slept on her couch for another hour and then went home. Dad was watching TV in the living room but was too drunk to hear me walking past. I went downstairs and fell asleep after reading for a few minutes.

The next day though, I woke up happy. I couldn't wait to get up to Mike's and then onto Mt Evans. I fed the twins, talked with Mom, worked for a few hours and then headed to Mike's. I'd told Mom I was going over to Julia's to study and would be back Sunday morning. She'd given me the evil, evil eye but she'd nodded.

"Hey!" Mike said when I arrived. "Come in! I think I have everything. My parents bought a bunch of outdoors-y shit they've never used when we moved here." He walked into the living room and I followed. There was a monstrously large blue cooler, two sleeping bags and a tent in their sacks, and a ginormous camping backpack, complete with metal frame.

"Like I told you on the phone," he said, running his left hand through his hair maniacally, "you don't need anything. Except you," he said suddenly, bounding up to me and kissing me on the cheek. He was sweaty.

"You're really excited about this," I said, laughing.

"Oh yeah! My parents talked about doing this all the time but we never did. And my friends were never really that interested in it. And there were so many places in California that we could have camped, there really were. But no one would do it."

"We did when I was a kid. It was fun, but it was also kind of a nightmare. Dad would get drunk on cheap beer, and Mom would make s'mores. I don't know. I guess it was fun until Dad would either start crying or yelling. I liked being out there, listening to the birds and the trees in the wind, all that shit. Though there's always the possibility of bears or mountain lions.

Mike stared at me incredulously and then said, "Really? I assumed they left folks alone. I mean, with the hunting and all."

"Well, people don't hunt around here as much as they used to. And the mountain lions aren't as scared of us as they were. Fuck, a kid was killed just last year running past a lion's den."

Mike sat down and looked up at me. "You're shitting me. You're just shitting me," he said, shaking his head. "Really? Killed by a lion."

"Yep," I said.

"Well," Mike said, "that is pretty Hemingway of him. In a way, that's cool."

"I guess," I said, "I don't think his parents thought it was cool."

Mike seemed to not even hear me for a minute and then said, "What?"

"I said, his parents didn't think it was cool," I repeated.

"Oh. Oh. Yeah. But at least he died in nature, by nature's hands. Know what I mean?"

"Not really."

He sighed, heavy. He walked into the kitchen and brought back two beers. He handed one to me and I cracked it open and sipped. He cracked his open, clinked his beer against mine and sat down on the couch again and patted the spot next to him with one of his long, elegant brown hands.

"I'm not sitting next to you until you explain what you meant by that."

He sighed, impatiently. It was strange. He wasn't usually like this. I guessed he'd been hanging out with his track buddies. He was always a little keyed up and cold at the same time after he'd hung with them.

"Look. We're all going to die, right?"

I nodded.

"Well, at least he didn't die in some factory, or in some cubicle, after a long, boring, meaningless life."

I sighed and plopped down next to him on the couch and then turned to him and smiled. I put my beer down on the floor and then took his out of his hand and put it down next to mine. I put one leg over him.

He laughed. "I see you agree with me after all."

"Maybe," I said.

Driving up, I couldn't believe how beautiful it was. It was late May, and although the mountains still had some snow on the peaks, it had been a hard but short winter and things had been warming up for some time. We had packed Mike's big, blue SUV and were on our way up 103. His right hand was resting on my leg and he was driving with his left. Our windows were rolled down, and Mike was playing another one of his white noise bands that I didn't recognize, and I closed my eyes and let the raspberry, deep green, pine, dirt smell roll over me. It didn't take too long to get to the foot of the mountain. We were planning on camping somewhere around the lake, but we decided to drive to the top of the mountain first. They had just opened the road up for the season and we drove, things getting bumpier and bumpier, which just made us laugh as we rocked back and forth in our seats, firmly buckled in.

Goats appeared on the side of the mountain, clinging miraculously to the edge. It always looked so death defying. Goats fucking killed me. They were everywhere around here, on the mountains, in people's yards. Lots of folks had billy goats in the area, and they were always greeting you with their funky yellow eyes, hungrily eyeing your backpack, their necks encircled with string that they were inevitably going to chew through.

"Wow, look at the trees," Mike said, pointing out his window.

The trees here grew low to the ground and were wildly crooked. They looked like abstract art, their grey, funky bark zigzagging up into sparse explosions of pine needles.

"Yeah, we're about to hit a point where trees don't grow at all, actually," I said.

"God. Those trees look like they belong in a science fiction movie," Mike said.

"I think they're very old, too," I said.

"Ah. Like the Redwoods in California. Man, I'd really like to show you those someday," he said and I pulled nervously on my white tank. It always made me feel funny when he talked about shit he was going to show me or shit we were going to do in the future. I couldn't figure out if I wasn't brave enough to believe him or if I was too stupid to see that he was just talking.

"Yeah?"

"Yeah."

We were silent then looking out the window at the landscape which grew more and more bereft and strangely beautiful by the minute. Finally we reached the top and parked. We opened our doors and I could feel the hard, cold wind immediately. I reached for my hoodie. I could see that Mike was doing the same. We shut our doors and walked closer to the edge. There was a guardrail and I took hold of it and looked down, feeling dizzy. Mike stood by me and put his arm around my waist.

"Ha, goats," he said, pointing. Sure enough, I could see some clinging to the mountain, walking up and down, occasionally bending to chew at a tiny plant growing out of the mountainside.

We were next to a family and the kids were laughing and pointing at the goats. I looked at Mike and we smiled.

"Dad! Gimmie my Twinkie for the goat, OK?" one of the kids said, a little girl who looked about eight or so. She looked up at her dad with her big, green eyes. I shook my head.

"OK," he said, handing one over.

"Excuse me?" I said, "You can't feed the goats. And especially not that kind of thing," I said, pointing to the Twinkie.

The girl pulled the Twinkie out of her dad's hand and he looked me and Mike and narrowed his eyes. "I'm sure it won't hurt him. And my little girl wants to feed the goat."

I sighed and pointed to the sign not five feet from him that said, "Don't feed the goats."

He looked at it and blinked a few times and then said, "I pay my taxes."

Mike and I looked at each other and then Mike started laughing and the guy looked at him suspiciously. The little girl was already leaning down, her tiny body halfway over the rail.

"Your kid?" I said and he turned around, and picked her up, her Twinkie falling out of her hand. Her legs kicked, hard and she yelled, "Noooo! Dad, nooo!" He set her down and said, "Let me help you. You could get hurt." She just started crying angrily and I rolled my eyes.

"Do you want another Twinkie?" The dad asked the little girl and in response, she cried harder, her tiny, sparkly pink sneakers flashing in the light as she stomped.

Mike looked at me, his long black eyes mirroring my disgust.

"Let's go look at the sun dial, drive back down and drink beer and touch each other's naughty parts," I said, a little loudly.

Mike laughed his little, sophisticated laugh and the man whose daughter had been trying to feed Twinkies to goats looked at me and covered his kid's ears, his large, white hands clapping nearly audibly over the sides of her tiny little face. He looked at me angrily and I said, "Just feed her another Twinkie. I'm sure that will fix everything."

Mike and me held hands, and the guy yelled, "You... assholes!" at our backs as we walked away.

"God. And I think my parents fucked me up," I said, yanking the zipper of my thick hoodie up further.

"I know," Mike said thoughtfully. It was beginning to rain and I pulled my hood up and around my head. The wind was strong at this elevation and I shivered. Mike squeezed my hand. "Thank you for suggesting we come up here."

"'Course," I said, and we walked over to the dial.

"It just occurred to me how useless this dial is right now. Without any, you know, sun," I said.

"Quite true," Mike said. Let's just sit on this temporarily useless device, look at the view, throw some Twinkies at goats, and go." I nodded and we sat down.

Wave after wave of mountain range unfolded in front of us, the clouds moving quickly, the rain coming and then going, spots of sun hitting us then fading.

"Have we had enough beauty?" I asked.

"Yes, though I'm not sure about our truth quotient," Mike said and we stood up. I looked over at the dad who we'd argued with and he was looking real intent at a map, his kid hanging precariously over the rail, a ranger striding angrily towards them.

We walked over to Mike's car. I thought about how big, blue, and shiny it looked, like some sort of prehistoric dragonfly. He unlocked the doors for us with his clicker and we got in, the sun coming out, fading, Mike's car starting in one, crisp turn of his key. The ride down was just as bumpy as the ride up and we laughed again, bouncing and bouncing and looking forward to getting down the mountain and setting up camp.

We parked near the camp, paid our fee and carried all of our stuff to the site. Setting up a tent was usually torture during any kind of family excursion, not only because Dad was drunk and crappy about it, but also because when my family used to camp, we had old, bad shit. Mike's shit was new, expensive. His sleek grey and blue tent nearly sprung up on its own, looking like some bizarre variety of gorgeous, muscular mushroom.

While Mike had been setting the tent up, I'd been dealing with the food. I turned the stereo we'd brought up, Nirvana being the one band Mike and me could really agree on, and opened the cooler next to the grill.

"Hey," Mike said. He'd just finished stuffing the sleeping bags and backpacks in the tent.

"Yeah?"

"Do you want to get high and walk around before we eat? It's only 3:00. I don't know about you, but I'm not hungry yet, and it's really nice out," he said, looking at me and squinting in the sun.

"Sure. I don't know why I was so into this grill anyway. Probably because anything to do with fire really excites me."

"Note to self," Mike said, and I walked over to him and lightly punched him in the stomach, a one-two routine. He caught my arms and held them.

"Come on, baby. Light my fire," he said stoically.

"OK, Jim, will do. As long as you don't die at twenty-seven."

"Deal," Mike said, taking my hand. We walked towards a path that led around the lake, the silvery water rippling lightly in the wind. We could hear birds and I pointed out a male Grosbeak doing it's little Hammer Time-like mating dance on a branch, the less colorful looking female looking on apathetically from a nearby branch.

"I guess that's how it goes," Mike said.

"How's that?" I said, leaning over and pulling a fallen stick up from the wet, brown ground and slapping Mike lightly on the right side of his face. He pulled it from my hand and stuck it quickly through my hair. I stopped, blinked dramatically and pulled it out, throwing it at him. I missed.

"Well, I get all dressed up pretty for you, dance, and just like that bird there, you don't even care. And this is a new dress!"

"Well, if you'd just learn a different freaking dance. You only know the one, and it's getting, you know, old, OK?"

"You misogynist asshole," Mike said.

Yeah, I am," I said, thinking that I would look that misogynist word up at home.

"I'm really very shallow, so you'd better stay pretty," I said.

"Note to self," he said and I laughed. I loved it when he used that expression.

"It really is amazing here," Mike said. "I miss California, I do. I miss my friends and the culture and everything. But this is nice." He squeezed my hand.

"I'm glad you're here," I said, and he stopped and looked at me.

"I'm glad you're glad. I am too," he said and kissed me.

We broke and started walking again, the rich green forest all around us. We stopped by the water, threw rocks in. Looked at a nest in a tree, the tiny, fuzzy robin heads poking out, bright orange beaks first, the peeping noise urgent.

"Spring, spring, springtime," I said. We walked all the way around to the restaurant and Mike said that we should go in and get drinks. Both of us had fake IDs.

We walked inside the old wooden building, the goofy gift store full of plastic tomahawks, fool's gold in little baggies and aspen leaf jewelry. We walked through the restaurant and up to the big wooden bar and sat down. There were a few tourists at the bar, though most were families sitting out in the restaurant section. I wondered if Twinkie Dad would show up at some point. The tall, paunchy, white bartender came over and asked what he could get us. He seemed tired, a long white bleach-smelling towel thrown over his right shoulder.

"Gin and tonics," Mike said. He had a thing for those. The guy asked for our IDs and, after looking at them with a bored expression on his face, asked if well was OK and Mike said yes. The guy nodded. He walked to the middle of the bar, plucked a couple of thick glasses from under it and set them down. He yanked a bottle of vodka out, poured, squirted tonic into the glasses, pulled a couple of limes out of the condiment dish, squeezed them into our drinks and brought them to us.

"This be all?" He asked and Mike nodded. We'd brought plenty of beer and were ready to cook and drink and listen to music after this.

We sipped at our gin and tonics and talked and looked around, laughing under our hands at all of the tourists with their fanny packs and plastic Indian shit and pounds and pounds of expensive hiking gear.

"Look, if I'm going to hike, I'm going to do it gangster," Mike was saying. There was a big, white, yuppie-looking family all dressed in puffy jackets and expensive jeans but their teenaged kid was in a big, black, Tupac t-shirt, his oversized jeans falling far below his butt.

"Oh, leave him alone," I said. "At least he's rebelling against his yuppie-ass parents."

Mike took a drink from his glass and looked over at the kid. The kid looked back, narrowed his eyes, and adjusted the red bandanna carefully tied around his head.

"Should I get gangster? Would you like that?" he asked, taking a drink and then sitting back and posing with one hand over his shoulder and the other crossed over his waist, a disaffected smirk on his lips.

"That is so hot. Fill me with your hardcore babies," I said, and he broke his pose and laughed, practically snorting gin and tonic out of his nose. I looked over at the kid. He was staring moodily at his hamburger. He was probably twelve or thirteen years old.

I sipped the last of my drink and looked over at Mike. "It blows to be a teenager, it really does."

Mike looked over at the kid. "Yeah. I mean, being sixteen isn't so bad. I guess, at least I'm not a thirteen anymore. And I've got this girlfriend, who is like, OK, I guess." He looked at me. I was quiet, so he looked down at the bar and rubbed his fingers over the wood.

"Who said I was your girlfriend?" I said and Mike blinked rapidly. I realized that he didn't know that I was teasing him, so I said, "I have to tell you something." He looked really nervous. I leaned over and whispered, "I'm really a man. A hardcore man." He laughed and shook his head.

"You're one lucky man," he said. "A lucky man with a vagina." It was my turn to laugh.

"Let's get my hardcore vagina out of here before she bitch-slaps everyone," I said.

"Your vagina is so West Coast," Mike said. The withered old fucker sitting at the bar a few stools down looked at us both incredulously, shook his head and ordered another shot.

Mike motioned for the bartender, who was wiping the bar down not far from us, listening to some guy talk about hiking as if it was the most amazing, spiritual, awesome, life-changing thing he'd ever done for mankind. The bartender kept saying, "Uh-huh." He told the guy he'd be back, and came over.

"Cash out?"

"Yeah."

He went over to the register, got our bill, came back, handed it to us and Mike put a twenty down. The bartender picked it up, the bleach smell radiating from his worn looking hands, and came back with our change. We walked out, and I couldn't help but look over at the kid in the hip-hop getup. He was still looking angrily down at his hamburger, his parents not talking to one another, his younger sister filling the air with talk of Barbies and ponies and all things sparkly.

We walked back through the woods, laughing the whole way. At our campsite, I pulled the grill open, and quickly threw hamburgers onto the hot metal.

"Unlike that kid, I'm not going to stare moodily at my meat," Mike said, cracking two beers open and handing one to me.

"Now that is hot," I said, and we clanked cans.

We finished grilling, ate, and made a fire as the light began to dim.

"This is amazing," Mike said. It was getting cold, and was now almost completely dark. It had gotten dark fast. Mike was looking into the woods and I could hear the sound of crickets starting up.

"Soon we'll be able to see the stars," I said, putting my hoodie on.

"That will make this perfect," Mike said, sitting down in one of the chairs we'd brought.

"Except one of us needs to learn to play the guitar," I said, spearing a marshmallow on a stick and handing the bag over to Mike. "And it's not going to be me. I'm too lazy."

"How about we just turn the radio up?" Mike moved his chair closer to mine and put his arm around my shoulders. We sat like that, the sound of the fire comforting, the stars coming out, the marshmallows blackening on our sticks like something ripening on the vine. I felt so content, so beautiful parts of me felt like they were dying off, exploding.

"I don't think I've ever felt so good," I whispered into Mike's ear, my lips brushing the delicate brown edge of it.

"Me too," he whispered. He took my hand, led me into the tent. He took my clothes off slowly, his hand running down my hip, over my thunderbird tattoo. "I love this thing," he said and kissed it. He looked back up at me, and everything slowed down. My stomach turned with too much feeling and urgency, his voice in my ear, our clothes all around us, the faint heat and light of the fire, Mike telling me he loved me.

Mike put the fire out as I was fading into sleep, the sound of the tent unzipping and zipping, the water hissing on the fire. Mike crawled back in and curled up next to me. I dreamt.

CHAPTER 6

I was staring at it. Like I had stared at the ten ones before it, the big, blue plus signs sitting in a ring around me. I was sitting on the toilet, staring at them, my head swimming. I knew this was my fault. Mike had told me that he hated condoms, that he was clean, that he had only slept with one girl before me, his girlfriend in California, and that they had never used a condom and never gotten pregnant.

"Shit!" I whispered to myself. I gathered all of the tests together and buried them beneath a pile of tissue paper in the trash. I pulled my pants up, drained the bathtub I had been sitting in after the eighth test and opened the bathroom door like everything was fanfuckingtastick. Like I wasn't sixteen and pregnant and a total fucking statistic. I walked out into the living room and sat down in front of the TV with the twins. I was watching them until Mom got home. She had some sort of lame-ass meeting that was going to keep her late. I sat in front of the afternoon cartoons and tried not to feel like I was drowning. I'd been due for my period about a week after Mike and me had been camping, and when I hadn't gotten it and had started getting sick in the mornings, I had known. I had just known. I watched TV, the colors swirling, the twins clapping, my stomach moving further and further into a deep, dark hole. I thought about what I had to do and went blank.

A few hours later, Mom came in. I was still sitting by the TV. She put her bags down, let the twins rush at her and looked over at me.

"I thought you were going to start dinner?" she said, looking exhausted, her button-down white blouse wilted like an old flower about to rot away and blow into the wind.

"What?" I asked.

"Dinner? I swear sometimes, Margaritte, that you're getting high down there."

I laughed uneasily. "Dinner, yeah, I was distracted."

"By homework I hope," she said, walking into the kitchen. She came out a few minutes later and plopped down on the couch next to me, smiled, put her long, dark arm around me. "Forget it. Let's order pizza, OK?" She said. "Your call. Whatever you want. As long as you get a plain cheese pizza for the twins."

Carrie broke eye contact with the TV. "Pizza?" She asked.

"Pizza!" Mary echoed and started jumping up and down.

Mom laughed. "Oh, to be a child again. To be that happy over pizza."

"Huh, yeah." I said, and picked the phone up. I ordered pizza and we waited, all of us watching TV together. There was a knock at the door. The pizza guy was a tall, skinny kid with bright pink acne in his junior year who had bought weed from me on multiple occasions. We had exchanged an awkward *hi* when I opened the door. I gave him money and he placed the pizza box into my hands, and we laughed at the ironic role reversal.

It was nice without Dad home. Sometimes he was fine, sometimes he was silent, sometimes he laughed too much, but we were always waiting. When he finally came home, Mom and me had put the twins to bed and we were sitting on the couch, watching *Quincy* together.

"Hi girls," he said, shutting the door.

"Leftover pizza," Mom said.

"Great, thanks."

He got himself several slices from the kitchen and then sat down next to us. He'd poured himself a large glass of scotch to go with it. During the break Mom told Dad that Jake was getting out of juvie tomorrow.

"His parents letting him come home?" Dad asked.

"Yes. Though they have all kinds of conditions."

"I was going to suggest that we all go to the Spaghetti Factory for dinner Friday night. How about we take Jake along?"

"Really?" I said, looking over at Dad.

"Yes. We all need a break. Let's go out."

"Thanks, Dad," I said, and Mom took his hand.

We watched TV together that night, and although I was aching inside over what I was going to do about the thing inside me that was only going to be a bigger and bigger issue, literally, it was nice to feel like a family, instead of all of us sequestered in our usual spots, Dad in the office, Mom in the bedroom, me downstairs. I went to bed scared, happy, picking my pipe up, putting it down, picking it up, putting it down. Trying to read and failing.

The next day, pouring myself a cup of coffee, I looked out the window and saw Jake leaning against my car. I ran out the door.

"Jake!" I yelled, running over to him. He caught me in a big hug, and his smell: motorcycle oil, hair tonic, and some strange indefinable spice enfolded me along with his arms and I felt good. I pulled back after a minute and he smiled down at me.

"How was time in the joint?" I asked, and we piled into my car.

"Great!" he said. "I feel like I've grown. As a person."

"In other words, you sold a lot of drugs," I said, turning onto the main street.

"Exactly."

"Jake," I said, shaking my head. "You need to be more careful."

"Oh, little cousin," he said, turning and giving my head a pet and then a twist until I told him to cut it out. "I missed you. How are things with your new loveeeeeerrrrr," Jake said mockingly. My stomach twisted. I had almost been able to forget about my problem for a second there.

"Great," I said nervously.

Jake's eyes narrowed with concern. "Something tells me that it's not great. You sound funny."

"No. Really. He and I are totally cash," I said in what I hoped was a convincing tone. It wasn't.

"What did he do? He fuck around on you? I'll kick his little Colombian ass—"

"No! No. It's fine. He's fine. It's really good. It's fine."

Jake was silent. He knew I wasn't telling him something and this was new for us. I told Jake everything. And I wanted to tell Jake, I really did. I knew that he would help me, no matter what I decided. And I knew what I had to do. I just, you know, didn't want to face it. And telling Jake was facing it. I didn't even want to tell Mike because it would change things. I wanted to just, I don't know, do what I had to do and then maybe it wouldn't. Or something like that. I was confused.

Jake and Mike and me spent that week hanging out, laughing, doing deals together and it felt like the most perfect thing in the world. But hanging with Mike was weird. We had fun but I felt the whole time like I was hiding something huge from him, because I was. I figured he would know something was wrong but for some reason, he didn't. And that was best because I needed badly to figure this out in my head, for me, before I let anyone, even Mike, in on it.

But I was really looking forward to Saturday. Dad was behaving that week, and Mom was looking less wilted and the twins were not annoying the living crap out of me. The only thing wrong was that I was fucking, fucking pregnant.

Saturday, all of us piled into Dad's giant, blue suburban. It had been sitting like a ancient submarine in our yard for years, half buried in the dirt but, for some reason, lately, he'd kicked it into high gear and had actually fixed it.

Dad was obviously drunk, but not too drunk to drive of course and the twins were cute as hell, buckled into their car seats, Barbies in grimy light brown fists. On the way there, Jake made funny faces at the twins and they laughed, and Mom and Dad talked up front. They didn't argue once. Dad didn't growl or yell, or tell everyone to *be quiet!* He seemed happy, laughing at Mom's jokes and reaching up to scratch at his light brown beard whenever she said something interesting.

Coming into Denver was always cool, the city appearing like parts of a cloud drifting into view until the whole city was around you, the buildings glittering upwards. I stared up and then closed my eyes. I thought about what it would be like to be older, to have a job in a city like this, to do something important, or meaningful. I couldn't really imagine it. Sometimes though, when I would buy a magazine, usually some women's fashion magazine, and I looked through all of the glossy pages at the women dressed in clothing that cost more than what my parents' monthly mortgage was, I did picture myself as one of them. I'd even go to my closet occasionally and try to put something together like the women in the magazine, but I pretty much failed every time. My collection of Walmart tank tops and jeans and tennis shoes just couldn't add up to anything resembling what those women's lives looked like. Julia bought those magazines too. She was cool and knew things about music that I didn't and also bought magazines like *Rolling Stone* and *Spin*. And even though she was poorer than me, knew how to find things in the thrift stores that fit her lovely, thin body and made her look like an alternative version of the women that I so envied.

Jake was making both of the Barbies dance to La Cucaracha for the twins and it was hilarious. Even Mom and Dad were watching here and there and cracking up. It was good to hear my dad laugh. He did it so rarely. Sometimes my sadness for him overwhelmed my resentment and that was even worse. I worried that he would die horribly, either walking around drunk one day, freezing to death, or in a car wreck, or he'd just die in his bed when the alcohol finally took him. He was focused on the road ahead, still smiling slightly. I sighed deeply and with a slight rumble in my chest from the smokes.

Dad had to circle about a trillion fucking times before he found a parking spot. He'd offered to drop us all off at the front door, but for some reason, Mom kept telling him no. The twins were starting to get restless in their car seats, and nothing Jake did to entertain them was working anymore.

"I gotta pee!" Carrie said, looking over at me urgently. Mary nodded.

I looked over at Mary nodding and said, "Mary, do you have to pee too?" She just kept nodding. She always did what Carrie did, wanted what Carrie wanted, said what Carrie said. I had no idea if she really needed to pee, or if it was, as usual, a situation where she was just echoing Carrie's sentiments.

"Margaritte, do the twins need to pee?"

"Yeah."

"Oh, no. Doug—"

"Everyone just calm down."

"Doug, you calm down."

"Shut up Christine! Let me focus."

Mom folded her arms in front of her chest and I began to feel sick. It had been going so well. About fifteen minutes later, after more and more circling, further and further away from the restaurant, Dad found a spot and parked. We filed out of the car. Carrie had been crying for ten minutes. Dad kept telling her to stop and Mom kept telling him to quit telling Carrie to stop, and then Mary had started crying, too. I felt like joining.

As we walked and the twins cried, Dad walked ahead, nearly losing us. Jake tried to keep an even distance between all of us, while Mom yelled, "Doug! Slow down!"

"If all of you would just move it!"

"Dad," I said.

"Margaritte, if you would just hurry up, this wouldn't be an issue."

"Dad, your legs are longer than mine and we're—"

"Let's go!"

I sighed deeply and thought about all the walks we'd taken up in the mountains when I was kid, before his body became too fucked up to handle long periods of exercise. He would make me walk in front of him, and when I would lag, he would swat me on the ass. I would cry and keep trying.

Finally, we all made it to the restaurant, as I had picked up one scratching, angry twin and Jake the other. Jake was silent.

I could tell that he was furious. Though Dad had been in an unusually good mood, in the week since he got back from juvie, Jake spent as much time as he could with me, but he'd disappeared a few times, as he always had, and I knew he wasn't at his parents' place. When he showed back up, he'd sit in my basement listening to his heavy metal Christian rock on my old boom box, the one Dad had taped up with duct tape to ensure its survival.

Dad was already at the front, and we walked up behind him and waited until someone came to lead us to our table. We settled the twins into their booster seats and made our drink orders. I thought things might be over but I was wrong. As soon as Dad had his second scotch in hand, he set into Mom.

"You need to learn to control them, Christine. They need discipline. And if you'd only plan ahead—"

"Don't start in with me. I take care of them, you don't."

"I work."

"I work too!"

"Guys!" I yelled. Jake looked at us and went to the bathroom. I knew he was going to get high. That's how he dealt with his life at home. His parents never fought, but his father quietly controlled everything. Being in their house was like being in cold, windy tunnel. Sometimes though they would joke and laugh and it was fun being there, like in the days they used to powwow.

Dad ordered yet another scotch and I vibrated with expectation. Mom and I watched him drink scotch after scotch, as the twins chattered and laughed. Once Jake had gotten back from the bathroom, I went and got high myself. I knew that that was wrong, considering my situation, but I figured that since it wasn't going to be my situation for long, who the fuck cared. Though I felt funny doing it. Real funny. I only took one hit.

Mom and Dad bickered and Jake and me tried to talk about school shit, but neither of us gave enough of a fuck about school to really make much of a conversation. It was the only half safe subject matter we had to talk about in front of my parents, not that they were listening. I wondered how had they gotten to this place, where there was no love, no seeing the other. Only anger, pain; the unfulfillable desire to win. I knew that I would kill myself if I ended up in a place like that. My stomach was in knots.

Jake added to the tension but I was glad he was around. I looked over at his long, dark, muscular body and felt sad. It wasn't his job to protect us. He was only a kid. A big tough kid, but a kid.

By the time we got the bill Dad was drunk as fuck and the twins were squirming out of their chairs every few seconds. As we walked back outside, and into the darkness, it began to thunder.

"Oh for God's sake," Mom said, closing her eyes briefly and then pausing to look up at the sky.

Dad mercilessly barreled through the rain, and Jake and I quickly scooped the twins up and began after him, Mom trailing behind and complaining the whole way.

"Move it!" Dad said, nearly disappearing around a corner. My arms were already killing me and Carrie was weeping and tearing her claws into me. I didn't even have the energy to tell her to stop and hoped she would wear herself out.

We made it to the car mainly through memory, as Dad finally managed to move too quickly around one too many corners, and lose us.

"Goddamn him," Mom said before she opened the door.

We filed in. By this time, the rain was pouring in sheets. Mom and Dad began to argue in earnest.

"Why do you do that!"

"I was just trying to get through the rain, Christine, if you'd only move it."

"We're not as fast as you are, and we had the twins."

Dad pulled sharply out of the parking spot, barely checking on his left to see if there were any incoming cars. I winced. Jake patted my shoulder.

"It's going to be OK," he whispered. I nodded and my eyes began to well up.

"Doug! You're going to kill us. Watch where you're going."

"Shut up Christine and let me drive."

"Doug, please. It's raining and you need to watch where you're going. And you had so many scotches—"

"I'm fine Christine! What the hell is wrong with you? I have one little drink, so that I can put up with your incessant bitching, and you make an issue out of it!" He pumped the wheel with his left fist, to make his point. The car moved jerkily with each stomp of his fist and on the last one, skidded a little in the rain, which was now coming down much more wildly than it had when we left the restaurant.

I grabbed Jake's arm and squeezed. I closed my eyes. "Do something," I whispered.

"Auntie Christine and Uncle Doug, maybe you guys could talk about this once we get home," Jake said, and I opened my eyes. I had a pretty good idea this wasn't going to go over well. I wish I hadn't asked Jake to do anything.

Both of them were silent for a little while and I thought they might just let it go.

"Shut up!" Dad screamed. "Just shut up!" He began to move his arms up and down violently, keeping his hands on the wheel but causing the car to skid around in the rain with each pulse of his elbows.

"Dad! Calm down!"

"You calm down! I'm fine!" The twins began to cry in the back again, and I turned around and tried to comfort them as best I could.

"I'm just sick of putting up with a family that won't take responsibility!"

Mom snorted at this.

"You fucking bitch," Dad said in low, grumbling voice.

"Don't you dare talk that way in front of the kids," she said, crossing her arms and shaking her head. "Don't you dare."

"Don't you *dare* talk to me like that!"

"Shut up."

Dad's fist shot out from his right side and connected sloppily to the right side of Mom's face.

"You bastard!" she said, putting her hand up to the side of her face. "You goddamn bastard!"

"Maybe now you'll shut the fuck up and let me drive!"

Mom began to cry.

"You need to learn to respect me!" Dad said, hitting the wheel with his left hand.

"This is not how you get respect Doug, from bullying and drinking and hitting. What is wrong with you? You used to be reasonable, kind."

"That was before I knew you were a bitch."

"You bastard," Mom murmured again and Dad's hand shot out once more, but this time, Jake caught it.

"You need to stop," Jake said. Dad looked at his arm, taking his eyes off the road. He began to shake at Jake's hand violently, and the car started to swerve. Jake let go of his arm, but it was too late, we were already headed for the side of the road. We hit the ditch and started to go down a hill and the last thing I remember before I passed out was the sound of crying from all sides.

I woke to sirens outside the car and voices seeming to come from a great distance. The twins were wailing and I lifted and then shook my head. We were at an angle. The car had gone into a large ditch and it looked as if we'd slid until we hit the bottom of it. And although the voices had sounded distant, they were not. There were men outside of our car, prying doors open, asking if we were all right.

"Is everyone OK?"

"We're OK, I think!" Mom yelled.

"Try not to move," one of the men outside the car said.

I felt a faint throbbing in my left thigh and looked down. Some kind of piece of metal had lodged itself in my thigh, though it didn't look very deep. I looked over at Jake and he was just waking up.

"Margaritte, are the twins OK? Can you see them?" Mom asked.

"I... I can't get out of my seatbelt without falling forward but I think if they're crying, they're OK."

"Carrie! Mary! Are you OK?" she asked, and I could hear the anguish in her voice.

"Moommmyy," Carrie wailed.

"It's OK, it's gonna be OK," she said, and Carrie and Mary began to cry harder.

I looked over at Jake. He was awake. "Did you pass out?"

"No. We both swung forward when the car hit the bottom of the ditch, but I stayed conscious."

"Mom, are you OK?"

"Yes," she said, her hand coming back into the space between the seats. I grabbed her hand and we squeezed briefly.

"Dad?"

"He's out. His head hit the steering wheel. I think he's alright though. I hear him breathing."

The men outside were finally successful in prying our doors open. They got us out one by one, Dad coming to during the process. We were all examined. I was the only one that they decided had to go to the hospital, though I'd seen Dad failing his breathalyzer on my way out. I knew Mom would have to bail him out. Again. On the way to Saint Lutheran's, I listened to the men talking in the front of the ambulance, Metallica blaring from the speakers. One of them was talking about a woman he had fucked and both of them were laughing. His story went on and on with details that made my stomach turn. I briefly considered pushing the thing sticking into my thigh further in just so I might pass out.

I had to have the metal removed from my thigh under local anesthetic, and then needed to be watched for a day. I was given a tetanus shot, and antibiotics intravenously. Then I received stiches. I was pissed. I wanted to go home and sleep in my own bed. And I was worried about Jake. I knew that Dad wouldn't want him near the house for a good long time, if ever again. He would have to start fully sneaking in through the window. And then there was the baby. I wondered if it was OK, though it felt strange wondering that.

I couldn't sleep for a long time. It was very dark outside. I had the TV on, like my mom did at night, but it wasn't helping. The TV rarely helped me sleep but I didn't have a book here, and the place smelled of pain, rubbing alcohol and underneath everything, an almost rotting flesh smell. A nurse came in every few hours to check on me and take my blood. I turned the channels and found an old episode of *The Jeffersons.* I loved that show. The housekeeper always reminded me of my auntie and Weezy was like my mom, always taking George's bullshit.

I wasn't in any real pain. The wound had been pretty minor, but they had given me some painkillers, and they were adding to the strange, sleepless state I was in. I wished my dad was like the next door neighbor in *The Jeffersons*, big and friendly and kinda dumb, but nice. I wondered what it was like to have a dad who drank a couple of beers here and there and gave you good advice. Even George, though an asshole in a lot of ways, at least didn't drink, and eventually listened to Weezy. George reminded me of my uncles, the kind of ego that has had to fight for everything to survive and is all puffed up but could be deflated at any moment, especially when women were involved. My dad was more like a big, angry brick wall, one that you could never reason with, one that grew the more you tried to get around it, like a maze where there was no exit. He'd gotten to the point where nothing you said would be met with anything but some fantastically twisted, paranoid reaction.

"Why won't she just leave him?" I whispered to myself, watching a tiny TV George jump around his apartment building, Weezy standing off at the side in a silky red dress, an expression of amusement on her face. I thought about Mike. I thought about the baby inside me. I thought about Mom. I thought about what it had been like for her when she got pregnant the first time. I put my hands on my stomach and wondered. Felt strange, sure of nothing. I looked outside at the dark. I slept before I knew that I was closing my eyes.

I woke up surprised that I had gone to sleep. Mom was sitting in a chair next to the bed.

"Hi," I said, and stretched and then sat up. "Can I get outta here?"

"Yes, soon. The doctor has to come and check you out and that could take a while, but they tell me you're fine. And you can order breakfast."

"I'm sure that's deeeelicious in this joint," I said, adjusting my thin white blanket and thinking about the fact that this was the second set of stitches I'd had in two months. The other wound had healed, the stitches taken out, and the whole thing was nothing but a brownish scar on my side and a shitty memory. But it did strike me that one way or another, I really was sick of hospitals, stitches, and the cause of said things.

"Oh, Margaritte, just order something."

I looked at the menu and ordered cereal. When I finished and the orderly had gone, I looked up at Mom.

"Is everyone OK?"

"Yes."

"And Dad? And Jake?"

"Dad got a DUI and this morning, I had to go and bail him out. Jake is missing and your dad has already started drinking."

"Oh, God," I said and drank out of the Styrofoam cup of coffee in front of me. Mom must have brought it in for me. I shook my head. "Well, Jake has friends. Not great friends, but places he can stay, at least for a while. But damn Mom, it's eleven in the morning." There was a clock on the nightstand next to the bed. "Not that Dad has many borders but he usually at least waits until four. And doesn't he work today?" I sighed and ran my hand down my hair. I couldn't wait to shower the stink of this place off me.

"I called and told them about the accident and then dropped the twins off at Auntie Justine's before I came here. I had to. The minute he got home, he headed for his office. I could hear him laughing in there, and crying and mumbling. I thought he'd come after me but he didn't."

"Mom… "

"Don't say it."

"Why don't we just leave him?" I couldn't help it. I guess it was the lack of sleep, and the accident and the late night TV and this place. This white, sterile place that smelled of alcohol and death.

"If I leave him, he'll die, Margaritte. We don't have the money for rehab and he won't admit he has a problem."

"He's going to kill us someday, Mom. He almost did last night."

Mom took a breath. "That's not true. That was also Jake's fault."

I looked at her incredulously. "Are you crazy? He was trying to get Dad to stop hitting you! And he was driving all of us around totally drunk, as usual!"

"He's a good driver, Margaritte. And before tonight, he was doing better."

"I don't want to talk about this anymore. I can't."

I turned my head away from her and started crying, silently. She tried to come around to me after a few minutes, tell me to stop, but I just put my arm over my eyes to block her out. She whispered my name. She began crying too. I almost wanted to tell her, confess everything, tell her that I had a child inside of me, feel her long brown arms around me, because I was her child. Tell her that I didn't know what to do. Ask her, because she was my mother, what I should do. Because I always had asked her. But I couldn't. I just couldn't. I stopped crying. I began to feel hard, cold as the steel armrests beneath me.

We waited in silence for the doctor. She came in with a nurse and they stitched the small wound in my leg up. It only needed two stitches. When she was finished, the nurse left and the doctor told my mother that I had to fill a few forms out and that hospital policy was I had to fill them out alone, as there were some confidential things that she had to ask me. My mom cocked her head at the doctor suspiciously.

"But she's a minor. And I'm her mother."

The doctor smiled tiredly and said, "I know. Hospital policy."

My mom sighed and pet my head, looked down at me, her dark eyes deep with concern. She left.

The doctor pulled one of those goofy looking pastel colored hospital chairs over and sat down by my bed. She smiled, her light brown eyes large, sweet. She had freckles all across her nose, and I thought about how young it made her look.

"I think you know why I asked your mother to leave."

"Yeah. Is it… OK?"

"Yes. But you're sixteen. And I was sixteen too once and I remember how that felt. And I want you to know that you have options."

I nodded. "I know. I've been meaning to make an appointment. To, well, to not have it."

"I somehow thought so," she said. She pat my hand reassuringly, and I noticed that she had freckles on her hands too.

"You're a good doctor," I said, feeling sad. "I'm glad that I got you."

"Me too Margaritte," she said. "I like your name."

"Thanks. It was my grandmother's."

"You know, I'm Cuban. Are you Latina? That was my auntie's name."

"No. I'm Indian. Dad's white though."

"Oh, I see. Well, in any case, smart brown girls need their lives, their whole lives. Someone helped me back when I was a kid in Florida. A teacher. He gave me a copy of this," she said, pulling the book that Mike had let me borrow out of my Salvation Army book bag. The corner of it had been peeking out the top. I looked at it and laughed and she laughed with me and she pulled a card out of the pocket of her lab coat. Handed it to me. Women's Clinic, it read. I held it. This card I would keep.

"I have a friend there, a good friend. Her name is Lisa. Tell her Cristina sent you. Not that they wouldn't treat you right even if you didn't. And if you need a ride, here's my card." I took that too and looked up at her. "Thank you," I said.

"Of course. Well, I'm going to sign you out and you can walk out that door. Well, wheel out the door. Here's a prescription for antibiotics. Make sure to pick them up, OK? That wound in your leg isn't too bad, but things like this can develop infections."

"I will."

"Bye, now." She smiled and left. I got dressed.

I liked that lady and had slid her cards into my book bag after I'd gotten dressed, feeling cold, determined. I loved Mike, but I was not going to be trapped. But as determined as I felt, I felt strange too. As I was leaving I checked myself out in the mirror above the sink, the antiseptic smell of the soap drifting up. It was sharp. It smelled like something that cleaned death out of things. The whole hospital smelled like that, like that and alcohol. A clean, silver, cold smell. You could nearly taste its metal on your tongue. I slid my hands onto my stomach. I squinted, looking into my own dark, wide eyes and turned to the side. I pulled my hands off of my stomach and inhaled the smell of death. I walked out the door.

CHAPTER 7

I lay in my bed, turning the card that the doctor had given me over and over in my hands until it was crinkled and worn. Until it looked like I'd had it for forever, stuffed into the back of a wooden drawer somewhere. Mom and me had barely talked on the drive home from Saint Lutheran's, more out of exhaustion than anger, filling my prescription at the Safeway and getting home to Dad snoring lustily from their bedroom. I told Mom that I was going downstairs and she nodded silently, walking like a soldier at the end of a long, winter war to her bedroom and shutting her door with her head down. Jake was downstairs, sitting on my futon, his face in his brown-black hands. When he heard me he lifted his head up and out of them and we hugged. We talked for a while. Jake had wandered around that night, finally ending up at Megan's around 4:00 AM, though he told me he couldn't sleep at all for worrying about me. It showed. His eyes were red, bloodshot, like he'd been smoking weed for hours and hours. He told me that his parents knew that it hadn't been his fault. They knew how my dad was. My auntie was always telling my mom that she was praying for him. Jake asked me if I was OK and again, I thought about telling him about the baby, about what I was going to do about it. But something stopped me and I let Jake hug me and leave. I knew what I had to do first. I knew that I had to tell Mike before anyone. I picked up the phone and dialed his number, my heart hammering in my chest. His mother picked up and as usual, sounded extremely displeased to hear my voice. Mike picked up in his room.

"Hey."

"Hey! How are you? I tried calling earlier but no one answered. I thought we were going to hang today? I was all set to come down the mountain and get high with my hardcore girlfriend."

"I'm sorry, Mike. I got in an accident."

I could hear Mike sitting up in bed, fast, his bedsprings jostling noisily. "Holy shit! What happened?"

"Well—"

"Hold on," Mike said, irritation in his voice. And though he clearly attempted to muffle the phone with his hand I could hear every word.

"Mom, no. Mom, I'm on the phone. Mom, something just happened to my, uh, my friend, she got into an accident so can I just not come to dinner tonight? I'll eat leftovers. Mom, I don't know yet, for God's sake, I just got on the phone. Mom... really. Later." I heard the door shut, hard. "I'm sorry. Go on."

"Well, so remember we were all going to dinner last night?"

"Yeah. The family affair."

"Right, so, my dad got rotten drunk, as usual and hit my mom while he was driving in a rainstorm and Jake tried to stop him and we ended up in a ditch. I had to spend the night in the hospital and Dad got a DUI but we're all OK." I could hear Mike sighing deeply on the other end.

"I hate, *hate* that your father does this to you. And I hate that your mother won't leave him."

"I know. I tried to talk about that with her in the hospital but she wasn't having it."

Mike was silent for a while and then he said, "Something has to change."

I took a deep breath and my stomach turned, hard. "The thing is, something has. Mike, what are you doing tomorrow? We should hang out." I could hear breath on the other end. A heavy, pained silence.

"Are you—are you breaking up with me?"

I laughed. "No, no that's not it at all. It's just that we gotta talk."

"Sure. Well, my parents will be gone all day tomorrow; they're off for another couple of days actually on another one of my father's business trips. So come up anytime you want."

"Cool. Well, I'll have to sneak out, so, ten at night OK?"

"Sure. We'll have gin and tonics and talk about whatever your lovely little head wants to talk about."

I laughed weakly. I knew he was going to freak the fuck out. That nothing would ever be the same between us. That all of this unexpected beauty was over.

"OK. Well, I'm gonna get some sleep. See you tomorrow."

"OK. Night. Love you."

"Love you too." I said, and hung up.

After a day of staying in the basement as much as I could, I crawled out the window around 9:00 and drove up towards Mike's house, the twists and turns on 103 mirroring my insides; my head, gut. It was dark and I felt dark, ominous, like somehow all of this was my fault and I was about to spoil everything. I felt like a rotten, stupid thing.

I found myself at Mike's door about thirty minutes later,

barely remembering the majority of my drive, my hand hovering over the knob and then floating down. I had been standing there for ten minutes, doing the same thing, over and over like the crazy-ass motherfucker I was when the door swung open. It was Mike.

"Margaritte! You weirdo. How long have you been standing here?" he rubbed his nose, sniffed and took my hand, drew me in and shut the door.

"I—do you have a cold?" he looked sweaty and high strung.

"Oh, yeah, no... no—well, actually, yes I do. But I'm fine. You're the one to worry about! Sit down."

"OK," I said, walking over to the couch and sitting down.

"You want a drink?"

"No! Well, I mean, yes. I don't know. OK... " I said.

He laughed that little sophisticated laugh of his and walked into the kitchen. He came back with two drinks and handed me one. I set it down on one of the big, pale, wooden end tables. Mike scooted over towards me and put his arm around my shoulders and leaned his head against mine.

"My poor girl. I wish you could just live with me."

"Yeah."

"So what happened to you that you had to spend the night in the hospital?" He asked, lifting his head and kissing me on the cheek.

"I'll show you," I said, pulling away from him a bit. I felt strange, like I was letting him kiss me when I knew that his affection didn't belong to me anymore. I stood up, pushed my jeans down enough so that he could see the stitches. He touched the area around it, gently. I pulled my jeans up.

He shook his head and looked into my eyes, which began to narrow with anger.

"I want to punch him, I really do."

"I know," I said. "I know."

"What is wrong with your mother?"

"I don't know. She's always telling me that he's getting better. Hardly. He just lets up occasionally, before he totally blows."

"I think I should tell my parents," Mike said, taking my hand. "We could... do something."

I looked back at him in horror. "No. Please don't do that."

He looked confused. "Are you protecting him? I don't understand."

I sighed. Closed my eyes. Put my head in my hands. So much was wrong. Mike put his hands over mine. He pulled me to him. I couldn't believe that he didn't know that I was pregnant. I felt like I was carrying it around on my face. Maybe he did know. But he probably would have pulled away from me if he did. I felt so confused.

"Mike, what would happen is that social services would be called. And then they would take all of us, me, the twins, and put us in foster homes. Ask Julia about those. They're horrible. Most people take as many kids as they can for the money, and don't do a fucking thing but sit on their couches collecting checks and eating Ding Dongs. And that's if you're lucky."

"Lucky?"

"Julia was raped by one of her foster fathers. She was twelve. She got... pregnant." I'd forgotten this part of the story and now regretted bringing it up. "She had to get rid of it."

Mike looked sick. "I can't... there has to be... "

"I know. Why do you think me and Jake starting selling? There's no way out, unless you're smart and go to college, or find a way to make money. And we found a way."

"I'm afraid for you, Margaritte. You're only sixteen years old. What if he... before you make it out?"

"I know. I worry about that too. He loves us, he can be sweet, and sometimes I think he'll be fine. But then he blows. Something will set him off and he drinks and then shit goes down."

Mike was silent, pulling at a long piece of thread poking out of the couch. He pulled at it a few times and then with one violent yank, it came out. He rolled it between his fingers and then threw it on the floor and looked at me. I could feel his anxiety, his feelings of utter frustration.

"This is why I'm so angry at the world. Why I tell my parents that everything is useless. Why I think college is futile," Mike said. "They always say that if I want to change the world, if I'm so angry at it, well, I should become a lawyer. But they say that hoping that I'll change my mind and become a corporate lawyer. And what if I don't? What if I specialized in social law? It doesn't seem like much happens that can change anything. I'd just be one guy, fighting for some small aspect of the law that in the long run, would change something in such a miniscule, insignificant kind of way, that—"

"Mike," I said, interrupting him. "Wait. Stop. I have to tell you something before I lose my nerve."

He blinked, rapidly. "What?"

"Remember I told you on the phone that I had to tell you something."

"Oh. Yes. That. That's why I... that's what made me nervous," he said, sitting back and running his hands through his hair. "What's going on Margaritte? Just... tell me. I can take it."

I took a deep breath. I knew that I had to tell him. I knew that after I did, this was over. All of it was gone.

"Mike, I'm pregnant."

His smile melted from his face. I closed my eyes. He was gonna flip out completely.

"Really?" I opened my eyes. "Margaritte, really?" He got up off of the couch. He fell at my knees and looked up at me. I couldn't have been more surprised. This was not what I expected. This did not make sense. I thought we would cry, pretend that nothing would change, share the cost of an abortion, a ride to the women's clinic, a few weeks of awkwardness and then, awkward smiles in the hallways.

"You're not screwing with me, are you? Please tell me you're not!" He said, tears in his eyes.

"I'm-I'm not... " I looked down at him. I didn't know what else to say, he had shocked me into silence. I put my hands on his head and he leaned into my lap.

"This is wonderful. I'm going to go get some of my dad's cigars!" He jumped up and ran over to the hallway, disappearing. I just sat there. A few minutes later Mike came out with a cigar in hand.

"I know you can't have one but," he said, sitting next to me, "here's to us!"

"But Mike—"

"No! Wait! Let me light this first," he said desperately, his hands shaking.

"OK." That's when I noticed something on his nose. I leaned in. It was white powder. I stood up.

"Are you fucking doing coke?" I asked, horrified.

"What? Oh, Margaritte!" he said, laughing, "C'mon. It's just a little nose candy. It's no big deal."

"Mike, how much of this have you been doing?"

"Margaritte, stop fussing and sit down. You're making more

of this than you should. Coke is nothing. And we should be celebrating!"

I sat back down, hard. My head began to swim.

"Mike... " I said, trying to focus and rubbing my forehead, my eyes down, "We can't keep it. I can't."

"What?" he sounded desperate, insane. "Don't you dare say that! How could you even say that! Tell me you're lying." He pulled anxiously at my arm.

"Let go!" I yelled angrily. "I'm sorry Mike, but you and me are too young. And the coke... I can't believe I didn't... why now, I... "

"Just say you won't do it!" he looked crazy, wild-eyed.

"Let go of me!" I pushed him away.

"No Margaritte! No! Please!"

I put my hands over my eyes and shook my head. I was exasperated. "Let's just calm down," I said, removing my hands and looking at Mike. He was breathing hard, sweating.

"And for fuck's sake, no more fucking coke while I'm here."

He kept staring at me, into me, desperation in his long black eyes. He sat down on the couch. We were silent. I sighed heavily and pulled a pack of cigarettes out of the pocket of my jacket and just so I wouldn't have to hear it, didn't light one up, but handed one to Mike.

He took it, walked into the kitchen for an ashtray, and smoked while I sat back with my eyes closed. After I felt like he'd calmed down, I turned to him.

"Mike. Why do you want me to have a baby? We're sixteen."

He was silent for a while longer, finishing his cigarette. He ground it out on the ashtray and sat back. "Because... because it would be mine... ours, I mean. Just ours."

"Yes, of course it would be ours but how would we afford it?

Where would we live? How would we go to school and make it through the next two years with a child? Not to mention that we could… either one of us… I mean, have one later in life. When things are better. Safer."

"Safer?" Mike said incredulously. "When are they ever going to be safer? This world is not safe."

"Mike, I love how smart you are and I agree with you, but these are important questions I'm asking. How would we live?"

Mike shifted around on the couch and looked away. He was silent for a while. Then he turned to me. "I don't know. But I don't care. I want this Margaritte, and our parents will just have to deal with it. We could get on some kind of… assistance if they won't."

My stomach turned. This was my nightmare. I saw those women at the grocery store. Fat, tired, their children reaching up at them, yelling. The women buying the cheap, shitty food the government allotted them. Either commodity or food stamp. I had spent my whole life knowing that I didn't want that. No matter what.

"You don't understand, Mike. It's bad. You don't get it."

"I don't care. Please, Margaritte."

I wanted a cigarette, badly. But I knew it would make things worse. I sat for a while, thinking, looking for strings of my own to pull.

"Mike? Why do you want this so badly? Most boys your age would be tearing their wallets out of their pockets and shoving money at their girlfriend's faces in the hope that they would get an abortion. But you, you really want this. I don't understand."

He was silent and I could feel the pain radiating out of him. It felt like waves of heat coming from every part of his body. Tears were beginning in the corner of his eyes and so I took his hand.

"I don't have anything here," he said.

My eyebrows knitted together in confusion, hurt. “You have me. You have your parents.”

“It’s not the same.”

“Not the same?”

“There is no one here that is really my family. You don’t understand that. You have a huge family.”

“OK, but Jake is who I’m closest to. And he’s adopted. I feel closer to him than any of my family.”

Mike nodded.

“You know Mike, Jake looked his biological family up once. They were fucking awful. His dad was a deadbeat, never there, drunk when he was. His mom is full-blooded. An enrolled Cheyenne. Jake thought that alone was reason enough to contact her. She wasn’t just a drunk, she was a junkie. He would come over and there were needles all over the floor, her kids all running around wild. He’d try to feed them, help her. It didn’t work. One time he came over and she was holding the kids hostage with a knife. They were all huddled in the corner, stinking of pee. Jake had to call the cops and social services took the kids. I’m not saying it’d be the same for you. But it doesn’t always turn out so great. Sometimes your biological family, well, sometimes they suck.”

Mike stood up and went to the kitchen, his glass in his hand. He came back with a drink for himself and sat back down again. He sipped.

“It’s funny, I used to think that all of my bad qualities came from my dad. I used to picture him as Indian. I used to picture my mom as more Spanish. I know how that sounds now.”

“I thought you didn’t think about what you were.”

“Well. I didn’t. I don’t. But, well, I did. Just not the way you would. It’s hard to explain.”

I nodded. "Well… I used to want blue eyes."

"Really?" Mike asked, looking at me with amusement. "I can't even picture it."

"I know."

Mike drank again, looked out into the living room, at all of his parents' beautiful, expensive, meaningless furniture.

"My mom wasn't our age you know."

"Our age?"

"When she abandoned me."

"How old was she?"

"Nineteen. That's not young. That's old enough to keep a baby. Sometimes I hate her. I fucking hate her."

"You don't know the story, Mike, what it was like for her, or what she was going through."

"I guess."

I put my arm around him. "Well, maybe it's selfish of me, but I'm glad you were adopted. Because otherwise I would have never known you."

Mike turned to me, took my hand. "That's not selfish. That's how my parents feel."

My stomach began to hurt and he pulled me toward him, the animal thing between us yearning until we began to kiss, and he began to cry and lead me to his bedroom.

He made love to me gently, as if I were days away from having our child instead of months and months, whispering *Please Margaritte* and *I love you so much* over and over. I kept telling him I loved him too, and I did, and it terrified me how much I did because Mike was a boy who had gotten so much and was used to getting it, but he was someone who had been ignored too. For all of his affection and tenderness towards me, I knew there was anger and immaturity there and it frightened me to think about what would happen if I said no to him. But it frightened me much more to think about what would happen to us, to me, if I said yes. When we were finished, he passed out into a deep sleep, his arms and legs wrapped around me as if he were my child. I watched him sleeping, his mouth in a long, peaceful line, his silky black eyelashes that slanted down over his eyes when he was awake making him look shy and devilish at the same time, almost like a doll's. I touched them gently and he sighed. I could not sleep. This was too much, too much.

I woke up to Mike's arms and legs still around me. I had finally slept a little, after staring at Mike, the walls and finally the light coming in through the window, and yet I still could not stay asleep. I disentangled myself and got up and made breakfast, wandering where his parents were now. I had never met them.

"Hey," Mike said, walking into the living room and stretching. "You made coffee? God, yes." He walked over to the machine and poured himself a cup and sat down. "Did you get something to eat?"

"Yeah. I made eggs and toast. I left some for you," I said, getting up and walking over to the plate I had made for him. "It's still pretty warm." I picked it up and walked it over to him, setting it down. He looked up at me.

"What?"

He was quiet, and then he put his hand on my arm and pulled me gently down towards him. He kissed me. I lifted back up and shook my head.

"You're an incredibly silly boy," I said, sitting down in front of my cup of coffee. He frowned.

"What?"

"That's not good for the baby."

"I… Mike, we talked about this."

Mike put his fork down, sat back, a pained expression on his face. "But I thought after last night… "

"Mike. I love you. But how in hell would we raise a baby?"

"Margaritte… we'll figure it out. Please."

"I can't live like the women in this town. My whole life I've promised myself I wouldn't be like my mother, or any other of the sad fucking women in this town, walking around with no lives of their own, trapped, fat, sad. Supporting their dead beat men."

Mike took a sharp breath. He looked angry. "I would never, ever be like that. Ever. And I can't believe you would even say that."

"No, no… Mike, I know you wouldn't but I don't want to be like that. I want to… I don't know what I want! I don't want to be a teenage mother just like every other girl in this town. And I *don't* want my mother's life."

"I am not your father."

"I know you're not! I'm not saying you're like my father. It's not about you."

"It is about me. This is my baby too. Please," he said, his lip trembling. "Let's just… I know you have to get back and my parents will be back in the next few days, but just tell me you'll think about this before you go and do something you know you'll regret."

"Why would I regret it, Mike? I don't understand."

"You do. I know you do. I can feel that you want this baby. Why else would you have told me?"

The force of his words released a tidal pain inside of me, ripping forward, wave after wave. "Don't do this to me. I love you so much."

We were quiet then, both of us eating our eggs and toast and sipping our coffee with little appetite. When we finished, I showered and got ready to leave. At the door he told me he would call me. We hugged.

"Don't do anything without talking to me first," he said, and I nodded. "Promise me."

"Yes," I said, and he looked at me like I was holding something of his, something he could not trust me with and I suppose that I was. But it was mine too. That's what he didn't seem to understand, that it was growing inside me. And the thing that I could not tell him, the thing that rose up in my throat, the thing that he could see as clearly as if it were written across my forehead was that he was right. I wanted it. I wanted it and him, and all of us together. But I knew where that kind of thinking led. To a doublewide trailer and miles and miles of cheap macaroni and cheese, ten for a dollar.

I drove down the mountain and snuck back through my window, hoping Mom would think that I'd slept in.

"Hey," Jake said, and I jumped. He was laying on the futon.

"What's up?" I was surprised to see him there.

"Arguing with the parents again. Where were you?"

I sat down on my bed, the springs creaking. "Mike's."

Jake nodded. "You really are in love, aren't you."

I took a deep breath. "Jake, I gotta tell you something. I'm not just in love, I'm pregnant."

Jake blinked a few times, like he couldn't comprehend what I was saying.

"You're... how... what?" He sat up on the futon, his mouth slack.

"Yeah."

"How did you get pregnant?"

"Well, when a boy and a girl get together and love each other very much—"

"Don't be funny. This isn't funny. At all. Have you told Mike?"

"Yes."

"What did he say."

"Fuck, I want a cigarette," I muttered, running my hands along the bedspread. I knew that I wasn't going to keep it, but smoking just seemed wrong.

"Margaritte, what did he say?"

"He said he wanted me to keep it."

"What?" Jake said incredulously. "He's crazy! I know he loves you but, well—is he talking about marriage? Is this what this is about?"

"No, I don't think so."

"Then what's going on? Why would he want you to have a baby at sixteen?

I thought about long drags of cigarettes and then reached into my bag and got one. I lit it, feeling perverse.

"I said the same thing. Not about marriage, about being sixteen, both of us. Frankly, his reaction shocked the fuck out of me. I thought he was going to freak out, make sure I was down with getting rid of it and that it would be the end of us as a couple." I smashed the half-finished cigarette down into the ashtray, as it was making me nauseated. "What he said was that, well, he wants it because he doesn't have any family here."

"Doesn't have any... of course he does. His mom and dad and oh, you mean because he was adopted," Jake said, a small breath coming from his nose. He nodded slightly and lit a cigarette. "Yeah. Well. Did you tell him about my fantastic biological family?"

"I did. But he's so emotional over this, I can't tell you. And there's something else."

"Oh, God. What."

"Remember that party he came to? The one where the cops got you?"

"Yeah?"

"Well, remember your friend saying something about Mike's friends all being cokeheads?"

"He's *not.*"

"Yeah. He is. He sure is. I caught him yesterday. And I couldn't believe I hadn't figured it out before. He's just all sweaty and high-strung and *fuck yeah!* after he hangs with his little track buddies. And sometimes he was like that when I came up to visit. I guess I didn't want to see it. But he was careless yesterday, after I told him about the baby, and I saw powder on his nose. Worst part is, he thinks it's no big deal."

"Margaritte, we can take the money out of our savings account for an abortion."

"Right. It'd barely cut into our savings, really. And I know it's the right thing to do. I am *not* living the Idaho Springs Lifestyle. Not this bitch. Hell no. But I know that it means Mike and I will break up. And I love him. And I'm so—" my voice broke and I began crying. Jake got off the futon and sat next to me. He held me as I cried.

"I'm sorry, Margaritte. I'm so sorry. I'll go with you."

I cried for a while and when I was finished, wiped my face with my sleeve and took a long, hard breath.

"We didn't use protection."

"Margaritte, Jesus."

"I know. I don't know why I did that. I know better. I know so much better. It's my fault."

"It's his fault too."

"I know."

I started to feel a little bit better. It was reaching towards lunchtime and I knew I had to put in an appearance upstairs.

"You gonna stay down here? I could bring you lunch."

Jake smiled. "Gotta go do some biiiidness."

"OK, you do that. I'm going to make the appointment. At the hospital a really cool doctor there gave me a card and a name."

Jake nodded, hugged me and squeezed out the window, which was always an amazing thing to watch. Fucker was lucky he was skinny, otherwise it would never happen. He knew if he was fighting with his parents, it'd take around two fucking seconds for that to get back to my mom via the moccasin telegraph.

I sighed and pulled the card out of the drawer of my end table. Looked at its faded letters in my hand. I pulled the telephone onto my lap and picked the receiver up and put it back down again. It was Sunday. They were probably not open anyway. And I was hungry. I wanted to go upstairs and eat a sandwich and hang out with my mother and the twins and watch TV and forget about all of this.

That night, around 10:00 the phone rang. Mom picked it up. She was in the kitchen grading, Dad was in his office. Mom yelled that it was for me, and I walked downstairs and picked up. I knew who it was before I heard his voice.

"Have you thought about this?" Mike asked, sounding wound up.

"Yes."

"And?"

"Mike, I told you. I can't have a baby. I'm sixteen. We can't have a baby."

There was silence on the other end. And then in the distance, "Mike, who are you talking to this late?"

"My girlfriend!"

"Your what? When did you get a girlfriend?" The voice was closer now.

"Mike, don't—" I said.

"Mom, I need to talk to her. Let me alone for a goddamn second, would you?"

"How dare you use that language with me!" Then footsteps and scrambling.

"Mom! Don't you hang the phone up! No!" And then more scrambling. The last thing I heard before the dial tone was Mike yelling, "Margaritte I will never forgive you if you do this! Don't you do—"

I looked at the receiver. I put my head in my hands. In the past, I would call Julia and whine my head off. And I knew she had been through this, and that what she had gone through had been much, much worse. But her strangeness with Mike made it seem too weird. I knew that all I really had was Jake. I looked down at my stomach and flopped on my bed. I closed my eyes.

The next week was hell. School was hell. Mike kept cornering me whenever he could, crying and begging, and then when that didn't work, he'd yell at me to not have an abortion. I told him I didn't want to talk about it at school, where people could hear, but he didn't care. He called me at home. Finally, Jake picked up for me.

"This Mike?" I watched him, his head nodding slightly at whatever Mike was saying. "Uh-huh. Well, she can't come to the phone right now." I put my hands over my eyes. "Oh, really? Well, you know what? You two are sixteen. And this isn't going to happen, buddy. Get that through your fucking head! Your fucking head which I will rip off and shit down if you don't leave her alone about this!" At this, he slammed the phone down.

That's when Mike stopped calling.

CHAPTER 8

"So, what's the plan for tonight? It's Friday. We survived another week in this town. Therefore, we deserve a little party-poo," Jake was saying. I had gone downstairs after dinner to find him sitting on the futon, his long, dark body sprawled out, McDonald's wrappers on the old coffee table in front of him. He was finishing a burger and fries.

"Want one?" he asked, holding the sleeve of fries out.

"Nah, I just had dinner." I sat down on the bed. "We have to have a plan?"

"Margaritte, you know I always have a plan."

I laughed. "OK, so what's your fantastic plan."

"Well, by plan, I mean party."

"Oh, God, I don't know," I said, putting my hands in my hair and looking at the old, beat up basement floor. There was something so cold and depressing about the painted concrete under my sneaks.

"Margaritte, you need some fun. Some distraction."

"Normally by that you'd mean booze."

"Well, yes. No. But... well. When's your appointment?"

"In a few weeks," I said.

Jake looked at me, his face radiating pity. "Has he called again?"

"No."

"OK, now I know you need a drink. That is, if you were drinking. Why aren't you drinking?"

"I can't explain it, but it just seems wrong. Creepy. I'm sure I will… after. But I'll go to the party if you really want me to. I could even call the moron twins up to see if they wanted to join us. Julia got a little pissy with me when I was with Mike, but I'm sure she's heard that we're not together anymore. I mean fuck, I've been trying to call her for weeks, but the foster kiddies always tell me that she's out and about."

Jake handed me the phone. I dialed and asked for Julia at her house, but the kid who answered told me she wasn't there. I looked at Jake and shrugged. I tried Treena's number but her mother, her voice heavy with years of cigarette smoking, told me she wasn't there either. That they had gone out together. I thanked her and hung the phone up. It was an old, red rotary style that had been in my parent's bedroom for years.

"Both of them aren't home. So, maybe they'll be at the party."

"I doubt it. This crowd is older," Jake said.

A few hours later, we were sneaking out the window. We started my car and pulled out of the driveway with the headlights off. The town went by in a near blur, and I felt pretty happy to be getting away from the house. Away from myself. I rolled the window down and let the smell of the green, wet season in. I turned the radio up and found that I still had one of Mike's mixtapes in the deck. One that he had made for me after the first time we'd been together. My throat tightened and I thought about ejecting the tape but I stayed my hand. I let the heavy, staticky, painful music into me and thought of Mike. His hands on me, his eyes closed, listening to the thrum of my heart as it sped up in response to his body. I had to feel this pain, I had to know it like I'd known him or I would never get through it, know what the fuck to do with myself after all of this was over. I looked over at Jake and he took his eyes off the road briefly, sensing my gaze. He smiled.

"What?"

"Nothing," I said. "Just happy to have you here and out of juvie and driving my car again."

"Me too."

We pulled into a side street, which led up sharply and quickly became dirt. The houses whipped by, and the smell of the night air became more specific. It was of pines, a lovely tangy smell. After about fifteen minutes we pulled into a short drive, parked in front of an old, pea-green house behind a bunch of other cars and a few bikes, the noise of the party already hitting us as soon as the sound of the car's engine died. A few people were outside, standing around a keg.

"This is new," I said.

"Yeah, I did a little business with them a week ago, and they seemed like cool guys and they asked me if I wanted to party with them."

I nodded. The wind picked up and I shivered, pulled my hoodie tighter. "It's colder than I thought."

We walked up and over to the keg. Jake pumped two and handed me one out of habit. I held it though, so that no one would think anything.

"Boy, I don't recognize anyone," I said, looking around. The handful of people outside really were a good amount older than Jake and me. A silver mullet crowd.

Jake looked around and took a drink from his beer. "That's why I proposed this. There really isn't a way to get away here, and half of these people are still probably related to the people we go to school with, but at least they're a little older and we don't have to mess with the usual drama."

"Yeah." I said. "Want to go inside?"

Jake shrugged. "Sure."

The old rusty screen door slammed shut behind us. The party was fairly low-key, music floating through the air from an old stereo system in the corner, though there were a couple of people doing coke at the kitchen table.

I tapped Jake on the shoulder. "Check it out. We've picked an upscale crew to hang with here. Coke, not crack."

Jake laughed. "It's always class with me."

"You so deliver. Class, that is."

"Class you can snort up your nose."

"God," I said, "speaking of class, where's the hard alcohol in case I decide to drink, even though I'm currently in the family way?"

Jake patted the pocket of his old black jeans. "Oh, I brought flasky. Don't you worry your crazy little head. I got us covered."

A couple of the dudes doing coke at the old, white kitchen table elbowed each other and got up. They walked over to us.

"Jake. My man."

"Hey."

"So, who's this?"

"This is my cousin, Margaritte."

"Hey cousin Margaritte." I looked up at him and smiled. His teeth were terrifying. Rotted to hell. I looked over at the other guy and he was nodding without speaking. Both of them smelled pretty ripe.

"This your house?"

"Yeah. It was my mom's, but she's dead."

"Oh. I'm sorry."

"I'm not. She was a bitch. The best thing she did was die."

"Well there's that," I said. "Hey, least you got a house though, am I right?"

"Damn right!" He said, giving his friend five. "Do you want some coke?"

"No thanks, I'm all coked out."

He looked at me suspiciously, and cocked his head.

Jake looked over at him and then said, "My cousin's just joking around. We like pot."

"Me too, dude."

"Yeah."

"Well, obviously," he said lamely. "So, speaking of that, I'm gonna need something to help me come down at the end of the night. You got any doobage for sale?"

"Of course."

Jake pulled a dime bag out and the guy handed him some money.

"Thanks man."

"Sure," Jake said, and he walked back over to the table he'd been sitting at when we came in.

"They're cool guys?" I said, looking at Jake incredulously. They looked anything but cool. They looked fucked up.

"They're OK."

"Yeah. Did you see homeboy's teeth?"

"Stop complaining, start drinking," Jake said and handed me the flask. We had picked it up at the thrift store a year ago. It was an old silver flask, and it was tarnished on the outside. I looked at the flask and felt a sharp spike of rebellion. What was I not drinking for anyway? I wasn't going to do this. I drank, feeling the rough, tarnished spots of the flask on my fingertips and then handed it back to Jake. He had been watching me the whole time I'd drank. I'd set my beer down as we'd come in and Jake had shaken his head.

"That's my cousin!" Jake said, whooping me and hitting me on the back hard enough to make me stumble forward.

"Jake, watch it!" I said, feeling sick.

I walked over to the couch at the other end of the living room and dropped my hoodie on it. TuPac's "California" came on and people began to move a little to the music. I joined them and let the small drink of whisky I'd taken get into me, through me. I closed my eyes. I felt a little nauseated, but the music was good. It was taking me somewhere, the base thumping in my stomach. My limbs felt fluid and the music was entering me the way the whisky was. More hip-hop came on, Biggie, Snoop; this crowd was into it. I felt Jake tapping my arm urgently. I stopped dancing and turned to him. He looked upset and took my elbow, leading me out of the group of dancers.

"Jake, what's going on?" I asked, but he was still trying to lead me further on. I dug my heels in and he stopped and turned around.

"I—I just wanted to tell you that I don't feel like being here anymore," he said.

I stared at him, feeling confused and irritated. "Jake. What are you talking about? We just got here. And I'm actually having a good time. What? Did those guys do something extra creepy?"

"No. I'm just suddenly—kind of tired, I don't know... is it OK if we just go?" He looked like he was in a panic. I sighed and shook my head. "Sure. Whatever you want Jake. It's not like this is the goddamn Emmy's or anything. Let's go."

“Great, great,” Jake said, grabbing my arm again and nearly dragging me towards the front door.

“Jake! Slow down and let go of my arm. What has gotten into you!”

“Nothing, nothing. I’m just ready to go.”

“Fine. Calm—wait a minute. I left my hoodie on the couch at the other end of the room. Hold on, let me—”

“No!” Jake said, forcibly turning me around. I’d turned away from him and was walking towards the couch.

“I’ll get it for you!” He said, walking, in fact nearly running past me.

“Jake—” I said and watched him disappear. I stood and watched the crowd of tired, sweaty people move, and that’s when I saw them. The crowd parted and I could see Jake picking my hoodie up from one end of the couch, Mike and Julia making out on the other. I felt sick. I couldn’t believe that I hadn’t seen them before. Had they seen me? I went through the crowd listening to the music and feeling sick. Jake had just picked my hoodie up and was on his way back to me when he saw that I’d spotted them. He slumped in defeat, the hand holding the hoodie nearly dropping it, but he quickly recovered and rushed over to me.

“Don’t—” he said and I shot him a look. “OK, but I’m coming with you.”

It felt like my legs weren’t even moving, as if I were moving through a net, but when I finally made my way over, they seemed to sense something was wrong, and at first Julia, then Mike looked up.

“Margaritte—” Julia said.

“Shut the fuck up,” I said. Her eyes moved to her hands.

“You are supposed to be my friend,” I said to Julia.

Julia continued to look down at her hands but Mike glanced

up at me with that look in his eyes that I now knew meant he'd shoveled a bunch of coke up his nose.

Mike kept staring up at me. "Have you done it already?" At this, Julia looked up sharply.

"Done what?" she asked.

"How can you ask me that here? When you're with her?"

"Oh, you think I'm betraying you? Let's talk about betrayal!" Mike screamed. "Let's talk about how you're killing me!" He said, sliding off the couch and onto his knees. He buried his head in my legs and wept violently.

I began to cry. I put my hands on his head. He wrapped his arms around my legs, started murmuring, "No, Margaritte, please don't. Please tell me you haven't."

"Don't you feel bad for him, " Jake said. "This is your decision. What you need to do. He's not thinking."

I tried to stop crying but I couldn't.

"What is going on here?" Julia asked, looking as if she'd stumbled into a horror show.

"I always respected you," Jake said. "I always... "

"Jake, please. I... "

"Please what? How could you do this to me? I mean, to Margaritte? Over some fucking guy? What is wrong with you?"

"I'm sorry. It's just, he called. And, I thought, well if they broke up, he's not really with her anymore and... "

"Does this look like they broke up?"

Julia looked over at us and I stared into her eyes.

"I'm pregnant," I said. "And he wants me to have it. And I don't want to. And even if I wasn't, you've been after him from the beginning and I don't know why." Her eyes widened in horror and she stared down at Mike and then staggered up and off the big, old red couch. She rubbed her forehead, her short, red nails like little harvest moons.

"I have to go," she said, starting to walk away. Jake grabbed her roughly by the arm.

"Is that all? Don't you have a fucking thing to say?"

Her lip trembled, and I could see even in that dim, dreamlike near darkness that her lipstick matched her nails.

"No. I have nothing to say for myself. Let me go. I only want out of here."

Jake shook his head, an expression of disgust on his face. "I loved you, you know. For years."

She looked back at him with an expression of pain on her face. "I know."

Jake looked at her in wonder. Mike was still wrapped around my legs, murmuring to himself.

"You know? That's all you have to say to that?"

She looked at him, a strange, not quite angry, not quite anything look in her eyes. "I can't afford to love anyone."

"You're inhuman," Jake said, shaking her arm free.

"I'm whatever I have to be to get out of here. If you can't understand that, I'm sorry. You'll be stuck here, then."

"At least I won't be stuck in your head," I said. And Julia turned to me, her lip trembling again.

"I'm sorry, Margaritte. I'm really sorry," she said, and with that she took off.

I tried to pull Mike up, but he was nearing a state of total shitfacery.

"How much coke did you do?" I asked him, and his eyes started to roll back in his head. I slapped his face and he seemed to be coming back.

"You can't do this to me!"

"Mike. How much coke? How much booze?"

He smiled at me. "A lot. Ever since you told me you were going to kill my baby."

"Mike. We're taking you home," I said.

"I'm not touching that asshole," Jake said.

I sighed. "Not now, Jake. Please."

Jake looked at me and shook his head. "Why do you care what happens to him? A few minutes ago he had his dirty paws all over your best friend."

"I know. But he looks bad. If he... really got bad I could never live with myself if I just walked off." I looked down at Mike and saw that he was slumped against my legs. It had only been a few weeks since I'd seen him, but his clothes and hair looked dirty, the black waves of his hair greasy and his jeans and blue t-shirt stained. I had never, ever seen Mike like this. He dressed casually, but fucking perfectly. He was always clean. He always smelled wonderful, like some spicy, expensive cologne. But looking at him now, I could see what a rough state he'd clearly been in for some time. I didn't know how he'd even managed to make out with Julia. He looked half dead.

"We should probably take him to the hospital, and not home."

"We should dump him off in a landfill," Jake said, and he took one side of Mike while I grabbed the other.

"Don't do it, Margaritte," Mike murmured in my ear.

"He seemed OK when I first started talking to him," I said. "He went down, fast."

"It's like that with coke sometimes. It feels like you're fucking invincible but when you come down off of it, if you don't do more immediately, you feel like shit. And he's been drinking too. And he's not a very big guy. And I hate this fucker."

I laughed despite myself but it turned quickly to tears as we dragged him towards the door. The guys doing coke at the kitchen table looked up and watched us drag Mike out, shaking their heads and laughing.

"Weak fucker," one of them said. The screen door shut behind us and we got him the short distance to the car, my tears flowing hard now. In my periphery, I spotted someone lurking near the keg.

"Hey, it's OK! Have a beer! Don't cry," the guy said. He was standing lonely at the keg. The party had moved inside by then, the keg totaled. People were either drinking the hard stuff or snorting it. He came stumbling up to us with a beer in his hand. I laughed a little and took the beer in my right hand. "Ever he is, not worth it! Men'r jerks, we really, really we, really are," he said, shaking his head and stumbling in place. "I definitely always fuck it up. Oh, yeah. I do. Definitely do... " and with that, he wandered out behind the house. I threw the beer into the woods. A few minutes later we could hear the guy peeing as Jake and me got the back door open and pushed Mike into the backseat.

"Hospital time. Again," I said. "At least it's not me this time."

Jake sighed and pulled out of the driveway. "OK. Saint Lutheran's. For you, not for him." He was silent for a few minutes, probably trying to think of what he could possibly say to make me feel better.

"Thanks, by the way, for trying to spare me."

"Of course little cousin," he said, reaching over to pat me gently on the head. "He seemed like a nice dude when we first met him."

"They always do, don't they?" I said, looking out the window and thinking of the drunk dude who handed me a beer outside,

"And they always fuck it up." I looked at Mike in the rearview mirror. He was passed out. And he was making a funny noise, which scared me.

"'Course, I fucked up too."

"But you wouldn't have done what he did. Or what Julia did."

"No."

I looked again at Mike.

"Hold that thought." I flipped the inside light on and maneuvered so that I could check him out. I let my hand hover a few centimeters over Mike's mouth. He was taking short, shallow breaths. I turned back around.

"Hurry."

"OK," Jake said, hitting the accelerator. We had gotten out of the mountains as the house hadn't been too far out, and through town, and were about to hit the highway. It was dark, and the lights of the town, the houses looked ominous, strange and white.

"I'm scared," I said and Jake patted my knee awkwardly.

About forty-five minutes later Jake was pulling up to the ER and Mike was looking worse. He had gained consciousness for a few seconds, only to vomit violently onto the floor of the car. I had done the best that I could to wipe him up with the Kleenexes that I had stuck in the side pockets of my door, but I noticed when I did that his lips were growing faintly blue, his skin paler and paler by the second.

Jake and I got Mike out of the back of the car and quickly, men in blue scrubs were there, pulling him onto a gurney and asking us questions, wheeling him away from us. I sat down in the waiting room and put my head in my hands, wanting to block out the white hallways and blue, buzzing florescent lights of the hospital. They were making me feel more nauseated than ever. Jake went to park the car and then came back in and sat next to me, his arm around my shoulders.

When I was finally able to pull my head out my hands, the white walls and cheesy paintings covering them came into focus. Across from us sat a miserable looking couple, with sour, resigned, angry expressions on their faces. They were wearing Harley t-shirts, ones that they had obviously picked up at the rally in Sturgis. Hers was an orange number, with a knife over her heart, consumed by flames. His, a long sleeved white one, with red flames going up the arms. I imagined that he also had, among his numerous bad-ass themed t-shirts, a t-shirt with "Big Dog" on it, and a picture of a bulldog in chains, breaking out of them. Both of them were big but they still somehow managed to look strangely weak, like it would take nothing to push them over. I wondered what gave them joy. Their bikes? Bike rallies? Did they even love each other? Had they ever? I felt sick.

"God, please don't let him die," I said, and Jake pulled me closer.

"He won't," Jake said. But I could hear unease in his voice.

Around twenty minutes later a doctor came out and asked if we had come in with Mike Walker. I told him that we had and he sat down next to us.

"Your friend will be OK. But his blood alcohol level, not to mention the level of cocaine... well... let me put it to you this way, if you hadn't brought him in, I seriously doubt he would have lived to see the morning."

I shook my head. "But he's going to be OK?"

"Well. Yes. Though it's clear that he is a habitual cocaine user and that, to say the least, is not good. He's young, but there is definitely damage. We've called his parents and they're on their way here. He's awake if you want to see him."

"Oh," I said. Hearing that Mike was going to make it had made me feel so good. But hearing that his parents were coming made that feeling drop away, quick. Mike had never introduced me.

I looked at Jake and he nodded for me to go ahead. I followed the doctor down a long, white hallway and into a room. Mike was in bed, the plain white blanket pulled up around him, making him look like a little boy. He looked weak. His eyes were closed. I went to him and took his hand gently. He opened his eyes, those soft dark eyelashes fluttering open and pulling me in.

"Fancy meeting you here," he said, and smiled weakly.

"Actually, I seem to be coming to this joint a lot lately."

"Cheap drinks?"

"Yeah, must be," I said, and we both went silent.

"I'm sorry, Margaritte."

"It's OK."

He was quiet again and then a tear started in the corner of his right eye and ran down his face.

"I just… don't want you to do this. It's tearing me up inside. The pain."

I swallowed. "I'm sorry, Mike."

He began to clench my hand. "Just tell me you'll think about it."

"God, Mike. Not now. Not when you're like this."

"I'm like this because of you!" He yelled, starting forward. He gasped and fell back, sweating. He closed his eyes.

"Mike. I don't understand this. Do you even love me? I feel like this isn't even about you and me. Like the baby is more important than I am to you."

Mike was silent.

"And the coke—"

"Don't start, Margaritte. I got that little speech from the doctor."

"Are you fucking kidding me? You want me to have your baby, but you're not willing to stop snorting coke? What the fuck are you thinking?"

Behind me I heard a woman take breath. I turned around. I saw two pristinely dressed, though disheveled, people hovering in the doorframe. His mom was tall, beautiful and thin, with large cornflower blue eyes and short, light brown hair. His dad looked like Businessman Ken, his coloring the same down to his slightly tanned skin. His mother looked at me and then closed her eyes as if she'd taken a bite of something rotten and was too classy to spit it out. She walked past me and up to Mike, her husband close behind her.

She looked down at him. "We discussed what would happen if you did this again."

"Again?" I echoed faintly. She ignored me. It was like I wasn't even in the room.

"Mom, no. I'm not going anywhere. I'm fine."

"You're fine? This is the second time I've had to come and get you in a hospital. You're anything but fine."

Mike sighed and looked over at his dad. "Talk to her, would you?"

His dad sighed and ran his hand through his perfectly coiffed hair.

"There's nothing I can say, Mike. For God's sake, we relocated in hopes that you would clean up. And you told us you would. And we hoped that living in a small town would put you far enough away from what had been dragging you down. But apparently not."

"I am not going to rehab. I'm not a junkie."

My head began to spin. Who was this person?

"Excuse me," I said, and his parents turned around. "What is going on?"

His mother looked at me with that sour expression she'd had when she'd first come in the room.

"Could you please leave us alone with our son? I don't know who you are, but the fact that you're still standing here as we're trying to have what's obviously a personal conversation with our son shows how rude you are."

"I'm his girlfriend."

She looked at me as if I'd sprouted another head and said, "No. His girlfriend is a girl named Julia. We met her this weekend."

I looked over at Mike and he turned his head away from me.

"Is this true? You introduced Julia to them? And never me? You fucking jerk."

His head snapped back to attention.

"You're the jerk. No. That's not the word. The word is whore."

I hadn't even seen Jake at the door, but before his parents could react, before I could say or do anything, Jake was flying past me and he was on Mike, punching him in the head. All three of us rushed over to Jake, tried to pull him off, but he was too strong, too angry, his long dark arms flashing under the fluorescence. I could hear myself begging him to stop. When security finally came, it took three of them to get him off of Mike and by the time they did, Mike was out cold, marks covering his face and arms.

I began to cry violently, and Mike's mother turned to me. "Get out!"

"You are why he's like this," I hissed angrily.

She drew back in shock. "You little piece of trash. *You* are why he's like this. And he will have nothing to do with that... thing inside you, should you chose to have it."

I shook my head. "You're the trash. You two leave Mike alone constantly, and then tell him who to be. Tell him what kind of an adult he should be. And God forbid he becomes the kind of adult you two are, with your love of things. It's disgusting the way you live."

"The way *we* live is disgusting?" She said, and began to laugh snottily. "How about you people, with your trailers and houses bursting with dirt and children—"

"Enough! Both of you!" Mike's father yelled. He was standing over Mike, his hand cupping the side of his face tenderly. He turned back to Mike. "I'm sorry son, I'm so, so sorry... " he said. Several men in scrubs came in and pushed Mike's dad gently out of the way. They began to work on Mike and though I still loved him, I went out into the hallway as hospital staff began rushing into his room. I could not stand to be in there with his mother one more second and I knew I had to find Jake. In the waiting room, I didn't see him. I went to the large windows, the flash of a blue and red light attracting my attention. Jake was being pushed into a police car outside. I ran out into the rain and tried to talk to the cops, but they only brushed me off by telling me that the appropriate people would be contacted. They drove away, their lights growing dim in the distance. I walked slowly back inside, now soaked, the sliding doors opening and closing behind me in a whoosh, and walked over to the chairs Jake and me had been sitting at only twenty minutes ago and sat down. My bag was still there. I picked it up, feeling sick and useless and exhausted.

Outside, it was dark, but the fluorescent lights of the hospital were good enough to see by. It took me a few minutes, and in that time I became even more soaked, but I found it. It was a small green beast, and the dent in the passenger side door made it at least sort of easy to find. I fumbled with the keys, my hair now streaming water, the keys falling through my hands. "Shit," I muttered, beginning to cry and trying not to completely lose it. I knew I had to get home, get out of there. I picked the keys up off the pavement and got the door open, threw my bag in the passenger seat and sat down. That's when the smell hit me. "Fuck!" I yelled, hitting the steering wheel. I'd forgotten that Mike had puked in the car and my stomach and sense of smell had been particularly sensitive ever since I'd gotten pregnant. I started the car, rolled the windows down and headed for the gas station I could see a few minutes down the road from the hospital. I parked in front, opened the door and headed straight for the bathroom. I pulled as many paper towels as I could from the dispenser, wet some of them, pumped soap on the wet towels and marched over to the car. After a few trips, things were next to tolerable in the car and the rain had started to let up some. I washed my hands in the bathroom, dried off as best as I could with more paper towels and got back into the car.

I pulled onto I-70 after a few turns, heading west, the mountains in front of me, their snow-capped blueness only reminding me of the wonderful time I had with Mike on Mount Evans. I began crying and hit the steering wheel, hard. I hit it again, until I heard a honk from off to my left and realized that I was swerving slightly. I took a few deep breaths and tried to calm down but all I could think about was Jake and Mike and Julia as the sun came up and I got closer and closer to Idaho Springs. I just had to hope that Mom had not noticed my absence. I looked at the clock on the dash. It was around 5:00 AM. I could probably get home in time to sneak through the window and get a few hours of sleep before Auntie Justine would wake my mother with the call. I didn't know what was going to happen to Jake this time. I remembered talking with Mom about him the last time he went to juvie, and she'd said that if he got caught again, he would be tried as an adult, but maybe she was just being dramatic to try to scare me. That would be something she'd do. And as to Mike, I would never be able to forgive him for calling me a... that. It had hurt me deeply, and the image of him lying in bed, his long brown arms sitting placidly on top of the thin, white hospital blanket, calling me that word, kept running through my head over and over like a torture device set to infinitely re-set. His mouth, the "o" of the word, his face twisting around it. And the coke. And the fact that his parents had moved him to get away from it. And the fact that he had lied to me about why they had moved here.

I pulled off the highway and into town, first passing the Derby, the cowboys who looked like cowboys but weren't cowboys but volunteer fireman still probably sitting inside, drinking cup after cup of watery coffee. The neon lights of the Safeway, the kids who basked in the brightness of its twenty-four hour promises. The streets mainly empty, a few lonely cars crossing the pavement to get their owners to work in the dawn. The trees looked like they were being set on fire, the sun just beginning to really move up and into the sky. I pulled into the driveway quietly and got out. I walked over to my window and slid in. I sat down on my bed, grabbed the baggie of weed out from under it, looked at it and my pipe and set them both down on my lap. I couldn't. I just couldn't. I slid them both back under my bed, pulled my clothes off and put an oversized white t-shirt on that had once been my mom's and crawled into bed, thinking that I would never sleep, never.

CHAPTER 9

"Margaritte!" Mom yelled from upstairs. "Get up here right now!"

I had been in a half-sleep state for a while and so when Mom yelled, I finally had good enough reason to open my eyes. I rubbed at my face.

"Margaritte do you hear me? If you don't get up here right now, I'm going to come down there!"

"Why don't you?" I muttered to myself, rolling out of bed and sitting on the edge of it. I pulled on a pair of old grey sweatpants and walked grudgingly upstairs. Mom was standing at the top of the stairs, her hands on her hips, her mouth in a small, thin, purple line.

"Mom—"

"Mom nothing. You come here, sit down. You have a lot, and I mean *a lot,* of explaining to do."

"I—"

"I said sit down!"

"I have to go to the bathroom!" I said, running.

"You come back here right now!" Mom yelled. I kept going. The nausea was unreal. I ran into the bathroom, threw the door closed, locked it and went down on my knees in front of the toilet. I was sick for about five mind-bending minutes. When I was done I had to rest my head on the edge of the seat before I could remember my own name. "Dear God," I muttered, lifting my head and standing up. I felt light-headed, but like I probably wasn't going to puke again. I opened the cabinet door under the sink and pulled a sponge and some spray out from under it and cleaned the toilet up. I put it away, and washed my face, hands. Looking into the mirror, I could see how pale I was, my eyes two angry black slits in the middle of a puddle of yellow. I shook my head and opened the door, ready to face the pain. Mom was sitting at the kitchen table, an expression of intense irritation on her face.

"I know why you were sick."

"Oh?" I said, panic rising in my voice.

"Your auntie called about thirty minutes ago."

"Uh huh," I said, sitting down and putting my face in my hands.

"She told me about that little incident of yours and Jake's at the hospital."

"Mom, I–"

"No. You don't understand. Your cousin is going to jail this time. Real jail. What he did to that boy... it's called aggravated assault. And his record is long. He'll go to court but it looks like he'll be in jail for a while, Margaritte. And right now, they've got him in juvie, again. What I can't figure out is why he hit that boy. Why you two were there, in that hospital, in the first place? Who is that boy?"

I lifted my head out of my hands and looked at her.

"I don't know."

She looked back at me angrily. "Why are you... who are you protecting? What's going on?"

I sighed. I had told the truth, in a way. I didn't know who he was. I had thought I did. At least she didn't seem to know that I was pregnant.

"Mom, his name is Mike. He's my... well, he was my boyfriend."

My mother blinked, rapidly. "You have a boyfriend?"

"Yes. Well I did, I guess. I didn't want to tell you because, well, I don't know. Because I didn't want you to worry about me," I said, and then laughed. I got up and went over to the counter and poured myself a cup of coffee, knowing that it probably wasn't the best thing for my stomach but wanting the comfort, the familiarity of it. I swirled cream and sugar into the coffee and sat back down, the irony of what I'd just said echoing inside my head.

"When did you meet him?"

"A few months ago. He seemed nice. But it turns out he has a drug problem. And he was mad at me because... because I didn't want to do something for him and he cheated on me with Julia. And well, you know how Jake feels about Julia. And then we saw them at a party together."

"You were at a party last night? Goddamnit, Margaritte. I guess grounding you wasn't enough. I don't understand why you insist on screwing up your life," Mom said, shaking her head. She looked down at the table, her distorted reflection looking back at her in the white plastic swirl of the tabletop.

I sighed, took a sip of my coffee. "Mom, let me just tell the story, OK?" She was silent and so I continued. "So then Mike, my... boyfriend, he looked really sick. So me and Jake took him to the hospital. Then he called me something really bad, and that's when Jake hit him."

Mom looked at me for a few seconds and then away, taking it all in. She stood up and walked over to the window. She looked out for a while, the cars zooming by, the white noise of late morning.

"Margaritte, you don't seem to understand the seriousness of this situation," she said, her back to me. It was a warm day and she was wearing shorts and a big white t-shirt, not unlike the one I'd slept in last night. The window was open and the wind came in, the curtains billowing up, her t-shirt blowing back against her body. Looking at her, so concerned and upset with me, only made me sad. She had no idea how serious the situation really was.

"This will be on his permanent record."

"But, what if I explain to the police… " I said, trailing off.

"I think you know better than to think that will mean anything," she said.

"But he was only defending me," I said. "Really it's my fault."

"No Margaritte, it's not your fault that he punched that boy. He shouldn't have done that. He shouldn't have done a lot of things. We've lost him, Margaritte, don't you understand that?"

I was silent. I could hear the traffic in our silence and it felt like little razors on my skin. I did feel like I'd lost him, like I had no one now. I loved my mom, and I knew she loved me, but her dedication to Dad at all costs made things very hard between us. Julia had betrayed me, Jake was in jail for who even knew how long, and Mike had turned out to be someone I didn't even know.

"You make it sound like he's dead."

Mom turned around and looked at me. "I'm sorry, Margaritte. I didn't mean to put it that way. I know you love your cousin. But maybe this is for the best. He always gets you into trouble. Maybe now you can stay out of it."

"Mom, you don't understand. Jake keeps me out of trouble."

"I guess we aren't going to agree here. But one thing is true. I don't want you going to parties. You're sixteen years old.

And your grades are terrible. You have only two more weeks of school before this year ends and I want you focusing on the books, do you understand?"

I nodded and looked down, and Mom turned back to the sink and started to do dishes. When she finished, she wiped her hands on the old blue dishrag we wrapped around the handle of the refrigerator door and sat down with me. We drank coffee, both of us trying to pretend that what she had just said to me was going to make a difference. We talked for a couple of minutes, trying to make everything OK, and then Mom went into the living room to check on the twins and I poured myself a bowl of cereal hoping it would stay down. After I was done and I had stuck my bowl in the sink, I walked downstairs and flopped onto my bed. Nothing was OK. I slid my hands down onto my stomach and looked, opening one eye and then the other and then both of them, feeling grateful that the nausea had at least stopped. It seemed like nothing had changed. It looked the same. But it wasn't. And now I didn't even have Jake. Poor Jake. I couldn't even imagine what he was going through. I would have to call my auntie tomorrow to see what I could do for him. I felt sad, empty and more exhausted than I could ever remember in my life. I closed my eyes and everything buzzed and then faded.

I woke up to the phone ringing and my eyes flickered open. I flopped one long arm over towards the phone and picked up.

"Hello?" I felt like I was talking from the end of a long, winding tunnel.

"What's up, girl?" It was Will. I laughed. I couldn't believe Megan hadn't killed him yet.

"How are you alive?"

It was his turn to laugh. "Oh, girl, you know I'm a survivor."

"That you are," I said and sat up. I felt better. At least as good as I could feel considering that my life had just somehow come up to the level of a telenovela.

I knew better than to confide in him as Will couldn't keep his mouth shut for nothing, and was also judgmental as hell. He could make you feel like shit in about two seconds flat.

"How's stuff?" I asked.

"It's OK. Megan's a fucking bitch, but she's gone for the day, so at least I don't have to deal with her ass."

"Right," I said, rolling my eyes.

"I gave her money for bills and she's still acting like a crack whore."

"I see," I said, trying not to laugh. I wasn't sure what was funnier, the fact that Will had even come up with that or the image of Megan as a crack whore. If anyone was coming close to crack whore-dom, it was Will. Who the hell knew how the crazy fucker had gotten some money for bills. He wasn't saying shit about a job.

"So bitch, what are you up to today? Wanna go to a movie in Denver? You know, at the Mayan?"

"Why not," I told him and got up off the bed. Will was the only person in my life who would go and see arty films with me, and I figured I might as well get out of the house and try to get out of my head, too. Dad was actually at work. Mom was taking the twins to hang at the pool because a bunch of people with babies were going to do that and then have some retarded picnic after. So she wouldn't know that I wasn't downstairs studying like a mo-fo.

"Cool. I just have to get out of this shitty fucking town."

"Hear that," I said. "See you in thirty minutes?"

"Sounds good," he said and hung up.

I marched upstairs for a shower. No one was around. I showered, went back downstairs and got dressed and tried to figure out if my jeans were actually tighter than they had been the day before or if it was just my head. I sighed and headed out of the house, picking my backpack up on the way. I unlocked my car door and threw my backpack onto the passenger seat and slid in. After a couple of turns of the key, the car started and I backed out of the driveway and onto the road. On the way there I tried as hard as I could to push Mike out of my head, but it was hard. Stupid memories of him kissing me, laughing, holding me crept in. And then the image of him at that party with Julia. Of him calling me a whore in the hospital bed. I felt sick. I thought about how I'd told my mom that it was my fault Jake had punched him. How she had said it was Jake's fault. The thing was, I knew that when you did shit, it was your shit. But if it *was* anyone's fault besides Jake's, it was Mike's. If someone had hurt Jake, had said that kind of thing to Jake, I would have lost it and wanted to punch that fucker too. I rolled the window down and the quick, green smell of spring hit me as I lit my cigarette, carefully balancing the steering wheel while doing so.

Pulling up to Megan and Will's place I could see that there was a pretty good parking lot party going, complete with mullets, tattoos and endless cases of Bud Light. I parked and got out and they shouted for me to join, one of them moodily slurring, "C'monnnnn," as I walked past. I rolled my eyes and wondered if I'd sold any of them weed. When I got up there, I knocked and waited. I could hear laughter behind the apartment door. I was confused. I thought Will had said that Megan was gone for the day. Maybe she'd come back and Jesus had granted a fucking miracle and they were actually getting along for once.

Will opened the door with a "Hey, girl" and I walked in. There was some strange dude sitting on the couch, smoking, leaning back and looking at me with an expression on his face like a sweet five-year-old girl's. I was surprised. He greeted me with another "Hey, girl" and I said hey back and sat down. Megan was going to be pissed as hell once she came home and smelled that Will had been smoking inside again. Will gathered his shit together and we left, walking down the steps and into my car, past the parking lot party dudes. I looked curiously at Will's new friend in the rear view mirror. This guy was more than a loud voice in Will's room that woke the baby at three in the morning. This one was sitting in the back seat, his hand sat casually on Will's shoulder, though Will seemed to be trying like hell to ignore that he was doing it.

His name was Miguel and he was one of those beautiful Mexican guys who look more Indian than anything, except for this really wavy hair. And he laughed funny, like a donkey, slapping the back of Will's seat whenever I cracked a nervous joke. You could tell Will hated that, though he mainly stayed silent while Miguel and me talked, occasionally grunting at something we said, though Miguel kept trying to get him to be involved in the conversation.

Once we got onto Broadway, a little spring rain came up and I hit the windshield wipers, glad for the distraction of the rain and the mini-drama in the car, though I didn't understand why Will had wanted to bring Miguel along if he was just going to ignore him. I parked where I usually did, in the parking lot behind the theater next to the Walgreens, and we walked around and onto Broadway. I loved that street. Every time I was there I felt intimidated by all of the cool, thin, expressionless white people, though I also felt like there was more to life than what

I saw in Idaho Springs. But I knew I wouldn't fit in with these people any more than I fit in with the mullets at home.

We bought our tickets and got in just in time for the movie, a French one called *White.* And I loved it. I just loved it, the images floating out in front of me, the whole deal with the chick who was mad at her husband was kinda confusing but somehow familiar at the same time. But I couldn't help feeling sorry for Miguel because he kept trying to hold Will's hand which was brave of him 'cause even though we were in a cool, hip place, it was still a few streets away from Colfax. Will kept moving away like it wasn't even happening, just like in the car. I could see Miguel's hand snaking over towards Will's in the dark, and Will throwing his hand into the popcorn every time it came near. And every time, a wave of fury and sadness would come over me. I'd seen it a million times with guys who treated their women like this, even when they really liked them, *especially* when they really liked them.

When the movie was over, Miguel and me sat for a minute while the credits rolled. Will had gotten up immediately and muttered something about going to the bathroom and meeting us up outside.

"He's so weird," Miguel said.

"You don't know the half of it," I said, standing up and gathering our trash.

Miguel stood up, sighing hard and pushing his long, wavy hair over one shoulder as we walked out. "I'm just so tired of guys treating me like shit."

"I understand," I said, and patted his shoulder. He turned and smiled at me.

"Please don't tell him I said that," Miguel said and I nodded.

"Of course."

I went to the bathroom and when I walked outside, I could see Miguel smoking nervously on the corner and Will looking at the posters, his goddamn hands behind his back.

"You guys wanna walk around for a while? Get a beer or something?"

Will shrugged. Miguel nodded and threw his cigarette into the street. We started walking and though the shit was tense between the guys and I could see the hip people rolling their eyes at us as we moved down the street with our Walmart t-shirts and jeans, I was still glad to be there.

"Well, that movie rocked," I said, looking over at Miguel and Will, hoping to distract them. Miguel was still trying to hold hands with Will. I couldn't believe it. Dude was fucking brave. It was getting dark, and the bums and the crazy drunk people were out, and though I did see a few other guys holding hands, I could also see people eyeballing them and it scared me. But Will just kept crossing his arms across his skinny chest, above that funny little beer belly he had, every time Miguel tried. Finally Miguel stopped trying.

Will was quiet, moving farther and farther away from Miguel every second until he was walking ahead of us, which irritated me 'cause I wanted to go into some of the used bookstores. Miguel kept acting like Will was doing it by accident, like it was a result of some movement of the street, instead of some movement of the heart. Will kept inching away and Miguel kept inching towards, which was making it more and more difficult to talk to him. I figured it wouldn't be long before I lost sight of them completely, the way they were going, though finally Miguel quit trying to catch up with Will and slowed until he was walking by me. I smiled and he looked over at me thoughtfully.

"Girl, you got great hair."

I pulled some of it over to my line of vision and said, "It's OK."

"No, it's straight and thick and dark."

"Not as thick as my auntie's. Plus, I love your hair. I used to get perms all the time, trying to get my hair to look like yours."

"Really? Well... it's OK, I guess."

"It's great. It's cool that you keep it long. So, you from here?" I asked.

"No, Albuquerque. You?"

"From here."

"What do you do?" he asked.

"I'm in high school."

"Cool... cool. I work at this restaurant, in the kitchen. Thirteen-hour days man, thirteen-hour days."

"Jeez, that's a lot," I said.

"Yeah. Gotta pay those bills. But I'm thinking of going to school to be a mechanic."

"You should. Do you like cars?"

He looked thoughtful. "More than I like the kitchen where I work."

I laughed. "Makes sense."

Finally Will slowed down and we caught up to him and I suggested we duck into a bookstore. I spent a little time wandering the shelves and I could hear Will and Miguel arguing in the next shelf over, Miguel's voice sweet and pleading and Will's hard and dismissive. I could not understand Will at all. He was being a royal fucking douche. I sighed and looked at the shelf in front of me. I felt weirdly proud of myself for avoiding the horror and science fiction sections and going into the one with all the classy books. The kind of books that Mike read. Though thinking about that made me feel conflicted. I mean, Mike had turned out to be such a fucking jerk, but then again, some of the stuff he had told me about was cool. And I had been getting tired of all the ghosts, and warlocks and planet Zegateron type stuff I'd been reading before I'd even met Mike. It didn't matter. I looked down at my stomach and my heart twisted, sharp and heavy in my chest, like some kind of dull kitchen knife was in there. I could hear Will and Miguel arguing again as I looked at the back of a few books and wondered what the fuck even mattered in this life. People were always treating other people like shit, even when they loved them, even when it was wrong and they knew it.

I had been holding a couple of books under my arm and looking at another. I put that one back and pulled the two out from under my arm and walked over to the cash register. Will and Miguel had made it to the couches up front. Miguel was looking at Will and Will at his flat fucking feet. In that moment, I truly hated him.

The cashier ringing me up had a blond Elvis 'do and big, black Buddy Holly glasses. These guys really killed me. I smiled and he smiled back and I shoved the lovely, dusty smelling books into my backpack and walked over to the couches. I sat down next to Will and looked at him with all the anger I could muster and he glared right back at me.

"Let's get a beer, you grumpy fucking fucker," I said.

He stared back at me like he was gonna slap my giant yellow head and then he cracked a smile.

"OK, girl," he said, getting up and putting his hand out at Miguel, his long, brown arm extending down as elegantly as a dancer's. Miguel looked up at him like he was his personal fucking savior and then took his hand and let himself be pulled up to his feet.

We walked out of the bookstore, the bell on the door jangling pleasantly, and onto the street. It was now fully dark, and the blue and red and yellow neon lights were shining through the bars on the windows, and the hum of it, the people, the smell of beer and smokes and sex was putting me in another world. Will looked over at Miguel and Miguel took that as a signal to try and take Will's hand again. I winced, thinking Will was going to throw a fucking shit fit, but he let him put his hand in his, though I could see that it was totally limp.

"So," Miguel said to Will. "What about your family?"

I nearly mouthed, *God no* but it was too late.

"What about them?" Will gave a little head snap and pulled his hand away from Miguel's.

Miguel looked real uneasy but kept going. "Well, I mean, do you have brothers and sisters?"

"Yeah," he said, rubbing the back of his neck.

"How many?"

"Lots."

"He's got seven, total," I said, instantaneously regretting it. I couldn't help it. I felt so bad for Miguel, and I knew he just wanted to bond with Will. A bum with a cardboard sign saying, *Hell, why lie, I need a drink*, was standing on the corner as we crossed the street. I laughed and gave him a dollar. He looked up at me with big, blue eyes, and smiled.

"Me too!" Miguel continued. "I got three sisters and four brothers. All crazier than the last." Miguel looked at Will for a response but Will stared ahead and said nothing. "Do you hang out with them?"

"No," Will said. "I ain't like them at all."

"Well," Miguel said, giggling, "neither am I. You know… "

"Yeah, yeah, whatever."

"Hey! The Skylark," I said. "Let's go in. I love this place," and I walked in under the neon, hoping that they'd follow me and we'd drink and bond and forget all of our pain. I'd been there plenty of times, but I always got a little nervous at the bar, especially when they were examining my fake ID. I watched as the scarred, old bartender held my ID in front of his face. He looked bored and passed it back to me without a word. I ordered two tall gin and tonics for the guys and one tonic for me. I paid before handing the drinks out and then led the way to a booth in the corner, the sound of CCR thundering around us.

We settled into a booth and Will began gulping at his drink, staring into space while Miguel watched him. I lit a cigarette and thought desperately of something to say, as the CCR had stopped. But before I could, Miguel sighed and flickered his long, beautiful eyelashes at Will. "You know, you got great hair," Miguel said, running his hands through it. Will's eyes got big and he slapped Miguel's hand, hard.

"What the fuck do you think you're doing!"

"Nothing—I mean, we... "

"Just stop that shit, OK?"

"OK," Miguel said and sighed. We were all quiet for a while and then Miguel turned to Will again. "Didn't you tell me that you're from a... reservation?" I shook my head, just a little.

"Yeah, so?"

Miguel laughed his little donkey laugh like it was a joke. "Well, I mean, that's kind of cool, don't you think?"

Will looked back at him like he was carved outta shit, his eyes narrowed into angry little slits and his head set back like a snake.

"No."

"No... well, why not?"

Will went silent and then we were all silent for a while. I looked out at the people in the bar as strange, angry music like the kind Mike liked started pumping out of the speakers. The bar was packed with people looking for drinks, and I'd never seen so many biker types combined with people with nose rings and dyed black hair in my life. I looked at all of the names carved into the wooden table and traced them with a finger.

"It's OK, baby, I want to hear about your family," Miguel finally said, breaking the silence and batting his eyes at Will. I took a long, long drink of my tonic water and prepared for Will to totally lose it.

Will looked all set to get crazy angry and then he leaned back and got this funny, kinda stoned look on his face.

"Wanna hear a story?" He asked.

"You know I do baby," Miguel said, looking real happy. I wasn't so sure.

"Well," Will said, sitting up and pulling a cigarette out of my pack and lighting it. "I had this one best friend when I was a kid. One. We was just a couple of stupid boys I guess, but we really talked, you know. We hung out every day. We'd talk about TV and school and what life could be like off the rez and comic books and everything, all the things boys talk about, but it was different with him." Will paused and Miguel nodded encouragingly.

"That kid was cool. We would always walk home from school together, kicking up dirt and making fun of the teacher, this wasichu bitch who hated all of us. Then we'd get home to my house and hang out in my room, or in the badlands behind my house... laugh about shit until our faces got numb. Things were fucking great. Until one of my uncles decided to get in our faces."

Will sighed, looked back at the two of us and took a long drink. He went on.

"We'd been sitting behind my house, drinking Pepsi and throwing the cans into the distance, drawing things in the dirt, when I saw my uncle coming up the driveway. He didn't live far away and he was always around. He was kind of an angry guy—not real nice to his wife and kids and always fucking yelling about something. I heard later he was elected to council." Will laughed roughly. "Figures. Anyways, it was hot and real dusty and I could see his shitkickers kicking up dust on the drive as he came walking up towards, real fast. *Hey,* I started to say, but then as he came up close I could see how pissed off he was. I looked over at my friend, George… yeah, George was his name… and shrugged and threw my stick down. *What's*—I said, kinda worried 'cause I hadn't seen my dad for a coupla days, but he interrupted me. Got real close to my face and grabbed me by my arms and started to shake me, hard. I started to cry. Finally, he stopped and said, *Listen to me! Listen to me!* And he dropped me on the ground. I was crying hard by then and snotting and I looked up at him, tall as he was, his big ol' belly standing out, his fists on his hips, waiting to see what I'd done wrong. I thought maybe he was gonna bust us for throwing black cats behind the trees by his house.

Are you two listening to me?

I told him yes.

You two are gonna listen good!

And I looked over at George whose eyes had gotten real big. Everyone was afraid of my uncle—I had been afraid of him for as long as I could remember.

Will stopped and took a drink, finishing it in one gulp.

"Then my uncle said, *Why don't you boys ever hang out with other boys?* and I looked over at George again and I shrugged 'cause I didn't want to say that it was because the other boys wouldn't hang out with us, not the other way around. All I could do was stutter, *I-I-I...* and then he yelled, *I don't want to see you two together ever again, you hear?* And he looked like he was gonna pick me up and shake me again. I wanted to say no but I was too scared. And then he said, *If I ever see you two winktes together again, I will knock the both of you out, do you understand?*

"'Then my uncle leaned in real close, his breath all nasty from that tobacco he was always chawing and he yelled, *And get girlfriends!* He turned around and walked away. George and I looked at each other. George got up and left. I watched him go down the driveway the whole way, until I couldn't see him any more. After that, I'd see him and he'd see me and we'd just look away. I thought about telling my mom... but I didn't."

Will put his cigarette out, got up, walked through the crowd and over to the long, dark wooden bar. After he got the bartender's attention and ordered, I could see him downing a couple of shots, one after another, the short, clear glasses winking in the light, all neatly lined up on the bar.

Miguel was looking down at the table, a sad, defeated expression on his face. He pulled listlessly at his black t-shirt.

"You know, I thought he was such a nice guy when I met him," he said and I nodded, though I wasn't sure he could see my nod with his eyes on the table. Poor bastard had really liked Will. Finally he looked up and I smiled.

"At least he opened up?" I said awkwardly.

"Girl, that shit's happened to all of us," he said, slamming the last of his drink, the ice cubes hitting him in the mouth as he tipped the cup all the way up. He set his drink down and sighed. He looked over towards Will, who was making his way back towards us, a drink in his hand, a serious wobble in his step.

We sat there for another torturous hour, Miguel and me talking to each other about random shit, Will clearly shitfaced beyond belief. We'd tried to involve him in our conversation but it just resulted in short, angry grunts, eventually devolving into Will falling face-first on the table.

"Is he actually fucking snoring?" I asked Miguel, Will's black, greasy hair all that we could see of his head.

"Let's go," I said, knowing that we were going to have to pull over on the way home. We tried waking Will up but it was impossible, and so we were forced to pick him up. We got him in between us and dragged him out, thin, hip white people outside looking on, one of them rolling his eyes. I could see the guy mouth, "Drunk Indian," and another one nodding, laughing. I looked over at them with an angry-ass expression and they looked away.

"I hate when he's like this," Miguel said. It surprised me because I didn't think they'd known each other for very long.

"When did you meet him?"

"About a month ago."

We got him outside and I told Miguel that I'd go and get the car and he nodded and propped Will against the building as best as he could, one arm around his waist. Will moaned and Miguel pet his head reassuringly with his free hand, Will waking up just enough to slap at him.

I walked down the street, the bums holding their wilted cardboard signs up, the print running from the light rain that must have hit while we were in the bar, the cracked white and brown hands of the bums out, the neon lights shining from under the metal bars on the windows telling me about *the high life*, the buzz-hum sound of them making me feel like some kind of strange animal alive for no good reason at all walking in a city familiar and unfamiliar in the middle of the night. A white guy with a big, brambly grey beard and bloodshot eyes stumbled out of one of the liquor stores on my right and said, "Baby *please*." I kept going, and tried not to pick my pace up, my heart hammering and my hand slipping into the pocket where I kept the little pocket knife Dad had given me for my last birthday. I shook my head and inhaled the deep, musty smell of rain soaked into city sidewalk. All I wanted was to get to the car and then home.

After what felt like an eternity, I got to the parking lot and it was wonderfully quiet and peaceful and drunk-free. I unlocked my junker, got in, pulled out and then around onto Broadway to the bar, which was only a few blocks from where we had started. I parked in front and helped Miguel get Will into the backseat. He woke up only to puke before we even got him in. I felt lucky he'd done it before we'd gotten moving. He slept most of the way, waking up occasionally to moan dramatically and mumble in Lakota. I shook my head. What a fucking waste.

Me and Miguel were quiet most of the way, each of us wrapped in our own thoughts, the rain starting and stopping again, the wipers making a quiet, rubbery rhythm. When I saw the exit sign for the Springs, I sighed with relief and thought about Julia, who'd always laughed at it, making it into *I-dah-Ho* Springs. I thought about her as we drove through town, the whole of it closed up and quiet.

I drove into the parking lot of Will's apartment and wondered if Megan was back and if she was going to give him hell, though I figured she'd see how fucking useless that was in his current state. I parked and asked Miguel if he needed help getting Will in, but Miguel said no. I told him that it was nice meeting him and he smiled sadly. He put Will's arm over his neck and Will slapped weakly at him with his free hand. They stumbled up and over to the steps that led to Will's apartment. As they were going, I thought about how cool Miguel was, and what a jerk Will was, and a shiver of anger came over me. It didn't matter.

As soon I could see that they were OK, I put the car in drive and pulled out of the parking lot. I picked up my pack of smokes that had been sitting in the passenger seat under Miguel and sighed and thought *fuck it* and lit one.

The streets on the way home were almost completely empty, though I passed a drunken walker here and there stumbling towards home and the last few Buds in the fridge until the final, pathetic, stinking collapse onto the bed. Again the feeling of anger and uselessness washed over me and I thought about Mike and about the baby and I rolled my window down and threw my cigarette forcefully out the window. I hit the steering wheel and started to cry, which only made me feel angrier and even more useless. Though I knew I wouldn't talk to him if he did, he hadn't called. I didn't know where he was and I wished that I didn't care. My appointment was coming up soon and I knew after that, I could start over if I wanted. And I did want to start over. I really did. Most of the time, though, it seemed like that was just something people said but nothing ever really changed. People were still the same fucked up, stupid, hypocritical assholes that they always were. I pulled into the driveway with my lights off, and opened and shut the car door as quietly as I could. The lights were off and I knew that I'd wake up to Mom wondering where my car had been, where I had been. I slid through the window and pulled my clothes off and got into bed, folding the covers over my body.

CHAPTER 10

The next week of school was a mess. Mike wasn't there, which should have been a relief of some kind, but it worried me like hell. Julia just kept avoiding me. Not that I was seeking Julia out, but she'd see me in the hallways and walk the other direction, her guilt folded over her shoulders like a powwow shawl from a dead relative. Treena would just roll her eyes and look away every time she saw me. God, Treena just did whatever Julia wanted her to do. Of course, she'd never liked me much in the first place. And Mom had glared at me and said nothing the next day after the whole Will incident, which was worse than her bitching me out. It was like she'd given up on me. And Dad was Dad, drinking and being grumpy and hiding in his office. What was ominous though was that he was being even more weird and reclusive than usual, and that generally signaled a blowout of the apocalyptic kind.

That weekend there was a powwow. I'd called Megan up to see if she was gonna go and she said yeah, and told me how much she hated Will, how she was ready to kick him out, as the money he'd given her was back, back rent and bills and when she'd asked him about whether he had any plans to pay more, he'd been a total bitch and left for two days. I told Mom that I was going up to Julia's to study and she told me that I was going to do whatever I wanted anyway.

I drove over to Megan's that Saturday, ready to try to forget everything. My appointment was in the back of my mind. And so was Jake's court date. There was so much happening that I wish wasn't happening at all.

I pulled up to Megan's apartment and when I'd made it up the stairs, I could see that she and Will had set chairs up outside and were sitting around smoking and laughing and drinking wine coolers. I wondered about what had gone down between my phone conversation and now to make them OK with one another again, but I wasn't going to ask. I sat down and grabbed a wine cooler. I figured if I just picked one up and had a few sips here and there, no one would start on questioning me. Megan was talking about being a kid on the rez in the eighties, about how had she dyed her hair pink with her dad's help.

"Girl, you'd look downright skeezy with pink hair," Will said. I rolled my eyes and thought about what a fucking idiot Will was. Motherfucker didn't know how to quit when he was ahead.

So I said, "I don't know. Maybe she'd look cool as hell."

"No," Will said.

"Whatever. I looked good," Megan said, looking at Will with her green-brown eyes slit. She took a long, hard drink of her Piña Colada wine cooler and set it down next to her on the cement. "And like I said, my dad helped me do it. He's a cool guy."

"Sucker," Will said.

We were quiet for a minute, drinking our wine coolers and appreciating the sun and temporary lack of responsibility, when Will turned to me and asked me if I'd ever been to a Sun Dance.

"No," I said.

"You know, I used to do Sun Dance every year," Will said, looking thoughtful. He ran his rough, long fingers through his greasy black hair and looked off for bit.

"I think you told me that once," I said. "That's hard-core."

"Yeah, it is. You're attached to that pole all day, and you can't eat. But I loved it. I waited for it every year. We even had guys from other tribes coming up and doing it with us," he said.

"That's awesome," I said.

"Pass me the cigs, girl," he said and I tossed them and a hot pink lighter into his lap. "Thanks," he said and lit one and then looked at it, rolled it slowly between his fingers, and took a long drag.

"Although... I have to admit, it isn't always so good sometimes. One summer all these whites came up. I don't know who invited them, but we let them hang out, though I don't think they would've done the full ceremony, even if we had let them. After the ceremony they wanted to crash at my mom's place. Guess my brother had been talking to them, all drunk, and wanted to help them out. They were real hippies, you know, with ponytails and that. And my mom, she just couldn't say no to any of us. She let them camp in our backyard. They had all this weird music going and smoked more pot than half the people on the rez, and danced around a bunch. Some of the chicks wanted to get naked, which was not a good idea. Me, I left pretty soon after Sun Dance, I had a job I had to get back to—I felt lucky they let me off for Sun Dance at all. But when I got back to Denver I found out they had given the job to somebody else, and so I decided to go back and visit with Mom for a while. She was sick that summer, real sick, had cancer. But when I got back they were still camped out in the backyard and they were eating her outta house and home. So I cleared them out, Crazy Horse style."

I smiled and laughed. But even though I felt bad about it, all I could think was, you're no Crazy Horse. Maybe Crazy Horse's *girlfriend.*

"So, Will, how hungover were you the day after I dropped you off?" I asked. I couldn't help it.

He was silent for a bit and then said, "Oh, I wasn't that bad."

"Huh," I said, the image of Miguel propping him up against the building coming into my mind.

"Yeah."

"Hmm," I said, letting it go.

We sat around for a while, Will getting more than a little buzzed, tipping Caribbean-themed cooler after cooler down his throat. He began to brag about himself more and I could tell Megan was getting irritated with him, shifting her baby around in her lap almost roughly.

Around noon, we decided to pile into my car and hit the powwow. Will was next door to totally shithoused, nearly tripping on every step as he walked down the steps, talking loudly about some girl he'd seen a few days before who was wearing something he thought made her look trashy. I rolled my eyes as I unlocked the car door and got in, and I could see that Megan was doing the same, steam practically shooting out of her nose.

The drive into Denver was clear, and me and Megan listened to Will yammer on about the chick who dressed bad, other chicks who dressed bad and what a great grassdancer he'd been when he was a kid; Megan silently, totally, losing it. Her baby was asleep in the backseat and once in a while, I could see Will petting her full head of black hair tenderly, mouthing words I knew had to be in Lakota.

Pulling into the parking lot, we could see that there was a pretty decent sized line, and loads of Indians in regalia coming in and out of the main building. After standing in line and paying, we went straight for the auditorium and sat for a bit, watching the dancers move. Occasionally I would Fancy Shawl, though I was really becoming too old for it. If I was going to continue to dance, I knew I needed to move onto Jingle Dress. My auntie used to take me with the cousins before they became born again and I'd never lost interest, except for lately. Will was still talking up a storm, pointing out who he thought was good and who he thought stunk. Megan was clearly losing any good feeling she had had for him and wasn't really even talking. I was nodding at what he was saying, hoping to keep the tension low. Occasionally, the baby would cry and Megan would pick her up and bounce her on her knee, or give her a bottle. I looked over at the baby. She really was cute. It made me feel funny to even think about it and when the tiny tots came on to dance, I felt even weirder, my stomach twisting around my heart.

"Hey, you guys wanna get up and walk around for a bit?" I asked. I had to move. "We could check some of the vendors out?"

"Well, I ain't got shit to spend," Megan said, looking at Will. He just gave her an *I'm so fucking innocent* look and then when she narrowed her eyes, he looked away.

"Hey, me either, but I love to look at stuff."

Megan sighed, long and heavy. "What the hell," she said, standing up. We got our shit together, and then got the blue mesh stroller into the right position and put the baby in it. The baby started clapping her hands and giggling.

I figured though I shouldn't spend, I had just made a bunch on sales, enough for a pair of earrings, maybe some long pow-wow style ones or some kick-ass Navajo turquoise ones. My Auntie used to trade her beadwork with silversmiths, so I know what to look for. I was elbowing my way through the crowd to get a good look at all the jewelry and I could hear the pow-wow MC laying his jokes on the crowd, the sound of it echoing throughout the hallway. "Ayyyyyyyyeee," he was saying at the end of every cheesy joke.

"Ayyyyyyeee," Will said in my ear, and I punched him in the arm.

"Ow!" He rubbed his arm.

"You big baby," I said jokingly, and he rolled his eyes.

He was clearly about to respond with something witty, his mouth already open, his hands on his hips, when Megan turned around and glared at him. "Cut that shit out," she said and Will tightened his lips and narrowed his eyes, but said nothing.

After that, Will went completely quiet. I was guessing he was starting to sober up and it had become more than obvious that whatever good feeling he had achieved with his cousin, it was already well on its way out. He looked restless and tired, his hands shoved deep into the pockets of his torn-up blue jeans.

We walked around for a while, stopping at different vendors and looking at the native hip-hop, the jewelry, but Will didn't seem to want to do anything but follow us around like a tired little boy. It was like he had expended all of his energy talking in the car. He would stand behind us every time we'd stop to look at something, and sort of nod at what we were saying, not even making his usual bitchy comments about people's hair or clothes.

Megan was craning her neck to get a good look at all the cute longhairs. Every few feet she'd see one and elbow me hard and say, "Check him out," and I'd laugh and tell her that she could snag him and she'd laugh and say, "Naw." I looked over at her, her large, tired body. I couldn't imagine what it was like for her, all on her own, her man in jail. I was sure that even if one of these guys really did want to hook up with her, she probably wouldn't have the energy, or the heart for that matter, to do it. I wasn't sure exactly what the status was with her man or why he'd gone to prison. She never said and I knew enough not to ask. Will had started to tell me once, but she came back in the room when he was doing it, and looked at him hard and he'd shut up. I figured if she really wanted to tell me, she'd tell me when she was ready.

We'd stopped at a vendor that sold Pendletons and Megan was fingering a Nav Steering Wheel cover. The crowd was heavy and thick with lots of Indians of all tribes, and of course, a good amount of white people there looking around at all the Indians with goofy ass smiles on all of their faces, cheap-ass Indian jewelry and amulets around their necks, their children carrying fake little tomahawks in their sweaty little hands.

"I'm thirsty," Will said. It was the first thing he'd said in thirty minutes.

"Well, let's go stand in line for a Pepsi," I said.

"Jeez, then I'll see you in a year," Megan said, shaking her head. "Those lines are long."

"But I'm thirsty," Will said, Megan narrowing her eyes at him. He lowered his gaze to his big, black sneaks.

"They charge a fuckload for drinks," Megan said.

"I'll pay," I said and started walking, turning around to see if Megan and Will were following me. They were.

On the way there, I found some sweetgrass and bought a strand. Then I saw an amazing green and white case for my Native American Church paraphernalia.

"It's beautiful," I said, Megan and Will stopping with me. The vendor smiled and gave me a price. I thought about my last one. I'd given it to Julia. When I started going to the Indian Center in Denver, I went to a few NAC meetings and then Julia started coming with me. Then she got pretty serious about it, even going when I didn't, whenever she could, getting people to come and pick her up in Idaho Springs. Then her mom came for one of her rare visits and for some reason, she liked the case I'd given her and Julia gave it to her. I shook my head. I ran my hands over the front of the case.

"I'll go get the drinks," Will said and I handed him some money.

"I gotta change the baby's diaper," Megan said. I watched them both go and turned around back to the vendor.

"I'll take it," I said and the guy put it in a plastic bag.

The vendor handed me the bag. Megan was coming from the bathroom so I went to meet her, and I spotted another vendor whose stuff I wanted to check out, an old lady selling jewelry. We stood there for a while, looking at all of the stuff, the silver sparkling in the fluorescent lights when we heard a rush of noise behind us. For a second, I ignored the noise. After all, we were in the middle of a crowd. But it got louder, and I realized that it was a group of male voices. And they sounded threatening.

I looked at Megan and she looked back, confused.

The vendor lady looked up and over our shoulders. "You get gone! Don't you make trouble!" We turned around. It was a group of guys, maybe five in all, staring at Will and yelling. Will was backed up against the wall, looking terrified, a cardboard tray of drinks in his hand. They came about two feet from him and stopped.

"Hey Will, you fucking faggot! How ya been? All your boyfriends up at Pine Ridge sure do miss ya!" a guy with short hair and a big belly said. All of his friends laughed.

"Yeah, man, they miss tapping that ass," another dude said. He was a skinny fucker with a long, scraggly mullet, a little older than the rest.

"Shoo! Shoo! You boys are only causing trouble!" the vendor said, whooshing her hands in their direction, which only made them laugh.

"Don't worry Grandma, we ain't gonna do you any harm," Mullet Boy said. She just said "Shooo!" one more time and of course, they burst into laughter.

"Quiet now, Grandma," Mullet Boy said and he looked like he meant it.

"Indian boys don't have any respect anymore!" She shook her head and looked almost teary. "No respect… " she said, trailing off.

Mullet boy shrugged and looked back over at Will, who was silent.

"Ain't you gonna tell us about your new boyfriends?" Two other boys stood in the background while their friends did all the work. All of them wore t-shirts with the names of different heavy metal bands on the front, Megadeth being the most popular.

"C'mon Will, ain't you gonna tell us about life in the big city? You must be scoring big at all the homo bars, idnit?" Big Belly said, and they all laughed again.

"Yeah, you're probably a regular stud out here," Mullet Boy said. "I tell you what, Will. Why don't you meet us outside and we can party, you know… you can show us exactly what kind of a stud you are, just like that one time on the rez," Mullet Boy said and smiled, his teeth yellow.

"Get lost," I said, and Mullet Boy looked over at me menacingly.

"Quiet now sister. You don't wanna get hurt over this faggot."

"You got girls defending you, you pussy?" Big Belly said.

Will stood there looking like he was choking, his face pale. He hadn't said anything back to them. I wanted to say something more but I was scared of them and I could see that Megan was too, though she was a pretty scary motherfucker, generally speaking.

"Come on Will, whatd'ya say?" Big Belly asked. Will shook his head, just a little and they all laughed wildly.

"Whatsa matter Willie? Didn't I treat you good? I'll buy you flowers this time, like a real lady," Mullet Boy said and they all laughed again.

"There's something wrong with you boys!" the vendor lady said.

"I told you to be *quiet* Grandmother. I might just break your hip if you're not careful," Mullet Boy said, and she drew breath.

I heard something on my right. A bunch of security guards were making their way through the crowd. The dude with the belly punched Mullet Boy in the arm. "What?" he said, annoyed.

"Look, cuz." He pointed towards the guards, who were getting pretty close. There were three of them and they were big.

"Aw shit, the cavalry," Mullet Boy said. "We better get the fuck outta Dodge."

The security guys could see that they had been spotted and started coming even faster, pushing people out of the way. Mullet Boy looked over at Will and said, "We'll see you again... and we can party, you know, just like that time on the rez. You can be my girlfriend again, faggot." Then he laughed, hard and mean, and they all cut out fast, the security guards making their way past us, following them.

"Damn," I said. Will was still up against the wall, clutching the drink tray, which was a goddamn miracle in my opinion.

"You OK?" I asked, and he swallowed and looked at the ground.

"Yeah," he whispered and licked his lips.

The vendor shook her head. "No respect!"

"I know," I said, and bought a pair of earrings 'cause I felt so bad for the lady, and we moved on, Will trailing behind us. We were silent, moving through the crowd, and after a while, I sighed hard and turned around to ask Will if he was really OK. I stopped and put my hand on Megan's shoulder. Will was nowhere in sight.

"What?"

"Megan, where's Will?"

"What do you mean, where's Will?" She asked.

"Megan, look behind you. He's fucking *gone*."

She looked behind her. "Motherfucker takes off all the time. Shit goes down in any capacity and he splits. I'll see his cheap, winkte ass in a few days."

"He's so weird," I said and told Megan about the night with Miguel. She told me she'd seen Miguel once herself.

"Really?"

"Yeah. I mean, you know, sometimes I see them."

"Well, not during the day," I said, looking around just to see if I could spot him. We had kept walking, stopping at vendors.

"Seriously, you know he'll just show up at the apartment later," she said, frowning with those long, thin lips of hers. "Stinking of ass and booze."

"Shit that's sad."

Megan stopped and looked at me. "Hell if it's fucking sad! What's sad is that he won't get his fucking shit together and pay bills. I'm not going to feel sorry for that asshole. You think it's sad he's a fucking winkte? Back home, you know what he used to call me in front of the other kids, over and over?" Her lip started to quiver. I had never, ever seen her cry. "He called me… I'm not going to say that word. It means half-breed. But the way he would say it… it was shitty, Margaritte. Fuck him! I should have never let him move in."

I took her hand and said, "I know."

I didn't know what to say. So many thoughts were racing through my head about who had what worse and why. We kept walking.

"I *don't* feel sorry for him. He's a jerk," she said, angrily wiping at her tears.

"I'm sorry Megan," I said. "Let's go sit down for a while, OK?"

She nodded and let me lead her to the bleachers and we sat down and watched the dancers for a few hours. I *was* worried about Will though, and I even went around to the vendors on my own to look for him but he was gone. We had to go home without him, and she raged the whole way, crying and yelling and telling me she would probably have to go back to the rez because of him. And I knew what it was like there. It was her home and she loved that, but there were no jobs, it was far from her man, people were living hard lives and it just wasn't what she wanted. I told her I was sorry again and again and thought about telling her what was going wrong in my life, but I just didn't. She knew Jake was heading to jail and that I wasn't talking to Julia, but she didn't know that I was about t-minus two seconds to being in a position pretty fucking close to hers if I didn't hit the ejector button.

I dropped her off and told her everything was going to be OK, though of course neither one of us believed that. I smiled at her guiltily, though the guilt wasn't mine. I drove home in a bigger funk than ever, dreading the potential clusterfuck at home. But things were OK; Mom seemed to be relieved that I was home for dinner, helping her cook and take care of the twins, Dad getting drunk and yelling at the TV and not at us, moving into his office at the end of the night, Mom into her room and me into mine.

The next day Megan called after lunch to tell me that she had woken up to Will on the couch. She begged me to come over that evening. She said she couldn't deal with him on her own, that she was going to hurt him if she did. I told her I would and lucky for me, by the evening Dad had retreated to his office and Mom was over at Auntie Justine's so I was able to just walk out the door and drive away without having to catch any hell or tell any lies. I needed to do a couple deals anyway.

I knocked, and Megan answered the door and let me in. Will was apparently still on the couch and I plopped down on the big old La-Z-Boy in the corner.

"We're watching a *Rocky* marathon," Megan said and Will grunted.

Megan was real into *Rocky* and we'd been through several Rocky marathons together, usually with Julia though. I thought about Julia. She hadn't called either.

"You gonna get emotional this time?" I asked Megan. She would always cry at the end and I'd tease her. I'd say things like, "AAAAAAdrian!" right during the emotional part and she'd get the look of rage and I'd shut it down.

"I brought Taco Bell," I said. It was cheap and I knew that Will eating food he wasn't paying for was a major issue and I wanted to help that issue go away, even if it was for a day. I opened my backpack and started distributing burritos and chalupas and such, first over to Megan and then to Will, who stood up to get his, smiling briefly and mumbling, "Thanks girl," before sitting down stiffly and eating fast. After he was done, he went to the kitchen, threw his empty wrappers in the trash and shuffled off to the back. I looked at Megan and we both shook our heads silently. I figured we wouldn't see him for the rest of the night, but after a few minutes, I heard the shower going, and then later, the sound of his door opening and closing.

"I need a smoke," Will said. "Can I bum one offa you?"

"Sure," I said. *Rocky* had just gone to commercial. Will and me got up and shuffled outside.

"Will... Megan is about to full on freak out," I said in between drags.

"Yeah, I know," he said. I was surprised at his honesty, his calmness. We both puffed silently for a while. I figured I might as well smoke a cigarette. Weird as I felt doing it, I knew it didn't matter. My appointment was coming up.

I didn't know what to say, so I started do a few Fancy Shawl steps.

"Girl, you gonna fall flat on your flat Indian ass," Will said, laughing. Even though he was insulting me, as usual, I was glad he was laughing.

"Probably," I said. "And if I crack my head open, I leave all of my smokes to you."

"Well, that's good."

"I tell you what, I'll also leave you my jacket," I said, and Will rolled his eyes. "Also, my ass is not that flat," I said, and he shrugged.

I stopped dancing and looked out at the highway.

"I gotta get out of this town."

"Hear that," Will said. "Yeah. I gotta get outta here. I mean,

I got away from home, and that's good, 'cause I didn't belong there. But I don't think I belong here either. I don't know where I belong. But not here. And not home," he said, looking off into the night.

"Yep," I said.

"You know where I would like to go? Europe. But I think it's a little outta my financial means, at least for now."

"Yeah," I said. "Another smoke?"

"Sure," he said, and I handed him one and he lit up.

"I want to go to Paris," he said, looking off. "I think maybe I'd find what I'm looking for there, on top of the Eiffel Tower. I've seen all of these pictures of the Eiffel Tower and it's always seemed right. And all of those little cafés. I want to sit outside in a café in Paris and drink espresso and wine and fall in love," he said, laughing. It was at that point that I realized that though the shower and food had done Will good, he was still on something. Or coming off of something, crazy fucker that he was.

"That sounds great," I said.

"Girl, you wouldn't even know what to do in Paris," Will said and I frowned.

"How's that?"

"Probably wear damn wife-beaters and Kmart jeans and they'd run you out of the city."

"Whatever Will," I said. "Like you've ever been to Europe, or know anything about it besides what you've seen on TV." Will didn't answer. I sat down in one of the beat up lawn chairs in the dark and looked up into the sky, at the setting sun and thought about Paris. About Mike. How I wish I could be in Paris with Mike. I ran my fingers over the little bit of grass growing in one of the cracked pots on the landing, the empty field in the lot across from the complex. It was full of rusting car parts and old furniture but the sun was setting and everything was golden and it was beautiful, even in Idaho Springs.

"I will make it to Paris someday," Will said. "Right now, since I'm kinda in between jobs, though I've been making a little money doing some jobs on the side, I have to put my plans on hold. But I think I'm close to something good. I mean, I've had a lot of good jobs, you know, business-type jobs, and I've got a pretty good resume."

"That's cool." I said. I knew that starting anything up with Will would just be a waste of time.

We walked back in and settled back onto the couch. I promised Megan I wouldn't yell "AAAAdrian!" in her ear during the emotional parts.

"Good," she said.

"Oh, God, it's nice outside," I said. "Let's keep the door open until it's just too cold to keep it open any longer."

"Hey, do you want some beer?" I asked Megan and Will.

"Sure," Megan said. I looked over at Will.

"Ummmm," he mumbled under his breath.

"It's on me. So let's go," I said and got up. I slung my backpack over my shoulder and Will stood up. I shut the door as quietly as I could behind me, so as to not wake the baby.

It took a couple turns of the ignition for it to catch, and I let it warm up a bit before we took off.

"Will, where did you get the idea to go to Paris?" I asked.

"Well, it's where all the cool people are."

"Sure. OK. But what's up with you wanting to go there?"

Will looked out the window and I thought he wasn't going to answer me. But after a bit he looked over at me and pursed his long, purple lips moodily at me.

"Girl, you think I'm not cool enough to know about Paris?"

"You're very cool."

"Don't cop an attitude with me, woman."

I laughed despite myself. "You're a fucking nut, Will. You really are."

"I'm not the only nut in the car, hey," he said and I agreed. I was a nut.

We pulled into the liquor store and I handed my little nutty accomplice some money.

"Cheap beer," I said. "I want to class this night up."

"Right," he said. He got out of the car and walked into the store behind an old, sad-looking white guy in overalls. Will reappeared a few minutes later, cradling a case of Bud in his arms.

"Mission accomplished," he said, pulling his belt over his lap and buckling it.

"You mean *classy* mission accomplished."

"Yeah. Bud's gonna class this night up good," he said.

I put the car in drive and took off.

"You know the only baguette I've ever had is from the grocery store. Something tells me that's not what they taste like in France."

"Fuck no. They bake that shit fresh every day," Will said, pulling a smoke from my pack and lighting up.

"The only thing I have that's baked and fresh is weed," I said. "That's fucking sad."

Will looked at me thoughtfully. "You got any weed on you?"

"Sure. Though I'm not in the mood to smoke."

"Occupational hazard."

"You could say that," I said, pulling into the parking lot. We got out and Will pulled the case of beer out of the back seat and we made our way back up the stairs and into the apartment.

Megan was watching some crazy horror film, the sound of a woman, probably blonde, screaming her crappy guts out echoing throughout the place.

"Good God, what is this?" I asked. Will had put the case of beer in the fridge and grabbed one for me and Megan. He handed me one and then Megan.

"Dunno. *Rocky* finished and this came on and I thought, why not? Don't you like scary movies?"

"Sure," I said, sitting down.

"Do you guys want to smoke some weed?" I asked.

Megan looked at me. "Well, the baby's asleep for the night. And I haven't in a long time." She looked at Will. "And I really do need to chill. Are you?"

"Nah. But you and Will should. Really."

"OK," she said, shrugging.

I had forgotten my pipe at home, so we had to dig out some old zigzags of Will's. He had gone through this phase of rolling his own cigarettes. I rolled a fatty and handed it to Megan, who took a deep hit and coughed hard after.

"Good one," I said, and she handed it to Will and pounded on her chest.

Will took a hit, a big hit, and then held the joint a distance in front of him, between two long, brown fingers, and leaned against the couch, this faraway look in his eyes. "Shit," he said.

I laughed. He passed it back to Megan but she shook her head and Will took it back, hitting it again, hard.

"Cool it, tiger," I said and he shrugged, held it in, exhaled and took another hit, blowing it out in a long, smoky stream.

We were quiet, watching TV, when Will said, "You know Margaritte, you're alright."

"Gee, thanks Will," I said, which cracked him up.

"No really, you're cool. You have a Mexican name and you kind of look like a Mexican but you're OK."

"Uh, sure Will," I said and looked over at Megan. She rolled her eyes and gestured for the joint. I handed it to her.

"Idn't she a little tall for a Mexican?" Megan said.

Will looked like Megan had said something totally profound and then said, "Yeah, yeah she is, come to think of it."

"I'm fine with looking Mexican," I said, wanting to hit that joint but still feeling creepy about it. Will laughed uproariously.

"Yeah, that's fucking hilarious," Megan said, going into the bedroom to check on the baby. She came back a few minutes later, shutting her door quietly.

"I need another beer," he said, and got up. When he got back, he had two beers in his hands. He plopped down in front of the TV and immediately opened the first one, drinking hard and long, his Adam's apple moving quick and hard. Pretty soon he was done with the first and onto the second, and then he started laughing real wild at the TV.

"What's so funny?" I asked and Will just held his stomach and pointed.

"You're weird," Megan said, getting up to grab another beer. She came back and cracked it open, plopping down hard on the couch.

Will then started to get real talkative, but he wasn't making any sense. He'd try to say something and just sputter out, like an old car. So Megan and me started laughing because as awful and stupid as it was, it was fucking funny and Will kept laughing harder and harder. Then, when he'd get up to walk, he'd fall straight down.

"You want some water?" I asked him and he looked over at

me and whacked me on the chest. Lucky for Will, Jake was in jail, 'cause if he had seen that, Will would have been upended. I got up and sat at the table.

"Megan. Wanna wrestle?"

She looked over at Will incredulously.

"No," she said, and he laughed hysterically.

"Just a lil' joke."

Finally, Will passed out on the couch like it was his final resting place. He hardly looked like he was breathing. I shook my head thinking, Jesus, I can't believe this guy. No matter where he goes, he's still on Pine Ridge.

"He looks dead," I said.

"He's not," Megan said. "Too bad."

"Jeez, Megan," I said.

"Well."

"You know what? Tomorrow morning, I'm telling that fucker to get the fuck out and never come back. He has fucked me over so many times."

I nodded. She was right. I knew she was right. He used everyone around her. He really did. I looked over at him, passed out and pathetic.

"I think he was already on something else before we started drinking and smoking," I said.

Megan rolled her eyes. "I'm gonna go check on the baby," she said.

I nodded and when she went into the bedroom, I went for a beer and drank it fast. I was angry. So angry. I could hear the baby crying. I leaned against the counter and finished the beer and cracked another one open. Put it down. Men were shit. They treated everyone around them like they'd been born to serve their stupid, childish needs.

I looked over at Will. I shook my head and though I felt like I hated him, I did hope for Megan's sake that his final resting place wouldn't be her couch.

I went over and sat next to him and I watched TV, feeling shitty and self-righteous. I looked over at Will. He was just sitting there, his expression nearly pompous. Something about that pissed me off. I walked over to my bag, this great brown and white Pendleton my old teacher gave me and I started digging through it. I heard the baby crying in Megan's room and Megan saying, "Shhh, shhhh." I kept on digging.

Finally I found what I was looking for and I walked over to Will and started to draw on his face, praying to God that he wouldn't wake up. I wrote, *Kiss me, I'm stupid* and *Here Comes the Apple.* I finished and laughed, then took a couple of steps back and then sat in a rocking chair across from that ratty old couch and looked at Will in the near darkness, admiring my work and laughing again. Then I pulled out my lipstick and gave him big, red lips.

I could still hear the baby crying but with all of that alcohol in my brain, it all seemed distant, meaningless. I sat there for a long time, waiting for Megan to come out of her room and I remember watching him like that I thought of one of his goddamn stories. It was about this dog he had found when he was a kid on his rez. It wasn't even a ratty rez dog or nothing, it was this poodle that his dad found wandering the streets in the town off of Pine Ridge. All his little girl cousins wanted the poodle 'cause it looked just like the dogs on TV that all the little rich white girls had. But for some reason that dog took to Will like nothing else, it just loved him and curled up with him at night and everything. Then one time, Will got really sick, thought he was gonna die he felt so bad, and that dog wouldn't leave him for nothing, not even to eat. Said his dad had to take the dog's food into Will's room until Will got better. About a year after that the dog got sick. It was old anyways. So they took the dog to the vet 'cause Will begged and begged and the vet said the dog was on its last leg but to leave it overnight so that they could observe it and everything. But the worst part is, when they went back the next morning, the dog was dead. Will told me he never felt so bad in his life, said he couldn't believe he had let his dad convince him to leave it overnight when that dog wouldn't leave him for nothing when he was sick.

I was thinking about Will and his poodle when Megan finally came out and saw what I had done. She started laughing, though by that time I felt like shit for doing it. Will didn't even move, but he was breathing pretty regular. We joked for a while and then started watching a movie. I looked over at Will. He was still passed out. I had never seen him asleep before and even with all that makeup on, he was still beautiful with his face like some kind of Sioux Jesus, his hands all spread across his chest. But he just throws all of that in the trash... he's nothing, really.

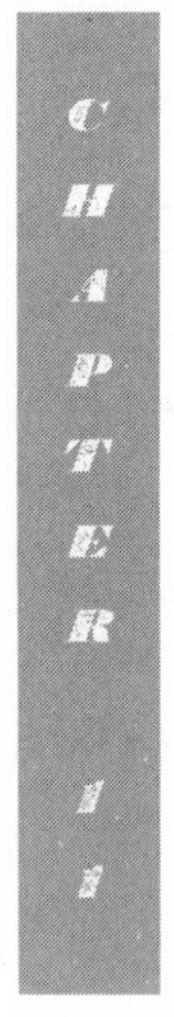

I drove home around 11:00, hoping that everyone was asleep. But when I got in the door, I could hear the TV blaring in the living room and sighed. I walked past as quickly and quietly as I could, thinking maybe Dad wouldn't hear me, so I wouldn't have to deal with his *please watch this program with me* thing. When I was a kid, I thought that his attention showed how much he loved me. But when I got older, I realized that he was just lonely and fucked up.

"Margaritte?" he said, his voice slurring, his back still to me. I had almost made it.

I was silent. I thought about just staying silent, tip toe-ing past as quietly as I could.

"Yes?"

"Where you... been?" he asked, turning around on the couch to face me.

"Studying with Julia," I said, hoping it was over.

"Oh."

"I'm just gonna go to bed Dad, OK?"

"No—no, waita minute," he said, standing up.

"Jeez, Dad." He was in his underwear, his thick, freckled legs and torso looking more white and freckled than ever.

"Whaaa?"

"You're... never mind." Normally he was a pretty modest dude and I didn't want to embarrass him by pointing out that he had somehow lost his robe in the process of the evening's entertainment, especially since he was drunk. He looked so drunk he made *me* feel drunk.

"Where you been?"

"Remember, Dad, I just told you. Julia's house." I arched an eyebrow.

"Dontchu tell me to member!" he yelled, slipping a little and then recovering. I flinched.

"Sorry, Dad."

He shook his head in an exaggerated motion and said, "Sorry, sorry, I—"

"It's OK, Dad."

"Is just, I find that hard to believe." He sounded almost sober.

"Believe it," I said and he laughed and cocked his eyebrows back in that funny way he always did. I stared at his drunk ass for a while, just wanting to take my clothes off, brush my teeth and sleep.

"Dad. I was studying all afternoon. I just wanna go to sleep, OK?" I sounded whiny. I was practically praying for him to leave me the fuck alone.

"Julia's."

"Yes, Dad, Julia's. Remember Julia?"

He seemed to be thinking about that for a while. I was afraid he'd forget again and we'd have to go through the whole fucking thing one more time when I heard Mom yelling from the bedroom.

"Doug! Come to bed!"

"Jus a minute Christine!"

I felt guilty. I'd left Mom and the twins alone with him.

Then I could hear the bedroom door opening and the sound of Mom stomping down the hallway. I sighed and pulled on the edge of my tank top. I really wasn't ready for drama. I was ready for sleep. The whole thing with Will and Megan had worn me out.

Mom appeared a few seconds later, her hands on her hips, her lips pursed. She looked over at Dad and rolled her eyes. "Jesus Christ, Doug! You're in your underwear!"

He swerved his head towards her. "Shut up Christine! I'm tryina talk to Margaritte."

Mom sighed real heavy. "Come to bed, Doug."

He waggled his head and I looked over at Mom and she looked back. We both looked over at Dad and then Mom went over and put her hand on his shoulder.

"Just come to bed, Doug."

He looked down at her hand, slowly, and then swatted it off.

"Doug, be reasonable."

"You be reasonable." He lurched past me.

"Doug… " Mom called, but he was already halfway to his office.

"Great. Now he'll be there all night," she said.

"Mom, you know how he is," I said moodily. "I just want to go to bed."

"Well, first of all, I don't know where you were all day, but when we got home, we had to deal with him on our own. And then he got really drunk." Her mouth was in a little, angry line.

I closed my eyes and put my head in my hands. Mom sighed, and we listened to Dad rooting around in the office. The twins' bedroom door opened and they walked out slowly, holding hands, Mary's thumb in her mouth. They were wearing Care Bear sleep shirts and they looked like the little Indian porcelain dolls that you can buy at gas stations.

"Is Dad mad?' Carrie asked.

"Yes. He's mad. And drunk," Mom said, and I worried Dad would hear her. "Let's all just go to bed." I got up and took Mary's hand, and Mary was still holding Carrie's hand. Mary let go of my hand and looked up at me. She delicately fingered the silver turquoise bracelet I was wearing that Auntie Justine had traded for her beadwork years ago, when she still used to do that.

"Can I get a bracelet like yours?" She asked.

"Sure, someday. We could maybe get you one at powwow."

"Yeah," she said.

"You should dance. You could do Fancy Shawl."

"OK." She stuck her thumb back in her mouth.

"I want to do... the fancy!" Carrie said. Mary frowned around her thumb and let go of Carrie's hand. I sighed. "You can both do Fancy Shawl someday. Now let's go." I took both of their hands. Mom followed behind.

"Is Dad in his office?" Carrie asked.

"Yes," I said, herding them both.

"Why?"

"I don't know."

"He sure does like that office."

"Yeah," Mary said, taking her thumb out for a second and then sticking it back in.

We were almost to the twins' room when we heard Dad behind us.

"Christine," he said, real soft. I kept walking but the hair on the back of my neck stood up.

"Doug, for... " and then she trailed off. And then, "Oh God, oh Doug, oh God," and I turned around. He was holding one of his guns.

"I jus' wanna talk."

"Doug. We're putting the twins to bed," Mom said.

"Does Dad have a gun?" Carrie asked, and I pulled them both close.

"I jus' wanna talk," he said again. His eyes were bloodshot and the gun was lying at his side, looking strangely like a dead snake hanging from his hand.

"Oh Doug," Mom said. We were all still.

"Dad… " I said finally, and he swerved his head drunkenly. He stared at me like he didn't really recognize me for a second, then said, "I wanna talk."

"Let me handle this, Margaritte." Mom didn't even look at me. She kept her eyes on Dad.

"Doug. If you want to talk, that's OK. But we were just going to bed. Can't we talk tomorrow?"

He looked over at all of us, and shook his head messily, sadly. "Why won't any of you talk to me?" He sighed heavily, his large nearly-naked frame moving solidly up, then down.

"We'll talk, Dad," I said.

"Margaritte! Let! Me! Handle! This!"

"OK."

"Are you gonna go back into your office?" Carrie asked and Dad looked over at her.

"I don't wannu, I don' wannu." He put his hand over his eyes.

"We'll talk Doug, but what do you need the gun for?" Mom asked.

Dad looked down at the gun like he'd almost forgotten he was holding it.

"Well, I thought we could talk, and then take a walk." He nodded then, like what he'd just said made perfect sense.

"Doug, we're tired. Could we take a walk tomorrow?" Mom

asked and Dad shook his head. "No. We should take a walk now, and we should take the gun. It's jus not safe out there anymore." He pushed his Kmart glasses further up his nose, which looked real funny on him, considering they were the only thing he had on besides his underwear.

"But Doug, it's late. We could talk, but I don't think we should take a walk. The girls need to go to sleep and you don't really want to walk this late, do you? It's dark outside."

He looked at her for a while with this funny, sad little expression on his face.

"Why won't you talk to me?"

"We can talk, Doug."

He switched the gun from his left to his right hand and looked down at it and then up.

"You jus' don't care."

"I care—" she said, but he interrupted her.

"You don't!"

"I do care, Doug, and we can talk. Just come to bed, OK?"

He shook his head again and looked down at the gun.

"Doug... can't you see you're scaring the kids?'

He looked up sharply. "You're scaring the kids, Christine!"

"Please, Doug. Please put the gun away, Doug."

"You don't love me." Tears were running down his face.

"I love you, Doug," Mom said.

"I love you, Daddy," Carrie said, and he looked at her and wiped his tears with one hand, roughly.

"I have to pee," Mary said.

"Just a minute," I whispered, and patted her on the head.

"Doug, aren't you tired? The kids are tired. They want to go to bed. Can't we just go to bed? Aren't you tired, Doug?"

He sighed. "Yes... I'm very tired."

He looked away, down at the gun and then at Mom with this real suspicious look on his face.

"Why don't you put that away and go to bed?"

He narrowed his eyes. "Why?"

"Because I think we're all tired Doug, can't you see that?"

"No. I think you all don't care." Mom closed her eyes. "I think—" he started, and raised the gun slightly. Mom and me stepped back.

"I have to pee!" Mary said.

"I know," I said, and Mary started to whine.

He raised it a little more. "None of you care!"

"Doug… " Mom said.

"No! No!" He pulled the gun almost all the way up.

"Margaritte, follow me," Mom said and I nodded for a full minute before I realized that she wasn't looking at me.

"Yes," I said finally, gripping Mary and Carrie's hands, hard.

"Good."

"I have to pee!" Mary said again. I reached down and patted her head without looking at her. I started to back towards the bathroom and Dad turned the gun towards us. We froze. Mary began to pee.

"Nooooooooo," she said, crying.

"It's OK," Carrie said. "I peed once too."

"Doug, if you don't put the gun away and let us go to bed, we're going to have to leave."

"Noooooo," he said, sounding like Mary. "We have to talk."

"No, Doug." She looked at him. He held tightly to the gun.

"Let's go." Mom started walking towards the stairs, watching Dad the whole time. "Doug," she said, pausing near him. "We're going to go. But we will be back tomorrow." And she motioned for me to follow. I started walking with the twins.

"No, Christine, no." He moved the gun in her direction. She didn't stop, but I did. She looked over at me, "Come on Margaritte," she said, and I looked over at Dad and started moving. He looked panicky but he trailed off, and the gun wilted in his hand.

As me and the twins walked past, I thought of the time that he had made me hold the gun. I had screamed that I didn't want to, but he made me, yelling angrily the whole time. It had sat limply in my hand, tears running down my face until he took it from me, shaking his head in disgust. The funny thing was, Dad had no real use for guns. He wasn't like my uncles, who were hunters. He didn't even know how to shoot proper really, he just had them. A lot of them.

We made it past him, behind Mom who grabbed her old tooled-leather purse that was always sitting on the stand by the door. I could feel the gun at my back. I didn't know whether he would shoot, or put the gun down, or whether he would shoot and miss, or hit... but I could feel his anger and loneliness mixing behind me and moving out towards us. I waited for the gun to go off, for it to hit me right between my shoulder blades. I thought of the little, tiny person growing inside of me. At the door, I looked back. He was standing there, the gun against his leg, his eyes on us. I turned and followed Mom. I closed the door.

On the car ride to the hotel, the twins cried for their Barbies, and Mom slapped me because I'd left them with Dad the whole day and that meant the whole thing had been my fault. When she slapped me, she split my lip, and blood began running down my face and mixing with my tears. I knew why we were heading towards a hotel and not over to Auntie Justine's. She knew what Dad was like and would have been happy to take us in, but then Mom would have had to bear the humiliation of having to tell her what had happened and hear another long, ranting speech about leaving Dad.

At the hotel the guy at the counter stared at us: two children in pajamas, one with pee stains drying on her Care Bear sleep shirt, one teenager looking like exactly what she was, a drug dealer in a white wifebeater, and a woman in pajamas. She handed the guy her credit card and he took it, ran it through, and handed us a hotel key.

The next morning, I went in to shower before anyone could get in the bathroom. I needed the comfort of the water on my face, anything to erase the image of Dad crying in his underwear, gun in his hand. I moved Mary's nightshirt, which we'd hand washed in the bathtub the night before, onto the edge of the sink and turned on the water. It sputtered to life, the white, moldy-looking shower curtain breezing in towards me. I moved as far away from it as I could and picked up the tiny white hotel soap. The place smelled funky, the combination of old cigarette smoke and carpet shampoo rising up from the faded blue and black carpet.

When I was done, I came out and could see that Mom and the twins were up, the twins cuddled up against Mom in her bed, watching TV. After a few minutes, Mom got up and showered, and when she was finished, asked me if I would bathe the twins. Even though we should have given Mary a bath the night before, we'd been so tired that all Mom could manage was a good swipe with a ratty hotel washcloth. So I nodded, and gave them a bath. Carrie didn't even fuss and in fact, the two of them played as if nothing had happened, as if we were on vacation, though both of them talked about their Barbies, wanting to know when they would be reunited with them.

"Soon," I told them. It broke my heart to see how easily they could push their confusion down, how quick they were to let it all go and play in the bathtub like their dad wasn't a drunk who had held them at gunpoint the night before. They splashed in the murky water for around twenty minutes, while I soaped their hair and bodies and then I pulled them out, toweled them off and put them back in their pajamas. Mary's was still slightly damp, so I ran the crappy hotel hair dryer over her as she giggled.

When we got out of the bathroom, Mom was standing by the window, looking out. Without turning around she said, "Let's go."

"Where are we going?" I asked.

"Home."

I was silent for a minute. "What?"

"Don't question me Margaritte!" she said, turning around, her eyes narrowed. I shook my head and walked over to her. "It'll be fine. I don't want to hear anything from you."

I sighed and looked out the window.

"Alright, Margaritte?" Mom asked.

I was silent.

"Margaritte, you answer me!"

"Fine!"

"I don't need your approval."

I rolled my eyes.

"Don't roll your eyes at me! Don't you treat me that way. I get enough of it from your father."

I turned to her and looked into her eyes. "Then why don't you leave him?"

"How dare you! How dare you!" Before I could see what was happening, she slapped me in the face with the back of her hand. Hard. I walked backwards and sat down on the hotel bed, stunned. I raised my hand to my mouth. My lip was bleeding again. She was silent for a short time while I cried and then she started laughing. "Oh my God Margaritte, you're so overemotional," she said.

We both went silent then. I didn't even know what to say. We gathered the twins and walked out of the hotel, silent, tired, stinking of shitty hotel soap. In the car, as we took the exit into Idaho Springs, I looked out the window at the town waking up, the glow of the sun on the mountains. We passed the Sugar Plum and I realized that I hadn't been to work in weeks, and hadn't even thought about it. I was guessing I was fired.

"Mommy, are you OK?" Mary asked. I looked over at her. She was crying and trying not to, wiping at her tears with the back of her long, tapered, brown arm.

"Mommy is OK, as long as she has you," she said to them. I looked down at my old, stained sneaks.

"I'm sorry Margaritte."

"It's OK, Mom," I said.

"Margaritte. You're my heart."

I felt like dying then. I rolled the window down and wished for a cigarette, badly.

"Let's get cookies," Mary said. "That always makes me stop crying, Mommy."

Mom laughed. "Oh, Mary," she said. "Let's go to the Derby for breakfast. How about that?"

"Um, well, I don't think they have cookies there," Mary said and Mom laughed again. I handed her a dusty Dairy Queen napkin that had been stuck into the side pocket of the passenger seat door, and she blew her nose while I held the wheel.

"Thanks, Margaritte," she said.

I looked back at Mary and Carrie, secure in their car seats, and saw Carrie was asleep and Mary was looking out the window, her tiny little hands folded in her lap. Carrie was drooling, so I pulled another ancient napkin out of the side pocket and reached back and gently wiped at her mouth. They both looked so cute, but messy. I had used Mom's comb, the old beat-up blue one from Walmart she kept in her purse to pick at her perms to comb through their hair in the hotel after their baths. Their hair was already starting to thicken though, and it had been hard to get the comb through. Not to mention that they were still in their pajamas.

We pulled into the Derby parking lot and got out, tired, hungry and in love with one another, ready for eggs and bacon and a few more minutes away from Dad. We ate, Mom and me drinking coffee and not talking about Dad but about my last week of school, which was this next week. And though Mom was worried about my grades, and she wasn't the only one, she didn't push too hard. Mainly we focused on the twins, getting them to eat something decent, wiping their mouths, making sure they didn't fight or cry over the absence of their Barbies. Half-way through breakfast, Carrie began to sing the theme song for *Sesame Street* and Mary joined in and they were quiet about it, not yelling, just singing together happily, and me and Mom clapped our hands when they were done. I looked at them and thought about how cute and silly they were, thought of them in front of the TV, their mouths hanging open in wonder, the glow of it on their small, yellow-brown faces.

"Are we going home now?" Carrie asked.

"Yeah," Mom said.

"Is Dad going to still be mad?"

Mom sighed, heavily. "I'm betting Dad will be asleep."

"I hate it when he's mad," Carrie said. "He made Mary pee."

"I didn't!" Mary said, her little pink-purple lower lip trembling.

"You did! I saw you pee—"

"Enough," Mom said, folding her paper napkin onto her plate. "That doesn't matter." She gestured to the waitress and asked for the bill. I was silent. It did matter.

"What matters is that I love you," Mom said. "And... Dad loves you too. In his way."

Carrie took this in, picking up her fork and dancing it around for a while. She set it down. "Sometimes Dad is funny."

"Yeah," Mary said, looking at her own fork as if it might get up and dance on its own.

Sometimes Dad *was* funny. After a few drinks. That was the thing; half the time we couldn't wait for him to drink, the scotch or the beer beside him on the table, by the TV. After the first few he stopped being angry, tight, wound up like a tangled spring. That's when he was free. But the next few hours after that were a gamble. If we were lucky he'd set himself down in front of the TV to yell at it or shut himself in his office, all of us waiting, expectant, tense. When were not lucky, he did stuff like hold us at gunpoint.

The waitress came over with the bill, pulling a thick black pen with the local bank logo on it out from the top of her ear and setting it down with the bill. Mom looked at it, squinting.

"Hey, I can help," I said. "If you need me to."

Mom looked up at me. "I don't think I want your money," she said. I was silent. I guess she was right. I had denied it a million times, but she knew what I really did for money.

We sipped at the rest of our weak, lukewarm coffee and the waitress came back and got the bill from Mom.

"I worry about you, Margaritte," Mom said, turning to me. I could see the grey buried in her perm.

"I worry about me too," I said.

"You will never understand until you have a child," she said, and I flinched. "You will never understand until you feel your heart being torn at like there is an animal in your chest every time you think your child is doing something that could kill them. You die a little."

I began to cry.

"Please turn your life around before it's too late," she said, putting her rough, brown hand on my shoulder. "Before you can't."

I nodded and wiped at my tears. "Alright Mom."

"Are you OK, Margaritte?" Mary asked.

I looked at her and got up and hugged her. Her tiny, soft hands came up and around my neck. I felt better.

"We should have gotten cookies," she said.

"Can't we get some on the way back, Mommy?" Carrie asked.

"Aren't you full?" Mom asked.

"No," they said in unison.

"OK, we'll get cookies, but you can only have one, and I mean only one, after lunch."

The waitress came back and set the bill down and Mom looked at it, signed, and got up. We walked into the midmorning sun and down the stairs of the Derby, each of us with a twin in hand. The smell of pine trees was everywhere.

"You want to drive?" Mom asked.

"Sure," I said, helping Mom get the twins into their car seats and then settling in behind the wheel. I always had to pull the seat back, considering I was near a half a foot taller than her.

She called me her baby giraffe. She handed me the keys and we drove the short distance to the grocery store, where I went in for the cookies and some milk. The parking lot was bustling with families, children sitting in the front of shopping carts, moms pushing them, plucking things from the endless, shining rows of shelves. I saw this all the time but today it felt just so fucking weird. Like I was bathed in light, like I was underwater. Or had done a drug I'd never done before. I found the chocolate chip cookies the twins liked, the crunchy kind in the blue package and then walked to the cooler for the milk, feeling strange and tired; I really hadn't slept well the night before.

I walked back through the aisles and up to the register and stood in line for a few minutes, looking at the magazines, the celebrities being busted for bad behavior, the newspapers talking about alien babies. The cashier was a chick I'd gone to school with but we didn't really acknowledge each other. What was the point? Her hair was permed and frosted into a nest that looked like it hadn't been washed in a while, and her eyes had big, black bags underneath. I'd sold to her a couple of times, but she'd either gone to someone else or gone onto bigger shit. I was thinking it was probably the second one. She looked like she was halfway to being a waitress at the Derby.

"Have a nice day," she said, looking down at my receipt and handing it to me, "Mrs. Riggs." I'd used Mom's card.

"Thanks." I took it and my sack from the bagger, a dude who'd been in a major car accident years ago which had resulted in brain damage and one hell of a pirate-ass looking scar on his head, which he kept shaved. He seemed happy though, bagging away and handing people their shit. I walked out and into the parking lot and found Mom's car. She had rolled the windows down and I could hear the twins singing again, and I was glad. It was freaking torture when they fought. Mom was singing along, all three of them belting out the theme song to *Sesame Street.*

I got in and we took off and I sang along with them to push away the darkness, to push away the fact that we were all going to have face Dad. That he was going to want us to pretend nothing had happened, and that we would do that because Mom wanted that, until they argued again.

I pulled into the drive and parked and helped Mom get the twins out of the car, both of them still singing. Mom hushed them. "Daddy's probably sleeping. Let's be quiet, OK?"

They stopped, and Carrie asked about their Barbies. Mom said she was sure they were right inside. As we were walking to the house, Mom stopped for a second and looked at me.

"I meant what I said."

"I know you did."

"Without the twins and you, my life would have no meaning."

"I love you Mom," I said and she told me she loved me too. We hugged and led the twins back into the house, the sound of Dad's snoring echoing throughout.

I went downstairs and plopped down on my bed, and lay there for a while, trying to sleep. I couldn't. I read for a few minutes and then put the book down. I slid my hands down over my stomach and stared at the ceiling for a long time, then picked up the phone and called Megan and told her about my appointment and asked her to go with me. She said yes.

CHAPTER 12

That week, the last week of school, the phone began to ring in the middle of the night. Sometimes I would catch it, sometimes Mom would. I would hear it ring, and then nothing. After the third call, I could hear Dad screaming upstairs and Mom calming him down. When I caught it, it was just breathing on the other end and then the line would go dead. Of course I hoped it was Mike. My anger with him had turned into pain, and then right back to anger, and then right back again into pain. I kept thinking about what we had been together and then my goddamn head would go right to what he had said that night in the hospital, and then to what he used to whisper to me when we had been together in his bed. I felt a sharp pain turning in my stomach, over and over, especially after the calls. And then flashes of pure hatred. For him. For Julia. I felt so alone. School was a blur. I did deals, took final exams and came home every day, exhausted. I thought about what I was going to do. I talked to Jake on the phone. His trial was coming up. They were going to decide whether he was to be tried as an adult, and then depending on that decision, they would decide what would happen to him from there. I was filled with dread about that, about everything. I wished that he could be in the basement with me like usual, shooting the shit and smoking up.

Saturday, I told Mom that I was going to go up to Julia's. That she needed my help taking her pre-SATs. That she needed someone to quiz her. Mom didn't fight me. I drove over to Megan's house and picked her up. On the way to the clinic, my stomach turned and turned until I felt like I was going to pass out, like I was full of an ocean that I was drowning in from the inside out. Megan's baby slept, and she told me that she had kicked Will out for good. That at the end of the month she would go back home and try to figure out her life.

"Where is Will?"

"I don't give a shit. I changed the goddamn locks. Probably'll end up back on the rez or homeless."

I knew better than to argue with her, knew that she would only get mad at me, and that she had her reasons for feeling that way. Though I did wonder what would happen to him, if he'd shack up with one of the dudes he'd treated like shit, if he'd go home, if he *would* end up homeless. Another waste.

The drive to Denver was good, no rain, and Megan read the directions off for me and though I feared getting there to a bunch of people with signs throwing dead babies at my face, when we pulled in, it was eerily peaceful. We parked and I got out, tripping as I did, my heart hammering so hard in my head I thought my ears were gonna bust.

"Are you OK?" Megan asked me, putting one plump hand on my arm.

I leaned against the car and felt faint, sick, weak.

"Margaritte?"

"I don't feel so good. I need to sit down."

The next thing I knew there were faces above me and I blinked, trying to focus. I didn't want to be awake, with nurses pointing lights into my eyes and asking me questions. I felt like I'd been somewhere very, very far away. But I was still in the parking lot.

I sat up slowly, the gravel under my ass grinding into me. I felt weak. I put my shaking hand to my forehead. It was covered in sweat.

"What happened?"

"Girl, you looked pale and then you just fucking buckled. I barely caught you and then you started to you know, shake, and your eyes rolled back in your head and that's when I ran into the clinic for help."

"I feel so tired," I said. "But I think I'll be OK."

"Do you think you can walk?" A nurse asked. "I think you just fainted and had a minor seizure, but I'd like to get you into the clinic so the doctor can check you out."

"Yeah," I said, and they helped me up and into the clinic, my legs shaking, and into a back room. I lay on an examination table, and a nurse came in and gave me water. A few minutes later a doctor came in. He asked me if I'd been under any major stress. I laughed and told him that yes, you could say that.

I hadn't been out long and the seizure had only lasted around a minute, so the doctor told me that I was OK, but that I might consider having my procedure another day. I looked at him and asked if I could see my friend. He said yes and left. A few minutes later Megan came in and sat down next to me.

"How you doing?" she asked. She looked anxious.

"I—I'm not going to do this."

"What? The abortion?"

"Right. I'm not going to do this."

Megan was silent, nodding to herself. "You know I support you either way, but I'm glad. I was raised to think this is wrong."

"Well, I don't think it's wrong, but I can't. I'm just not going to do this."

Megan nodded again and took my hand. I began to tear up, just a little. I felt relief. Loads of fear too, but for some reason, I felt good. Better than I had in a long time. Megan held my hand quietly, until I was done. And then she handed me a box of tissues. I took one and she set it back on the table.

"Speaking of babies, where's yours?" I asked.

Megan laughed. "Well, when you fainted and then had a damn seizure, I pulled her out of the car and ran into the clinic and when I explained what was going down, one of the nurses came and took her out of my hands and said not to worry, that she would take care of her. I just went and checked on her. She's sleeping like a little angel. Even though she's a little devil with me."

I laughed.

"I think I'm OK," I said. "Let's get out of here."

"OK," Megan said and she helped me up, the white paper crinkling as I went. We walked out the door and into the waiting room, which was filled with women, some of them with expressions of determination on their faces, some of them young and terrified, some of them older, some of them alone and others with men sitting next to them. One woman was filing her nails, looking bored.

I told the lady at the desk that I'd call back, that I was going to take the doctor's advice and reschedule. I just didn't want to get into why I wasn't going to do it at all. *I* wasn't even sure why. She smiled and said that was fine, and we made our way into the parking lot, Megan of course stopping first to pick her baby up. One of the nurses was holding her on her lap and another one was cooing at her, while the baby laughed and drooled. I thought to myself how totally fucking weird this charming little scene was, considering where we were.

We got into the car and drove back home and talked about Will a little bit more, about Megan's plans for the future. She asked me what I was going to do, what my plan was, and I told her I wasn't sure, that I didn't know. She understood. Pulling into her parking lot, I thanked her for coming with me, and she said to call anytime. I said I would.

On the way home, I tried not think.

At the house, Dad was sleeping it off and Mom was grading at the table. The twins were in front of the TV. I went into the kitchen, opened the fridge and got myself stuff for a bologna sandwich.

I finished putting the sandwich together and turned around. Mom looked up at me. "You look pale," she said, her stack of papers piled high on the kitchen table.

I leaned against the counter and ate my sandwich. "Yeah. I'm tired."

Mom nodded. "I guess maybe you really were doing work."

"Yeah. I guess I was," I said, smiling.

Mom smiled back at me, an expression of true tenderness on her face, and I almost began crying, telling her what was really going on with me. But I decided that I needed sleep first. I went and plopped down on the couch behind the twins, and soon I was falling asleep to the sound of children's television, the twins' lovely, child smell of apple juice and crayons floating all around me.

I woke up to the phone ringing and Mom answering.

"It's Julia," she said, walking into the living room.

"Oh. Uh. OK. I'll take it downstairs," I said. I wanted Mom to tell her I wasn't there, or tell her that I didn't feel like talking to Julia, but she didn't know that Julia and I hadn't talked in a long time. I didn't want to provoke any feelings of suspicion, as studying at Julia's house had become my excuse for leaving the house. Also, I was curious. Very.

I walked downstairs and sat on my bed. I picked up the handle of the old, red rotary phone and told my mom that she could hang up. I was silent.

"Are you there?" she asked, finally.

"Yeah."

"Oh, um, good."

"What's up?" I asked, though I felt like yelling into the phone, ranting into it, telling her to never call me again.

"Can we... can we go to Java Mountain Roasters and talk?'

I was silent again.

"Please, Margaritte? I have so much to say, and I know you probably don't want to talk to me ever again, and I could just tell you over the phone, but I don't think that's right. I think we should talk face to face. Don't you?"

I sighed, heavily. "Well, I'm really tired. But OK, yeah. Sure."

"I'm so glad Margaritte, I really am. I know I have no right to ask you, but I knew I had to try. Even if you just want to clock me one and leave," she said, laughing nervously.

"Well, I won't hit you. Probably."

"That's good," she said, laughing nervously.

"Well, I'm gonna go do a deal. Meet you in an hour."

"Yes. Please."

"OK. See you soon," I said and she told me goodbye in a faint, whispery voice and we hung up. I walked up the stairs. Mom was making dinner. I told her that me and Julia needed to go over some stuff we'd forgotten, and that I'd be back in two hours.

"Will you be home for dinner?"

"Could you just save me a plate? Seriously, Julia's desperate."

"She's a smart girl," Mom said, shifting in her seat. We had an old, fifties style dining set we'd found at a thrift store in Denver, and it was cool-looking but the seats were kind of small.

"Yeah, she is."

"So are you Margaritte. You're a different girl. But you're smart."

"Thanks Mom," I said, wanting again to let it all pour out of me. To tell her. But I had to meet Julia. I figured I would tell Mom tomorrow. I couldn't imagine what Julia was going to say to me.

I walked over to her, leaned down and hugged her. She hugged me back and I felt the guilt move through my veins, and it felt like glass. I didn't feel very smart.

"See you later," I said. I went downstairs to get my backpack and keys and then back up, and out the door.

Driving into town, I could see the exit for I-70 on my right. I thought briefly about the exit and what it would be like to get on it, to keep going. To stop somewhere nobody knew me and start over. But that was what people did in the movies.

Julia was leaning against the side of the red brick of Java Mountain Roasters, smoking, looking like a model on some kind of shoot for Seventeen, her long, thin legs ending in tiny white jean shorts and a lacy top she'd probably found at the local thrift.

She smiled nervously and I smiled back, a short, quick line.

"Hey," I said.

"Hey," she said back.

"Mind if I finish this?" she asked, gesturing to her cigarette.

"No problem."

"Want one?" she asked.

"Uh... "

"Oh. Oh, God. Sorry. I... forgot. But I thought... well, never mind."

She took one long, last drag and pointed towards the coffee house with her lips and we walked in. I remembered that this was where Julia had met Mike, and I felt my stomach twist. I felt a sharp, painful yearning for a smoke and repressed it. We stood in line for coffee and when we got our mugs, we found somewhere near the back to sit down. It wasn't busy this time of day and we were almost alone. The only other person in the place, besides the guy that worked there, was an old fucker that practically lived in this joint.

"So, your classes went good?" I asked.

Julia wiped at her brow nervously. "Yeah. I think I'll have a 4.0 again this semester. I'll be in AP, you know, advanced classes, next year. And that should help me get into college and hopefully get myself a fat scholarship, which is cool."

"That's good."

"How about you?"

I laughed. "I'll be glad if I pass. That's how it goes for a pregnant drug dealer. Grades come last I guess." Julia looked uneasy. She frowned and looked over at the wall. I thought about the first place I'd gotten high. I was thirteen and a friend had asked me if I wanted to hang with her in the parking lot across from the school during lunch. I had closed my eyes and said yes.

"Things suck. But at least school is over. For the year anyways," I said.

"Yeah," Julia said.

I wondered what she wanted with me. If she wanted to apologize, or ask where Mike was. She had been a major fucking douchebag the last time we'd talked.

"You're more than just a pregnant drug dealer, you know. You could take the SATs with me and get out of here. You could stop dealing. You could... "

"So. You're talking to me again," I said, interrupting her. I sat back and folded my hands over my chest. "If you want to know where Mike is, I have no idea."

"I—no... I don't care about him."

"So? Why the cold shoulder in the hallways? I'm the one who should have been ignoring you. You did me fucking wrong, and you know it."

"I know," she said. She picked her cup up and drank from it and I watched her. She put it down, touching the rim of the cup with one of her slender fingers. Her nails were painted a delicate pink. She looked up at me again. "And I *am* sorry," she said, her voice trembling just a little. She looked into my eyes and back down at her cup.

I sat there for a while looking down at my own cup of coffee, thinking, when I realized that Julia was crying. Julia never cried. The only time I'd seen her cry was at the funeral of a kid who'd gotten in an accident. She had been in a foster home with him. They had started smoking and drinking when they were twelve and he was the first person she'd had sex with where it didn't start with a foster father's hands reaching for her in the endless dark. The boy's name had been Jason, and he had driven off a cliff one night on the edge of a mountain road, drunk and high out of his mind. After the funeral, she said she would never let anyone make her feel that way again.

"Julia, why did you do this to me?"

"Because I'm so, so stupid."

"Julia... "

"I don't know Margaritte. Maybe because I was jealous that you got him, and you know it's stupid but I pride myself on getting the guy. That's so stupid. I know. He hit on me and I just... said OK. I promise I will never, ever do anything like that to you again. And he is such a jerk, Margaritte. Really. He is."

"Julia, I shouldn't forgive you."

"I know. Margaritte, I know I've done a pathetic, unforgivable thing. But please, let's not throw our friendship away over it. We've been through a lot together. I was doing coke that night because Mike had some, and because I knew what I was doing with him was wrong. And when you're on coke, all kinds of garbage will come out of your mouth."

"I forgive you, Julia. But don't do anything like that to me ever again. I'm fucking serious."

Julia took my hand.

"I feel so alone," I said.

She looked at me with a serious expression on her face. "So... is that why you're having the baby?" she asked.

I blinked. That had never occurred to me.

"I have to tell you, Margaritte, I don't think you should do this. You know, you *know* I've been through this. You can change your mind. It's not too late."

I felt my heart hammering in my chest. "I can't," I whispered. "I don't know why."

"Margaritte, this isn't about Mike is it? I need to hear that."

"No."

"He doesn't love you. He doesn't love anyone."

"I don't think it's about him, and it's not because a book somewhere says that it's the right thing to do. I think probably it will be the wrong thing, in every thinking way. But I can't. I can't. I just can't." I whispered, my voice starting to tremble.

Julia nodded. She squeezed my hand. "I don't want you to do this. I really don't. I have to keep saying that. I know Jake wouldn't want this either."

"I know," I said, wiping at my face. "You know the reason he's going to jail, this time for real, is because he hit the fuck out of Mike the night we saw him with you. Mike passed out from too much coke, and we took him to the hospital, and his parents showed up. And he... he called me a whore."

Julia closed her eyes. Then opened them, slowly. "Why are you having this loser's baby, Margaritte? You could have a baby sometime later, in the future, when things are better for you. Instead of having a baby with someone who would call you... call you that."

"I'm not like you."

Julia narrowed her eyes in confusion. "What do you mean, not like me?"

"It's not about being smart, because I think I'm smart. Or about wanting out of here. It's about something else. I guess there's something wrong with me."

"There is nothing wrong with you! Why do you keep on saying this shit! It makes me so... so—" and here Julia started to cry again—"angry with you," she said, coming around and holding me. The old guy was looking at us now but I didn't care. I let Julia rock me and we both cried.

"I know. I know," I said, patting her hand. "It's not... I can't explain. I just can't. It's not like my life is going to be like yours. I'm not like you. Can't you understand that? Please understand that." I said, my voice wavering and fading.

"I will never, ever understand," she said. "I hope I never do."

"Oh, Julia," I said, "you're so strong. I'm not like you. I'm not strong the way you are. I'm strong in a different way."

"No," she said.

"Yes," I said, and she giggled. She hugged me hard, one more time, and sat down.

"I feel like if I hadn't done what I did, then I would have been there for you when you were making this decision and you would have made a different one."

"No," I said.

She looked at me, a smile, devilish smile on her lips. "Yes."

We giggled.

"I'm just afraid for you. What are you going to do? Have you told your mom? What is your dad going to say?"

I sighed. "I don't know what I'm going to do. Survive, I guess. Live a different way. I'm going to tell my mom tomorrow. She'll go apeshit, then Dad'll go apeshit. It'll be an apeshit factory. I don't know exactly how they'll react. And I am going to do it when Dad's more sober than drunk. You know how he is."

"I want you to tell me when you're going to talk to them, and then I want you to call me after."

"OK," I said.

"So, what's happening with Megan and Will, that crazy motherfucker."

"He finally pushed Megan over the edge. She kicked him out."

"Oh, shit," she said, drinking from her cup. "Hold on. I'm going to get a refill. Want one?"

"Yeah, thanks." I handed her my cup and she walked up to the long, wooden counter and asked for refills. The guy serving smiled at her like a child, running his long, white fingers through his short, punkish haircut, making nervous chatter as he gave her free refills which would normally cost an additional

50 cents. I laughed a little to myself. It was good to know that some things never changed.

She came back over and set my coffee down, turning the handle of the thick, brown mug over to face me. I picked my cup up and sipped, giving her a captain's salute with the other hand. "Thank you," I said and she saluted back, her long, elegant arm executing the move perfectly.

"You dah bomb, you know," I said.

"I am dah bomb," she said.

We giggled again and she looked at me. "I missed you. I missed this. I'm sorry. Truly."

"I know. And I did too."

I sighed. "Well, I should get home."

She nodded. "One more thing. When is Jake's trial? I heard..."

"Next week. It doesn't look good. They're talking aggravated battery. They're talking real time. Adult jail. I think part of the problem is his record. And they're not exactly going to listen to me when I say he punched someone just because they called me a whore."

"I see. No cowboy justice for the justice system."

"I wish there was a way they would listen. No one understands Jake. He's got a heart of pure fucking gold. And me and him, we sell drugs because it's the only way people like us can make money like that. And I wish I could say that both of us were like you, that we loved school, that we were right for it, that it was going to be our ticket out. But it's not. It's not. And wouldn't you feel like punching someone if they called someone you love a whore?"

"Yes. I want to punch Mike *now*."

"Well, thank you. But I already have one person I love in jail. I don't need two. And I just got you back."

"I don't know where I was."

I looked over at her and smiled. "You were in the trenches."

"I was," she said, a foggy, faraway expression on her face. Like she was staring into a retreating storm. She was so beautiful, composed, someone who seemed as if they'd made up their mind up a million years ago and hadn't looked back. It was good to know beneath that façade was all of the bubbling, wild, angry shit that we all felt.

"Well, the war's over and you can come home now. I always was one to support my troops," I said, and Julia laughed, a sharp, sweet sound that I'd missed. I wanted her in my life. I wanted as many fucked-up, awesome people in my life, and my baby's life, as I could squeeze in.

"Can I come to his trial?" She asked, expectantly, anxiously.

"Sure. I don't see why not. It's open to the public. And it will probably go terrifyingly fast."

"Yeah," Julia said. "Well." She picked up our cups and walked over to the counter and the guy ran over to her to ask her if she needed anything else. She smiled at him coyly and he laughed like a little girl. "No. But maybe another time." I could practically hear his heart thumping like a rabbit's leg from my seat.

"You walk?" I asked.

"I did."

"Ride?"

"Yeah."

We got in to my car, and I turned the music up and rolled the windows down and Julia stuck her hand out the window and waved it happily in the wind. She turned to me and smiled, her hair flying in her face. I smiled back. Hers faded and she turned the radio down.

"What?" I asked.

"I—I have something to confess."

"What? You're making me nervous."

"I slept with Jake, you know. About a year ago. After a party."

I was shocked. Jake told me everything. And I knew how he felt about her.

"And I pushed him away. I told him that we'd been drunk. But that wasn't true. I was scared. Scared of Jake. And I want to tell you something, and I want you not to judge me."

"OK," I said, turning onto the street that lead to Julia's foster home. It was a nice, tree-lined street that always seemed to have kids jumping rope and yelling on it.

"It was because... I felt like Jake was going nowhere. And I felt for him. A lot. And I wasn't going to be trapped. I wasn't going to let him, no matter how I felt about him, get in the way of what I wanted."

"Look, Julia, you and I are different, but that doesn't mean I don't get it. This place is sad. I don't know what the answer is. But I think you're going to do something amazing. And you're not right for this place."

"Neither are you."

I sighed. "We're not going to go through this again, are we?"

"I just feel like I'm having a nightmare where you're drowning and I'm in this tiny boat somewhere in the middle of a storm on the ocean, and I can hear you but I can't get to you."

"Oh, Julia. I know. But it doesn't have to be like that. Maybe it's not a nightmare; maybe it's a dream. And a dream can be anything. Maybe on the other side of the ocean is something else. Something I never would have thought possible."

"I think on the other side there are diapers and welfare and not pursuing what I know you should be pursuing."

"How do you know what I want when I don't?"

"I know."

I pulled up to her house and stopped.

"What do you know?"

"That you may be a little wacky, but you're not a loser. You're not going to be happy here."

"I agree. But having a baby isn't the end of the world."

"But it's going to make everything a hell of a lot harder."

"That's OK."

Julia hung her head and looked at me with a funny little smile on her glossed lips. "Well."

"Well."

She leaned over and hugged me, the citrus of her floating around me and then she pulled back and opened her door. "We have a long time to argue about this. And I'm glad we are."

"Me too," I said and she gave me her clever, sly little smile again and got out. I watched her walk slowly towards the door of her foster house, loads of kids outside, playing, stopping their games to come up to Julia and talk to her, rapid-fire. She took the hand of a tiny little girl with dark, curly hair and they walked to the house, opened the dog-scratched green wooden door, and went in.

Sunday morning I woke up full of hope and energy. I was ready to talk to Mom. She would have to understand. I crawled out of bed, walked up the stairs to the sound of the coffee maker percolating and *Sesame Street* on the television. I sat down at the table and smiled at Mom. She smiled back. Dad was sitting at the table too, the paper like a printed wall between us.

"You working today, Dad?"

The paper twitched. "No. I just want to relax. Can I do that, Margaritte? Can you please be quiet?"

"Yes, Dad. Sorry," I said, thinking that he was probably hungover as shit. I looked over at Mom, but she was grading, and seemed to be trying to ignore us both.

The paper twitched again, and I shook my head. I went and got a bowl of cereal and sat down.

The paper came down, and Dad looked into my eyes angrily, his light brown hair ruffled in such a way as to make him look like a big, brown peacock.

"What?" I asked, the spoon halfway to my mouth, the milk dripping into the bowl.

"Could you not chew so loudly?" he asked.

"Sorry. *Jesus*," I said, trying to chew quietly, the paper going back up again. How the fuck Mom had put up with this shit for years and years was beyond me. I was going to raise my child without this fucked up shit, without some giant, angry, red motherfucker telling her to chew quietly for fuck's sake. I looked over at Mom again, but she still had her head down, her pen in her hand.

I got up from the table nosily, and walked over to the TV to sit with the twins, their funky haircut Barbies settled in their chubby, sticky yellowy-brown fists, their mouths open, eyes affixed to the TV. I reached over and patted Carrie's head and then Mary's. Mary turned and smiled at me briefly, but Carrie just squiggled in irritation and scooted further towards the TV.

"No, Carrie, not that close," I said, pulling her back. She scooted back up towards the TV again as soon as my hands had left her stubborn little body, and I had to pull her back again. She was set to move forward yet again when I told her that if she did it one more time, I was gonna turn the TV off.

"No!" Mary whined.

"Margaritte!" Carrie said, "No!"

"Well, stop trying to scoot closer. You know it's bad for you."

"I'm tireda doing things good for me!" She yelled.

I looked at her and then laughed. "Yeah. I know. Me too."

She narrowed her eyes in anger and frustration but stayed put and I shook my head at her and smiled and patted her head. She ducked pissily as soon as my fingertips hit her hair and I laughed again, making her madder. I understood why she was like she was, I really did. But that was another thing; I was not gonna let my kid watch TV all fucking day. I understood why my mom felt she had to let them do it, with me, Dad, work, the fact that she had two little kids, but I was gonna have one job and one kid and I was gonna put all of my energy into just that.

I sat with the twins for an hour, watching *Sesame Street* and then *Electric Company* propped out on the floor, my head against the couch and a cup of watery black coffee on my stomach. Carrie looked over at me occasionally, clearly hoping that I'd leave so that she could get eye-shatteringly close to the TV. When the credits started to roll I got up from the floor and headed for the bathroom for a long, hot shower, telling the twins to behave as I got up to go. Carrie made an angry, muffled gummmpph noise and I laughed yet again. She was a kid after my own heart. Stubborn. Good. She'd need to be, in this life.

Dad had retreated into his office and Mom was at the table, still grading. I swear to God, if Mom ever murdered some poor fucker, and the crazy Christians like my uncle and auntie were right, and there really was some cheesy place like hell, she'd end up eternally grading. She looked down at the infinite pile of papers and then scribbled, squinting. She scribbled again and then set her pen down to the side of the pile and pulled one off the top of the stack and put it on the bottom.

I opened the door to the bathroom and shut it, locking it

behind me before I took off my pajamas. I turned the shower on and stepped in, the water on my body giving me the shivers. I looked down at my stomach and wondered when I was going to start showing. The idea that there was another person growing in me fully, finally hit me and I shivered again. All of the horrible stories about young moms in my town came flooding in, like lightning in the dark. The tall, skinny fifteen-year-old girl who'd told me without expression that since she couldn't afford an abortion, she'd had her boyfriend beat her until it came out. The silent, tiny, eternally black t-shirt clad fourteen-year-old with the face full of cystic acne who'd been pregnant for nine months, whose parents had not bothered to notice, who'd left her baby on her own doorstep early the next morning when she gave birth to it in her room alone one night.

I finished and dried myself off with one of the black and gold towels Mom and Dad had gotten on their wedding day. I held the towel out in front of me thoughtfully, thinking about my dad's mom. How she drank too. About her thick, white legs squeezed into a pair of pantyhose every day of her life. Her lamé sandals with fake jewels. Her shaking white face. Her sweating hand around her glass of scotch.

I walked down the stairs and changed into my uniform, a white wife-b and jeans. I painted long brown lines on my eyelids in the mirror. I combed my hair slowly. I walked up the stairs and told Mom I was going for a walk. I opened the door and went a few blocks, over to one of my regulars. They were a bunch of guys who lived in a house together. Sometimes I would see one of them working as a busboy in a restaurant, or behind the register in a gas station, their long, greasy hair hiding their eyes, hungover, high, smiling at me funny. I knocked. No one answered. I looked down at my hands and sighed impatiently.

And then knocked again. A few minutes later, a shuffling noise, the sound of someone tripping over something that made a tinny noise, *shit* muttered unhappily. Then a messy, sleepy looking white dude finally answered.

"Hey. Sorry. I was sleeping."

"S'cool." I walked in and he shut the door. The house was gross as hell, so I always stood. There were wrappers from every fast food place in town all over the floor and trash of every kind everywhere. I could see the kitchen from the living room and it was in even worse shape. The dude and his roommates were the guys you went to for fake IDs, license plates, all that kind of shit.

"So, the usual?" I asked and the dude nodded, handed me the money, and I handed him his baggie.

"You like, want anything to drink?" he asked me.

"Uh, no thanks. I'm supposed to meet someone in a few minutes."

"That's cool," he said, looking at me. "Hey. Are you like, Italian?"

"Indian."

"Really? Cool," he said, opening his bag and rolling a joint. "You wanna hit?"

"No thanks."

"Yeah, I was telling my roommate I thought you were Italian but he was saying that you looked white. I was like, white? What, bro? No way, maybe like a half Mexican, but not white. Or maybe Italian, but anyway, you're like really young to be a drug dealer, you know that?"

"Yeah." I was really trying to keep up with him.

He took a giant hit and then coughed like hell.

"Good one," he said. He looked up at me in his faded black

and white striped bathrobe and scratched at his chest, thick, wiry hair poking out through the center of the robe.

"You should really try to get out of your line of work."

I thought about how to answer him, but he switched subject matter in true pothead style. "Yeah. This town blows. I've lived in it my whole life. I mean, screw the mountains. People are always talking about how pretty the mountains are but what good have they ever done me, you know?"

"I guess that's true."

I wondered what he thought the mountains were supposed to do for him.

He looked around and then back up at me. "What was I saying?" He asked and then burst out laughing. "This is good shit!"

"I gotta go. Good talking with you though."

"Oh, sure, anytime. Same time next week?"

"Sure," I said, and went over to the door and opened it. "See you." I looked back. I could see he was taking another hit. He waved and I closed the door and started walking down the cement stairs that led up to his faded, white house. What a fucking life. I probably did need to quit dealing, once I had the baby. Too risky. Too fucked up.

I walked back home, enjoying the sun and thinking about how I should break the news to Mom. Maybe I could tell her that I'd really loved the boy I'd been with. She would understand that. She had loved, and did love, Dad very much. I would tell her that she wouldn't have to support me in any way, that I could get on welfare but that I didn't plan on staying on it. She talked shit about kids with kids on welfare, but she'd have to understand. I mean, we barely got by as it was. There was no way that I was gonna be able to do it without welfare.

I was working it all out in my head, mapping it out, but when it came to thinking about what Dad would say, what he would do, I had nothing.

I went over to a rock that was a few feet over from the cracked and shitty sidewalk and sat down, tracing the delicate, lacy growth of moss on the edge. I thought about how he'd been during the accident, about when he'd held us at gunpoint. I shuddered and pulled my arms around me.

I sat there for a while. And then I thought about Mike. And something broke, turned in me, like a key in a lock. I still loved him. Where was he? It occurred to me that he didn't know that I was keeping the baby. I wondered what he would think about that. I shook my head. I couldn't go there. This wasn't about him. He had acted like a douche, treated me like shit. I was having the baby because that's what *I* wanted.

I sat for a bit, thinking, until I couldn't take anymore. I stood up and started walking home, puzzling over how I could get around Dad, how I could deal with what he would do and how he would live with me pregnant. I could think of nothing. He was going to blow the fuck up. Maybe this would make Mom finally leave him. Maybe she and I could get a place together, or somehow make Dad leave, get an apartment on his own so he could finish drinking himself to death. That was an ugly thought. I felt a twinge of guilt. But he wasn't going to change. And maybe Mom could finally have a decent life.

I walked up the drive. I noticed Dad's car was gone. I hurried my pace. This was my chance to talk to her, while the big, hulking, sweating shadow that my father had become was out of the house. My heart hammered in my chest as I opened the door.

"Mom?" I called.

"In here," she said from the kitchen. I walked in, my heart clanking like a hard, angry machine.

"Keep it down. I finally got the twins down for a nap."

"Actually, that's perfect," I said, coming around the corner and into the kitchen. Mom was at the table, grading. I sat down at the table next to her.

"Perfect?" she asked, her head still down, her pen still in her hand.

"Yeah. 'Cause I need to talk."

The pen stopped moving and her head came up.

"About what?" she asked, setting the pen down. "Your grades? Margaritte, don't tell me you're going to have to repeat the eleventh grade, for God's sake."

"No, that's not it," I said. I felt lightheaded. This was going to be hard. But I needed to be brave.

"What then?"

"Well, you're not going to like it."

"What am I not going to like? You're starting to scare me," she said, lifting her short, shapely hand to her chest. "What am I not going to like Margaritte? You're not... "

I was silent.

"No! You're not! You didn't! How could you! Tell me I'm wrong."

"No, you're not wrong. I'm pregnant."

She got up, sharply, the chair falling back and onto the linoleum floor. She ignored it and began to pace, looking up at me occasionally, one hand still over her heart, the other on her forehead.

"I could kill you! What's wrong with you!"

"I—"

"Quiet! Let me think."

"But Mom—"

"I said, let me think!"

I was silent while she paced. She stopped. "OK, I know there's a clinic in Denver because Murna's kid went there last year. I can call her and get their number."

"Mom, I already know about that clinic. I was there."

She looked at me like I'd just told her that I'd grown another, funkier, head.

"What do you mean you've already been there?" She said, her brows knitting together.

"I went there a week ago. I couldn't go through with it."

Mom blinked a few times, staring at me uncomprehendingly. "You... "

"Mom, I couldn't go through with it. I broke up with Mike over this. I was sure that I was going to do it and he didn't want me to. But when it came time, I couldn't."

Mom came over to me and slapped me, hard. I squealed and put my hand to my face, feeling the sting of her slap resonate throughout my body.

"What is wrong with you! You think that boy is going to come around just because you're having his baby? Are you crazy?"

I pulled my hand slowly down from my face and looked up at her. She was standing above me, an expression of fury mixed with pain on her face.

"No."

"Yes you do. That's what you think, you idiot!" she said, beginning to cry.

"I don't, you know, think that. It's not about him. I just can't. Why won't you understand that? We can work it out. We can, I don't know, I can get on welfare, and—"

"Welfare?" she said, shaking her head. "No. No child of mine will be on welfare! You are not going to do that! You're going to call them back up and make another appointment and you are going to have this abortion, do you hear me? Or I am going to kick you out! Your father won't have it! He will kill you, don't you understand? I won't have it! I'll call them myself!" She said, going to the phone.

She talked to Murna first, shakily writing a number down on a pad next to the phone. Then she slammed the phone down and I watched her dial the clinic. I closed my eyes, tears running down my face as she dialed the number. I watched her talk to them, make an appointment I knew I would never keep. This had all gone terribly wrong. Mom finished the conversation and dropped the phone into the receiver. She walked over to me.

"OK, your appointment is next Saturday, ten AM. I'm assuming you're not that far along?"

"No. Mom, you don't understand. I'm not doing this."

She looked at me with so much fury in her face, I worried for my life.

"You *are* doing this. This is not a discussion. You are sixteen years old. You have your whole life ahead of you. You are not going to ruin it over some guy."

I slapped my forehead, hard. "Don't you get it? It's not about him! As far as he knows, I'm having the abortion! It's about me, about what I want, about making something different—"

"Different?" she said. Her tone was mocking. "You think you're going to be different? Than who, Margaritte?"

I sighed, heavily. "I'm not saying different than you, Mom, but just different. I'll be fine. If I get on welfare—"

"Don't you goddamn use that word again."

"Mom, I won't be like, trashy, or anything."

"How are you going to support this baby?"

"I'll get on welfare, finish school and then figure out what to do."

"I guess you've got it all figured out then."

"No, I don't. But what I'm saying is that this is not the end of the world. I can make it work. Why don't you leave Dad? We could live here together, you could get him an apartment in town, and—"

"No."

I stared at her, hard. "After all that he's put you through. After the shit he's done."

"This is not your choice, Margaritte."

"And this is not yours."

We stared at each other, nostrils flared, breathing heavily. She broke the silence.

"You cannot live here if you have that baby."

"You're going to kick me out," I said incredulously. "You would kick your own daughter out of your house."

"I will not be a part of this. And your father, you know what he'd do."

"I'm so sick of him! Why am I bothering. I've told you to leave him so many times I'm blue in the fucking face! And you know what? You realize you're choosing him over me, right?"

She looked shocked and then reached over to slap me again, but I pulled back.

"That's enough," I said, getting up. "I've had enough of this shit! I'm not going to live like this anymore!"

I started stomping angrily towards the stairs. I could feel Mom behind me and I wheeled around. She took both of my wrists and shook me, hard, once. "Don't do this!" She whispered. "Don't!"

I looked at her, her disheveled hair. Her anxious face. I knew that she was only doing what she thought was best for me, what she thought would spare me the life she'd lived. I sighed. I leaned over and hugged her, hard. "I love you."

"I love you too," she said quietly. "Just please, please keep that appointment. I know you'll do the right thing. I know you."

I smiled at her. There was no use in discussing this anymore. And I was exhausted.

"I'm going downstairs, Mom, OK? I need to rest."

She let me go and I walked down the stairs. I could see that she was still at the top when I got to the bottom. I sighed and closed the door. I could hear the shuffle of her feet a few minutes later and the sounds of dinner being started. Pots and pans clinking. The sound of the front door opening and closing, and a few minutes later what was surely the sound of a bottle of scotch being set down on an end table. The twins waking up. The TV going on. I felt a twinge of sadness move in my body like a fish in a bowl. I lay down on my bed and put my hands over my stomach. I could swear that I could feel the slightest of bumps and I imagined what I knew was my daughter, kicking for her life, playing in there, her dark, fuzzy head bent around my body. I wondered how big she was. I picked up the phone.

CHAPTER 13

Megan is calling me from the kitchen. She's wanting to know where I put the cereal. I yell back that it's in the cabinet over the sink. *Thanks* she yells back. I can hear her kid screaming and running happily across the floor, her feet making a clack-clack-clack sound across the linoleum that fills me with something good. Something that feels like light in a yellow room. I look over at Christine. She's in her crib and crying a little in her sleep, her tiny hands pushing around her little brown face. She makes one more kitteny mummppph sound and goes back to sleep. She's been fussy lately. But she's not quite six months old and well, a fucking baby. They're born to fuss and puke and shit and generally still look so cute that your heart kinda bursts like a big, red balloon at a carnival. I walk over to her in her crib and stroke her tiny face with my right index finger. So soft.

Living with Megan this last year has been good and Megan had been more than happy about me moving in; it meant that she didn't have to go back home to the Lakota rez. There were just no jobs for her there, there were hardly any jobs for anyone there. One weekend, she'd taken me home to hang with her family. They were great, funny, tough. Her mom especially was hilarious. She reminded me of my auntie. And the land: oh, wow, long green and brown stretches of plains that seemed to go on forever and ever until you felt parts of you pulling into something strange and deep and wide. But so many people sitting by the sides of buildings, wrecked, their eyes distant and sad. There was something about it all that reminded me of Idaho Springs. But there was something else, too. One thing Megan said, was that everyone's cousin could draw, had work in some gallery. She said that for all the shit the government had put them through, they had come out with at least one foot kicking, hard.

Megan was talking about getting her nursing degree and she knew that if she did, she could maybe work at IHS back home but she knew she'd have to think long and hard about that. She wanted her kid to learn the language, know her family, know her culture, but there were so many things that could bring the both of them down. I told her that they had language classes in Lakota at the Indian Center in Denver, that maybe we could move there next year, and she nodded and looked thoughtful. I knew though that her mom missed her and wanted her and the baby back home. When we left, Megan cried for a long time. Her little girl was in her lap and she kept saying, *It's OK, Momma, it's OK*, her little dark eyes filled with worry.

As to her husband, he wasn't going to get out of prison for a few more years and she wasn't even sure they'd be together once he did. She went and saw him less and less. He'd gone to prison on a rape charge, she finally told me. At first she'd believed that he was innocent, hated the bitch who'd charged him, but she said that over time, she'd added a few things up. And she was beginning to doubt him, doubt that she would be the same person she was when he went in, whether it would work between them anyway by the time he got out. Either way, she was starting to get pretty determined to go to nursing school, and I told her I thought that was a good idea. I even found a school listed in the phone book in Denver, and called them and asked them to mail us some brochures. They did and not long after, an envelope came in the mail with the name of the school on it. That night when she came home from waitressing at the Derby, after she'd thrown her shoes to the walls and we'd made some dinner, we sat down on the floor and poured over the brightly colored brochures. They were glossy as hell and though there were some brown people, it was mainly really happy-looking skinny white people being hovering over other happy-looking skinny white people who looked like they were telling them something important. Megan seemed kinda intimidated. But I told her that all she had to do was take it one day at a time. That brochures were always stupid, that they didn't really show what anything was really like. That she could just apply, and I'd help her with the application fee, and that she didn't have to take a full load at first and not to worry, 'cause sure as shit she was a lot smarter than most of the dumb bitches I was always encountering at the hospital. She laughed and punched me on the arm, hard. I laughed back and rubbed my arm where she'd punched me. Megan was strong, man.

Once she kicked Will out the last time, he'd never shown up at her place again. At least not during the day anyways. Megan said she coulda sworn that she'd heard the door handle jangling in the middle of the night a couple times right after their last big fight. But she'd changed the locks and honestly, there were a couple of fuckers in that complex I could see jangling handles of all kinds in the middle of the night. We'd heard that he'd gone home, that he'd shacked up with a boy somewhere in Albuquerque, that he'd gotten cancer. But then one day driving around Denver, we saw him under an underpass not far from the bar I'd been with him and his buddy Miguel, passing around a 40 with a bunch of Urban Skins. Megan was all set to spit on him. I told her not to. She did anyway, telling me to slow down, leaning out the passenger side window, yelling *winkte* as loud as she could and spitting hard in his direction. He looked up and narrowed his eyes, and then lowered his head, his hand still on the bottle that someone was passing to him, sorta frozen in that position as someone he was related to, someone he'd lived with, screamed faggot in his language and spit at him.

I only got a glance at him but he looked bad. Dirty. Clothes that had clearly either come out of dumpsters or off of other, dead bums. A pitiful collection of graying hairs that you could maybe call a beard. And he was skinny as shit, except for his belly. I couldn't imagine what his day-to-day life was like. And I couldn't help but feel bad for the poor fucker, though when I said as much, I thought Megan was gonna punch a hole in my throat. He just blew my mind, that's all. He just seemed to be unable to get anything right. And I felt that way sometimes. But I guess the difference was that I tried so hard not to take anyone down with me. Will seemed to do nothing but take anyone around him down into his darkness, into total shit. What else could you do with people like that but learn to get out of their way?

As for my mom, I'd called her up the day after I'd moved out while she was at work and told her where I was, that I was going to live with Megan, that I was going to have the baby, whether she thought I should or not. She'd yelled at me for a long time, her voice growing hoarse and hysterical. She told me I was going to keep that appointment, that she was going to tell Dad and that they were going to come get me. That I was underage and not a legal adult. That I didn't have any choice in the matter and not to make her involve the authorities. I went silent. Then I told her that if she did that, I would go to social services and tell them about Dad. About what went on in the house. About his drinking, his hitting me, her, about how he had held us at gunpoint. I told her that there would come a time when he would hurt the twins and that she would be very, very sad then. She made a noise of pure pain and fury and then I could hear her crying and she slammed the phone down. I had stared at the receiver for a long time, wondering if I'd done the right thing. But then I looked down at my stomach and knew that I had.

I called her every day after that. I wanted to see the twins again. I wanted my mom to know her grandchild. For a long time, every time I'd call and say *Mom?* she'd just hang up the phone and I'd cry and cry and put both of my hands over my stomach, feeling more alone than I ever had in my life. Darkness.

After a month of this, I called Auntie Justine. I told her that I was pregnant, that I'd moved out, which I was sure she already knew. She yelled at me for a long time too, and I feared for my life. I always told Mom that I knew that my life would end when Auntie Justine would finally kill me in my sleep. Mom would always laugh. But seriously, the woman scares the living hell outta me. She's tiny, but she packs one hell of a Jesus punch. After a long lecture about what an idiot I was, what a disappointment to my mom and Native women everywhere I was, she ran out of steam. That's when I told her that I was going to keep the baby. She seemed to calm down then. Then she began with the Jesus and Mary and God talk and I had to listen to a lot of praise all three of those fuckers shit. I didn't bother to tell her that that wasn't the reason I was keeping it. That if I was anything, I was

Native American Church and even that was a stretch. But she told me that she could see if her church could help me with the cost of the baby, and I told her thanks. I was able to get on assistance, and with help from Auntie Justine's church and the money I'd saved up from dealing, I had the baby in Saint Lutheran's in the summer, on a warm, windy, snowy day in January. My water broke the night before and Megan had piled me and her baby up in the car and drove as fast as she could without scaring either me or herself. I was so excited. So scared. I kept looking down at the hugeness that had become my body and thinking about how I couldn't wait to see her. To know her.

She came out fierce: her little brown fists clenched, her long, slanted black eyes like a panther's, her tiny, wicked mouth screaming—she looked like a little Aztec warrior. I laughed and I cried and Julia (who Megan called when I got to the hospital) and Megan hugged me and I held her in my arms and felt a big, fat, sloppy pile of happy encircle me. But I was scared too. Scared I would never give her the life I wanted to give her. But then I looked at the people around me and thought about how much I had. Justine came a few hours later, my mom behind her, tears in her eyes. I looked at her and held her grandchild out to her, and she cried so hard I thought my heart would just fucking up and break right there. She came up to me and plucked her out of my hands and leaned to breathe her sweet baby smell in, like she was a little brown flower.

Mom sat and we caught up, and I could tell she was still pissed at me for the shit I'd said, telling me that Dad was doing better and all that. I asked her if he'd quit drinking and she went silent and then said, *no but he really is doing much better.* I nodded and held my baby closer, breathed in her new, new smell. Mom had made some kind of choice years ago that I could never understand, a choice she kept making over and over and over. Most people were like that; they just couldn't imagine how to get out of their shit. But I worried hard for the twins. They were still innocent. I told Mom I'd really like it if she would come over with them sometimes and she asked me if I'd like to come back home. That I was welcome to move back in. I said no, but thank you. She seemed angry and sad but seemed to accept it after I leaned over and asked her to hold the baby while I went to the bathroom. I placed her carefully in her arms and the baby sort of looked up at her and put out one of her fists in greeting. Mom laughed and took it, shook it gently and put her finger into her tiny little fist. I smiled and Megan helped me up and into the bathroom. When I came out I could see that Mom was still holding the baby, Julia above them making little bluesy cooing noises. I lay back down and watched them. I knew Mom felt sad that I wasn't coming back, ever. But there was no way I was going to live with Dad again. I loved him and I wanted to see him, but only during the day, and only when I felt like it was safe for me and my baby. To cheer her up, I told her that I was going to have a celebration for the baby with all of my friends at the park as soon as the baby was old enough and I would like it if all of them came, including Dad. She seemed happy then. Then she looked up suddenly and asked what the baby's name was. *Christine* I said, and Mom's mouth trembled and she cried all over again. I leaned over and hugged her and my baby and felt good, good, very good.

I spent half the morning in the hospital, waiting for the doctor to come around and check me out. Megan and Julia had to go, they both had to work and Auntie Justine and Mom stayed to keep me company and take me home. About an hour later the doctor came, checked me and Little Christine out, and made a follow-up appointment. Mom and Justine helped me and Little Christine into the car, buckling the baby into the car seat I'd bought at the thrift. On the drive back, Mom let me sleep and Justine told her to drop her off at home, where the twins were being watched by her husband. She told us that she'd be happy to watch them for the day. Mom came back with me to my place and we talked, and I slept, and we fed the baby and Mom told me she could bring the twins over after school and help me while I adjusted to life with a new baby. I thanked her. I told her that I was studying for my GED and that I was thinking about community college. She told me she was glad.

I got my GED not long after. I'd heard as long as you're literate you could pass it, so I had figured that it was a go. I may not be fucking Einstein but I *can* fucking *read.* I made the appointment for a few weeks after the baby was born. Megan watched the baby while I took it. And I got *myself* some glossy brochures—for Red Rocks. I found out that you can get a few grants for college when you have a kid that you don't have to pay back, and the rest shouldn't be too expensive because it's community college and for that I can take loans out. I figured on Red Rocks since that's the community college closest to me, so it'll be the easiest to commute to from Idaho Springs. I mean, even though I'm not sure what I'm gonna do, I definitely want to go to college. I'll never be like Julia, some kind of Super Indian, but I'd be happy to make decent money. I figure I'll just register for a bunch of classes of different kinds and then go from there. I mean, I know you can't exactly major in Stephen King and even if you could, I can only imagine that it wouldn't exactly rake in the billions.

Jake's trial was held not long after I moved out of Mom's place and even though Julia had said that she wanted to come, she ended up having to work. Jake looked so sad, dressed up in some stupid, cheap suit I was sure his state appointed lawyer had dug up for him. It was too short on him, on account of the fact that Jake is ridiculously tall and the bottoms of his pants rose high up over his shoes, exposing his different colored socks. One black and one brown. I waved at him and he smiled back. He looked calm but I could tell he was anxious as shit.

The place was packed and smelly, and the dark wooden benches were hell on my ass. I squirmed like an old lady with a massive case of hemorrhoids and never got comfortable. I figured that was the way it should be in a courtroom, I guess. There were wild looking fuckers everywhere, and folks who looked like they were the most normal, average what-the-hell-did-that-guy-do? folks. I don't know. I guess you can never tell. There was a big white dude with serious tattoos making big, obnoxious kiss faces at me every time I even started to look in his direction. After a couple times, I looked over and mouthed, *I will fuck you up* and he sat back, hard, and cut it out. Stupid fucker. He was the kind of guy Mom would think was really scary and she'd yell at me for threatening him, telling me I was gonna die that way someday. But I'd found out that half the time, the toughness of these guys went about two inches deep. Plus, I was done taking that kind of shit from men. Done for the rest of my life.

I waited for Jake to come up and prayed hard the way they'd taught me to the few times I'd gone to NAC in Denver, asking the creator and my grandma for help. It seemed like forever before they got to Jake. All those episodes of *Court TV*, all of those pissy judges came to mind. In those shows there was always a lot of crazy back-talking and in the end, the judge getting to tell it like it is. But in real life, it's more like a Justice Factory than an exciting show, that's for sure. It was just one dude after another, fast, boring and sad. Guilty/Not Guilty. It was like it barely mattered because from what Jake had told me over the phone, the lawyers had pretty much done all the deals beforehand and there was very little that was gonna change. I knew that if the judge decided to try him as a juvenile, he was gonna try to plead down to simple battery from the original charge of aggravated battery, on account of the fact that Jake had not done any really permanent damage. But it did look bad because Mike had been in a hospital bed and though he said seriously awful shit, the courts didn't much care about stuff like that. But Jake had told me that aggravated battery was more when you'd hit a kid, or a chick, or a cop. Or if you'd fucked someone up really, really bad. But it could have still been really bad for Jake, especially if he'd ended up with aggravated battery. I mean, it could affect everything: jobs, school. It could have meant he'd serve a year in jail, and that scared the hell out of me.

So when they finally called for Jake, I started sweating. I knew it was gonna be over fast for him. No one seemed to understand what a good guy he was. That he was only defending me. I mean for fuck's sake, Mike called me a whore after we'd dragged the stupid fucker to the hospital and saved his goddamn life. And Jake deserved a second chance, he really did. Jake and me had talked about quitting selling after the baby was born, about how we still had a good chunk in the bank and that it was enough to retire. Jake talked about going to school to learn to be a mechanic and we had enough in the bank to get him started. I told him if my dad could do that job drunk as hell, Jake could do it. I mean, mechanics can make decent money.

Jake stood there, towering over his lawyer, who was also in a pretty crappy looking suit, not that I knew the difference really.

I could just see that the knees and elbows of it looked worn out and shiny. The guy looked tired and overwhelmed, shuffling the papers he'd pulled out of his briefcase around like someone had woken him up in the middle of the night for a rousing game of UNO.

My cousin shifted his feet awkwardly, the judge looking down at him with narrowed eyes, swathed in those crazy fucking robes they wear that make them look like giant babies more than anything else. He was an old white guy and he was balding, his remaining hairs combed back in a 'do that was rapidly sproinging out of place. He looked more like a mad scientist than a judge. My stomach began to turn as they talked. The lawyer asked for Jake to be tried as a juvenile, and for the charges to be pled down to simple battery from aggravated. The Judge looked at Jake and asked him if he was going to do this kind of thing again. Jake looked uncomfortable and wiped the sweat off of the back of his neck and told him *no sir.* The judge looked down at something in front of him and then back up again. He asked Jake how he could believe that since it was clear that Jake had been getting in trouble for a long time. Jake's lawyer whispered in his ear but Jake batted him away. *Because I want to grow up, sir,* he said. I started to cry. I wanted to grow up too. We both wanted to be better than our parents, better than the people in our town. We wanted to get out, not out of town or out of our skins, but out of that big black hole that so many people throw their lives down. I felt sick. I closed my eyes.

The judge ruled that Jake would be tried as a juvenile, and could plead down to simple battery, but he would still have to serve a year of probation and community service. But that was better than having jail time. Or going to juvie again. He moved in with a couple of buddies a few doors down from me and Megan, and though his dad didn't want anything to do with him, Auntie Justine would go there once a month to yell at him about the mess he'd made of his life. I knew that was just her way of letting him know she still loved him. He'd felt so guilty about not being able to be there the day that Christine was born, but he had been at work, and by the time he got the call, I was back at home again.

I look over at Christine. She's awake now and staring up at me, happily, bubbles coming out of her mouth as she picks up her little foot and places it in her mouth around the bubbles. She looks like me for sure, but she also looks like her daddy. Her brown skin smooth as a stone and her eyes long and dark. I stare at her, taking her sweetness in for a while and then pick her up and take her to the kitchen to make her a bottle. Those bitches at the hospital tried to make me feel shitty for not nursing her, but after three days, I couldn't handle it. And she likes the bottle.

She sucks at it contentedly, and I get her bag ready. I'm off to the welfare office today, to settle some paperwork. That is an infinite clusterfuck.

Christine finishes her bottle and I change her diaper and get everything together and walk down to the car, which is making more noise than ever. It still runs though, and Mom's been telling me lately that Dad would like to fix it up for me, which is cool.

The drive to Georgetown, where the Welfare Offices are, is good, relaxing, and it doesn't take too long to get to where I'm going, park, get Christine out of her seat and into the welfare office. The thing that takes a long time is waiting. You take a number and you sit in a room for around an hour, if you're lucky. So I sigh, and sit down next to another chick who looks about my age. Her hair is huge and her eyebrows are painted on. I look down at Christine who is sleeping contentedly in her carrier, thank God. Usually I bring a book to read. But today, I reach into the diaper bag and pull out the letter from Mike.

I'd gotten it about a week ago. Mom had forwarded it to me. He'd just disappeared after the night at the hospital. When I tried to call his house there was an automated voice telling me the number had been disconnected. I asked everyone who might know, even resorting to calling his creepy track buddies, but no one seemed to know anything. And the rumors were everything from he was dead to he'd moved back to California, though I remembered his parents talking about rehab, and I wondered if that wasn't where he was. I figured that I would think about it later, maybe a few years down the road. That I would focus on getting by and feeding my kid and getting my life right before I thought about him. But it just seemed wrong to not tell him about Christine. And... I missed him.

My heart had leapt into my throat when I'd gotten the letter. Megan had told me to tear it up and for a minute there, I almost did. She stirred up how mad I was at him. And she made some good points: that he was a fuck up, and that he would only fuck up my kid's life. That whatever child support I would get out of him wouldn't be worth having to go to court, if they ruled in favor of visitation. That he would only confuse my emotions because I'd loved him so much. Plus, I didn't really want to spend the money to go to court. I nodded as she yelled and then took me and Christine to my room and sat with it in front of me while she had a bottle. I thought for a while. I thought about how curious I was to see what he was going to say. That I'd probably regret not at least knowing. I thought about what Megan said. I thought about my mom.

How much shit she'd taken from Dad. I just figured I'd leave it alone for a week and then see how I felt. But I knew I was gonna read it eventually.

The address was from California, from a place called Teen Rescue. I sighed deep, pushed my number into my pocket, felt my heart thunder, and slid my finger through the envelope. I pulled the letter out. Placed it on my lap.

Dear Margaritte,
Hey. So. If you're reading this, IF you're reading this, you might have already guessed where I'm writing it from. Yes, that's right: rehab. My benevolent parents thought to give this a go. It's hilarious. I keep thinking about how funny you'd find it. It's full of rich white kids at the maturity level of bratty six year olds. It makes ME feel mature. And I think we both know how mature I am. They make us do group therapy. It's fantastic. The lead therapist is this cheesy woman who wears a bunch of Indian jewelry and looks at you so sincerely when you talk, she looks like she might explode. And she pretty much says the same three things, no matter what you say: Thank you for sharing! Negativity is NOT the answer! And the last is my personal favorite: Transform your story! The other day Margaritte, we were in group. Well, honestly, most of these kids are like me. They're spoiled. They've never encountered a thing in their lives that could be construed as a hardship in any way, unless you count having their credit cards rejected because Daddy finally figured out that all of those cash advances were going right up his precious princess' nose. In any case, we were sharing. That's what we do in this group, share. I've mainly turned to making things up. The first day was great, because I spoke the few words of Spanish I knew. So I didn't have to share anything and it was hilarious

to watch them look at each other, try to figure out how I'd gotten there. But of course, once my group therapist talked to my individual therapist, who had my case file, that bit of fun was over quickly. So I try just making a new thing up every time I'm forced to share. Sometimes I tell the group I was raised in a house full of Satanists. That I was forced to sacrifice babies with a long, bejeweled dagger. Sometimes I tell them I'm the kid of a rich, Mexican drug lord and that I've been smuggling drugs over the border since I can remember. Other days I just go silent. The other kids there are pretty much of two kinds: the hardcore druggies who've been there many times and really do want to get clean, or the kids who just want their parents to think so, so they can get out and do drugs again. Some of them like sharing. Some of them are like me, they think it's a waste of time and a load of shit. What we all have in common is parents who have always thrown money at their kids rather than take care of them. And this is a way to still do that. That's what really amazes me.

The whole place really kills me. We each have our own room and the place is like a pretty, sterile Mexican restaurant, complete with miniature waterfalls. We're not supposed to socialize with each other in our rooms though; the deal with that is theoretically, we could be planning how to get more drugs together. But I think why they really do that is because we scare them. We're rich and we don't care about our lives. So why would we care about anyone else's, including theirs?

I have made a friend. His name is Rick. I like him because he doesn't buy any of the shit they're selling either. He's been in boarding schools since he can remember. The guy barely knows his parents. But he's funny as hell. Says he likes to paint. I told him we should get a place together when we get out of here. We're thinking about moving to San Francisco. I've heard we'd fit right in.

My parents do visit me. My mom cries and asks me if I'm better and if it's her fault and then yells at me and tells me that I'm running out of chances. My dad sits there, looking like he could use a drink. Mainly he's silent. I'm sorry about the things my mom said to you Margaritte, by the way. She's... well, she's an asshole. A well-intentioned asshole who loves me, but an asshole nonetheless. She was raised to be a showpiece and has done nothing but be a showpiece. I think that's why she got into church the way she did. She had to bury herself in something that didn't have to do with shopping and decorating her home. And my dad has done nothing but be the person his dad thought he should be. And so on. It's not their fault. But it doesn't surprise me that they couldn't get pregnant. Do you know that they'd asked for a light-skinned kid? That any time I would get dark in the summer, my mom would tell me that? She used to tell me not to drink, too. That because I was Colombian I should watch out for that. Yeah. Right. Colombian. The irony of my true vice in relation to the county of my origin is not lost on me.

Speaking of assholes, Margaritte, I want you to know I know I'm an asshole. I'm an asshole, Margaritte, I'd say it a million times if it could take away how I treated you, what I called you. I had no right to tell you what to do, to do what I did with Julia. I told you, I don't even like that girl. She's Indian, and I'm sure you guys are pals again, but Margaritte, in her way, she's just like my mom. She is. She will go out in that big, bright, white world and she will get the job she wants and marry a white guy and be a suburban nightmare. Mark my words. I slept with her because she was there, because she kept coming around, because I was so angry with you. I know it was wrong. But I just want you to know I don't feel anything for her. I love you. And I'm sorry. And I know you'll never forgive me. Let me try to explain myself, if you're still reading this.

First of all, I want to tell you all about me. Because when I met you, I liked you so much, I didn't want you to know me. I have been fucking up all of my life. I started drinking as early as I could. I went to parties in California as soon as I knew about them and my parents were never around, so that was easy. The drinking wasn't much of a thrill after a while. Because all I thought I wanted out of life was a thrill. Something, anything to make me feel alive. Because as long as I could remember I feared dying, and I thought the only way to get over it was to try to die all the time, to see if I could. I've learned subsequently that I was depressed, that I was trying to get my parent's attention. In any case, I started with pot. That was boring. Then one day when I was fifteen and at some kid's party someone brought coke. It was wonderful. It was sailing, thrilling, pumping, killing, machine-gun, fucking, it was everything I'd ever wanted to feel and the best part was there was a way in which it made me not feel at all. The only problem was that it didn't last very long. And I wanted to be high all the time Margaritte. And my grades improved. And my parents loved that. They showered me with gifts, money —which was great, because I used the money for more coke, and sold the gifts so that I could buy more coke. CokeCokeCoke. It was like I was falling in love. Until one day I collapsed in class. It was pretty scary. One second I was sitting there feeling like I was the inside of a diamond and the next I feel a little trickle, and then nothing. Blackness. I passed out and nearly hemorrhaged from all the blood I lost. When the paramedics came, I was in bad shape. They took me to the hospital. That was the fall. It was easy for the doctor to tell what my problem was, and when my parents came down, I knew I was probably in trouble. My mom was furious, and blamed my father. She said that my dad should not have stopped going to church and should not have told me it was OK for me not to go. My dad rolled his eyes and told her he was so sick of that fire and brimstone bullshit he could vomit. And that lots of kids experimented. And to calm down. He looked at me like I'd been caught drinking one of his beers and chuckled and told me that he knew I would never do it again. I told him I wouldn't. I was good for a week. Then I started up again and this time, since the flow of money had stopped, I started selling. That's when things really got bad. I loved it though. I was high all the time, I had money, I drove around in beautiful cars, with beautiful women much older than I was. And it was thrilling. I felt like I could never die. That's when the cops caught me. I was doing ninety on the highway, a girl in the passenger seat. I couldn't see anything ahead of me and I didn't care. I ran into a truck. I woke up in the hospital. This time my dad didn't find it all so amusing. The girl I was with was in ICU for days. She lived, but barely. Her face will never be the same. That's when my parents decided to move to Colorado. Which was fine by me. I figured that I would just keep doing what I'd been doing before. That's when I met you.

When I was younger, I'd watch movies, and they always seemed to have the same message: boy meets girl. Boy finds soul. And though I don't think anyone finds anyone's soul for anyone else, Margaritte, you did open my eyes enough to begin to search for it, I guess. Part of it was your honesty. And your poverty. And the poverty of that place. Because I'd never had to want for anything, seeing that, seeing you struggle, that did something to me. 'Course, you know that it didn't make me stop doing coke. I slowed down though, I did. But stop, no.

This place is like Disneyland. It's fake and everyone comes back and it costs a lot of money. There is little to no point to being here, except to continue the game wherein parents throw money at their kid's problems so that the rest of the world feels sorry for them, so that the rest of the world thinks they had kids for any other reason beyond that they went with the furniture. But I will say that it's given me time to think. It's very hard to get drugs in here, though I've heard that there are ways. But I realized that I haven't been straight for more than a day in years. And I'm only seventeen. It occurred to me that although my parents are pathetic, that they are human. That they want what everyone else wants but they just don't know how to get it. It occurred to me that I wanted to live. And Margaritte, it occurred to me that I love you. That I want you to move to San Francisco and I want to write, and I want to live with Rick and watch him paint and I want you to meet him. And I think you should write too. Can you tell that I've been reading On the Road? *I can hear you laughing at me. I miss that. That and the fact that after you'd laugh at me, you'd read it and then tell me what you thought about it.*

I know you probably hate me. But so much of me hopes that you don't hate me so much that you won't write back. Margaritte, I'm getting out soon. And I'm going to turn eighteen in a year. And so are you. If I can just get through one more year with my parents, I can get out. I want to go to Colombia. I want to meet my parents, my biological parents. I want to go there with you. But I'm getting ahead of myself.

I have a few more things to tell you, and then I'm going to stop. I've probably overloaded you, I know and for that I am sorry. I'm so sorry, Margaritte. I hope you can trust me. Trust me just enough to write me one letter back. Even if it's to tell me how much you hate me. Margaritte, I've had this funny feeling for a long time. It's that you kept our baby. I don't know why I think it. I shouldn't. And it doesn't matter. And I'm not writ-

ing you because of that, I swear. You were right. But it's part of what's kept me alive in here. It's part of why I don't ever want coke again. I really don't. It's just another lie. I've been lied to all my life, and I'm tired of being angry at my parents, or the world. I want to see what else I can feel.

There's so much to tell you. So much I want to tell you. And you know I'm a complicated person Margaritte, you know I live in my head. That I dream too much. That I get too angry. That I'm so worried about what's real I can't even see what's in front of my face. That I talk about stripping it all away, but I'm the first to put the mask on. But I'll work it out. And I will understand if you don't want to talk to me. But I'm going to keep on trying, I want you to know that. I've met lots of funny people in my life, and smart people, and there are at least a couple of people I admire, or think are genuinely good. But it's different with you. I don't know why. I'm only seventeen. But I get that. I love you. Please write me. Please tell me you want to sit somewhere free.

—Mike

My hand drifted down into my lap with the letter. I looked up and then ahead, and then everything went fuzzy and my head filled with a kind of white noise. I don't know how long I was like that, but I came back to reality because the chick next to me was poking me in the arm with one of her long glittery nails. I looked over at her and she said, *Like, your number is being called?* I blinked and tried to get myself together. I pulled my number out of my pocket and looked at it. They called it again, the voice over the loudspeaker crackling with urgency and irritation. It was my number. I mouthed *Sorry, thanks* to Ms. Nails and picked Christine up and walked over to the counter. I looked at the lady, set Christine down beneath the counter between my feet and smiled. There was so much to think about. So much my heart could never contain. I had no hope. I had infinite hope. But first there was paperwork. Dear God, there was always paperwork.

THANKS

Thank you. To my family of course, and especially to my mom & my sister, because they have had to put up with my mad scientist head for so long. As in, their entire lives. I'm so glad I wasn't pitched into a dark, bad crack in the earth (yet!). Thanks to my community, because even though I was made fun of for my love of dork books, I know they were only trying to toughen me up for the journey ahead. Which took eleven years in the case of this book. Which brings me to the agents who tried so hard, especially the last, to school me & sell this book to a big press. Which the last one almost did, several times. GOD I'm so glad they didn't. But their feedback was invaluable & it taught me not only what I shouldn't compromise but what wasn't a compromise at all, but something that just needed to be fixed. Thank you, my readers: Eden Robinson, Barbara Harroun, Jon Davis & Darlene Deas. Without smart readers, where would any of us be? Thank you *Stand*, you lovely British magazine. You published the first short-story version of this, which I wrote when I was twenty-four, but wasn't published until ten years later. Thank you to every journal that's ever published me, actually. I have a big, bad scary mouth and you said that's OK, we like that here. Thank you to Western Illinois University (especially David Stevenson), you gave me a job where I had time to write! What? That still exists? Thank you to every Native writer who ever existed (especially, in my case, thanks to Eden Robinson & Susan Power, who are my lady-heros, big time). Without any of you, none of us. Thank you to my editor, Maired Case, who waded through my novel with a good, sharp knife. Thank you to Curbside Splendor & Victor Giron. JESUS American letters are lucky you exist. Thank you of course & definitely & mostly, to Jacob S. Knabb, who years ago I kept seeing on THE Facebook, saying all kinds of smart things on people's pages & who has kept saying incredibly smart things in person. I'm so lucky that he saw something in my monster baby, something he got behind with iron fists. Man, I'm so glad I missed that plane. And lastly, thank you M, again. M. My muse, my sadness, I guess this letter has to be sent to the sky.

ERIKA T. WURTH is Apache / Chickasaw / Cherokee and was raised on the outskirts of Denver. She teaches creative writing at Western Illinois University and was a writer-in-residence at the Institute of American Indian Arts. Her work has appeared or is forthcoming in numerous journals, including *Boulevard, Fiction, Pembroke, Florida Review, Stand, Cimarron Review, The Cape Rock, Southern California Review* and *Drunken Boat.* Her debut collection of poetry, *Indian Trains,* was published by The University of New Mexico's West End Press.